FOREVER
AND A DAY

Also by Anthony Horowitz

The House of Silk
Moriarty
Trigger Mortis
Magpie Murders
The Word Is Murder

FOREVER
AND A DAY

A JAMES BOND NOVEL

ANTHONY HOROWITZ

WITH ORIGINAL MATERIAL BY

IAN FLEMING

HARPER

An Imprint of HarperCollins*Publishers*

FOREVER AND A DAY. Copyright © 2018 Ian Fleming Publications Limited and The Ian Fleming Estate. All rights reserved. Printed in the United States of America. No part of this book may be used or reproduced in any manner whatsoever without written permission except in the case of brief quotations embodied in critical articles and reviews. For information in the U.S., address HarperCollins Publishers, 195 Broadway, New York, NY 10007, U.S.A. In Canada, address HarperCollins Publishers Ltd, Bay Adelaide Centre, East Tower, 22 Adelaide Street West, 41st Floor, Toronto, Ontario, M5H 4E3, Canada.

HarperCollins books may be purchased for educational, business, or sales promotional use. For information, please email the Special Markets Department in the U.S. at SPsales@harpercollins.com or in Canada at HCOrder@harpercollins.com.

Material from 'Russian Roulette' by Ian Fleming, copyright © The Ian Fleming Estate, 2018.

James Bond and 007 are registered trademarks of Danjaq LLC, used under licence by Ian Fleming Publications Ltd.

The Ian Fleming logo and the Ian Fleming signature are both trademarks owned by The Ian Fleming Estate, used under licence by Ian Fleming Publications Ltd.

First published in the United Kingdom in 2018 by Jonathan Cape, an imprint of Penguin Random House UK.

FIRST U.S. EDITION

Library of Congress Cataloging-in-Publication Data has been applied for.

Library and Archives Canada Cataloguing in Publication information is available upon request.

ISBN 978-0-06-287280-7
ISBN 978-1-4434-5769-9 (Canada)

18 19 20 21 22   OFF/LSC   10 9 8 7 6 5 4 3 2 1

Contents

CONTENTS

FOREVER
AND A DAY

1

Killing by Numbers

'So, 007 is dead.'

'Yes, sir. I'm afraid so.'

M took a last, fleeting look at the photographs that lay scattered across his desk and that had been sent to him by General André Anatonin, his counterpart at the SDECE, or the Service de Documentation Extérieure et de Contre-Espionnage, in Paris. They had been taken from different angles but showed the same bleak image. A dead man, lying face down in dark, glistening water, his hands stretched out limply above his head as if in one last futile attempt at surrender. The flashbulbs from the cameras had reflected back, producing balls of brilliant light that seemed to float on the surface.

Eventually, the police had pulled him out and laid him on the quayside so that closer pictures could be taken of his face, his hands, the three holes in the breast of his jacket where the bullets had penetrated. He had dressed expensively. M remembered him sitting in this very office only a month ago, wearing the suit that had been made for him by the tailor he liked to visit just off Savile Row. The suit had kept its shape, M reflected. It was the man who was lying there, dripping wet and lifeless, who had lost his.

'Are we sure it's him, Chief of Staff?' The evidence seemed

inescapable but M asked the question anyway. The camera can lie. In his world, it often did.

'I'm afraid so, sir. He was carrying no identity papers – no surprises there. And he didn't have his gun. But the French have Belinographed his fingerprints and there's no doubt. It's 007 all right.'

'And this was taken in Marseilles?'

'Yes, sir. The basin of La Joliette.'

Bill Tanner was closer to M than anyone in the building, although the distance between them was incalculable. They had never eaten together, never enquired about each other's private lives. M despised small talk anyway but it would not have occurred to either of them to discuss anything but current operations and the general work at hand. Even so, Tanner – previously a colonel in the Sappers until he had been sucked into the less formalised world of the Secret Intelligence Service – knew exactly what would be going on in the head of the older man. The death of an active agent was to be regretted and 007 had been effective on more than one occasion. More important was to find out what had happened and to take immediate, quite probably permanent, countermeasures. It wasn't just a question of revenge. The service had to demonstrate that killing one of its operatives was nothing less than an act of war.

He had actually been with M, in this very room, when the idea of a Double-O Section had first been mooted, the cipher being as blank and anonymous as possible: it was literally nothing and nothing again. And yet it meant everything to the elite group of men who were going to carry it and who would at once be promoted to the front line of the country's war against its many enemies. Tanner still remembered the reaction of Sir Charles Massinger, permanent secretary to the Minister of Defence, when the proposal had first been put to him. His lip had curled in evident distaste.

'Are you serious? What you're suggesting here is tantamount to a licence to kill.'

It was the same old-fashioned thinking that had hampered the efforts of the Special Operations Executive at the start of the war. At first, the RAF had refused even to provide planes to transport their agents, not wanting to dirty their hands with Churchill's 'ministry of ungentlemanly warfare'. And now, just five years after VE Day, how many of those same agents were to be found in the corridors and offices of the tall grey building next to Regent's Park? Still ungentlemanly. Still, whatever the public might think, at war.

Tanner had listened as M quietly explained the point which the civil servant had missed. Although it might not appear so, hostilities had not come to an end in 1945. There were a great many people dedicating themselves to the complete destruction of Great Britain and everything it stood for. Counter-intelligence agencies like SMERSH in the Soviet Union and the Special Activities Committee of the People's Liberation Army in China. Or rogue elements including Nazis who still refused to believe that their precious Third Reich hadn't quite made its promised thousand years. You had to fight fire with fire, which meant that there was an urgent need for men – and women, for that matter – who would be prepared to kill, if only in self-defence. Death was part of the job. And like it or not, there would be times when the service would have to strike first, when a state-sponsored assassination would be the only answer to a particular threat. M could not have his hands tied. He was the one making the decisions and he had to know that he could act with impunity. The licence was as much for him as it was for the people he commanded.

The Double-O Section had been kept deliberately small. In fact, after this recent loss it was now down to just two men – 008 and 0011. M had always rejected the idea of there being a sequence, 001, 002, 003 and so on. Patterns, in any shape or form, are the enemy of counter-intelligence. Tanner wondered how quickly 007 would be replaced.

'What exactly happened?' M reached for his pipe, which rested next to the ashtray made out of a twelve-inch shell base that never left his desk.

'We still don't have all the details, sir,' Tanner replied. 'As you know, we sent 007 to the south of France a little over three weeks ago. He was investigating the activity of the Corsican underworld in the area. Or rather, the lack of activity. Someone had noticed a sharp drop in the supply of drugs coming out of Marseilles and the natural assumption was that they must be up to something else.

'These Corsicans are loud and unpleasant, really nothing more than modern-day gangsters with fancy names and a proclivity for violence – Joseph Renucci, Jean-Paul Scipio, the Guerini brothers . . . to name just a few. Up until now, they've had none of the discipline of the Unione Siciliana or even the Unione Corse but that's exactly the point. This silence is worrying. If they've managed to organise themselves, that could make them a danger not just to the immediate area but to the whole of Europe and – inevitably – us.'

'Yes, yes, yes.' M had all the information in the cavernous filing cabinet that was his mind and didn't need it paraded in front of him now.

'007 went in under cover. We gave him a new name, new passport and an address in Nice. He was an academic working out of University College, writing a history of organised labour. That allowed him to ask all the right questions without raising too many eyebrows. At least, that was the idea. Part of the trouble is that the police – and that includes the SDECE – are riddled with informers. We thought he'd have a better chance on his own.'

'Did he come up with anything? Before he was killed?'

'Yes, sir.' The chief of staff cleared his throat. 'It seems that there was a woman involved.'

'There always is,' M growled into the bowl of his pipe.

'It's not quite what you're thinking, sir. 007 mentioned her in what would turn out to be his last radio transmission. He referred to her as Madame 16.'

'Sixteen? The number?'

'Yes, sir. It's not her real name, of course. You'll know her as Joanne Brochet – French father, English mother – started life in Paris before the first war and then moved to London where she grew up. She spent three years at Bletchley Park, working in the indexing hut, before she was selected by Special Operations, who trained her up and parachuted her into France under the code name Sixtine.' Tanner spelled it out. 'She was very highly regarded by both F Section and the Deuxième Bureau and there's no doubt that she provided us with useful intelligence in the build-up to Operation Overlord. She was captured and tortured by the Germans and after that she disappeared. We assumed, of course, that she had been killed. But she turned up again a few years ago, working in Europe, and by then she'd managed to lose her entire history . . . age, name, nationality and all the rest of it. She called herself Sixtine or Madame 16 and she'd gone into business for herself.'

'She was the woman who sold us the Kosovo file.'

Tanner nodded. Both men knew what he was talking about.

The Kosovo file was a feasibility study that had been put together by a low-grade civil servant with too much time on his hands and, worse still, a heightened imagination. It set out, in detail, the strategy to incite and support an armed uprising in Albania, which had become a communist state after the war. There was never any chance that the plan would be given a green light, but the file had gone into minute detail, identifying all the local operatives along with the royalists and the expatriates who might have lent themselves to the cause. The Kosovo file should have been shredded the moment its existence was known. Instead, it had been photostatted and circulated and then, unbelievably, a young man working as third secretary at the Prague embassy had left a briefcase with a copy under his seat one evening when he got off a tram.

'We never found out how Sixtine got her hands on it,' Tanner went on. 'But it was hardly surprising. By now, she'd reinvented herself as an agent for hire, dealing in pretty much anything that would make her money. She had a good-sized organisation behind her and contacts all over Europe . . . on both sides of the Atlantic as a matter of fact. Exactly the sort of person to act as a go-between in a business such as this. Anyway, she contacted us and agreed to sell the papers back for £2,000.'

'It was blackmail, pure and simple!' M made no attempt to hide his annoyance. 'We should never have agreed.'

'That may well be true, sir.' Tanner drew a hand over his chin. It was always risky, answering M back. 'But for what it's worth, our man in the Treasury thought she struck a remarkably fair deal. The Russians would have paid five times as much and we'd have ended up looking like complete fools if the file had come out. It may be that she felt some loyalty towards us, left over from the war. It's like I said: as an agent, Sixtine had been very useful.'

'And 007 met her in Marseilles,' M said.

'We don't know that, sir. But he was certainly interested in her. The very fact that she was in the south of France indicated that she was up to something. This is not the sort of woman who simply goes on holiday, and we know for certain that she'd been talking to the syndicates. In the last transmission he made, a week before his death, 007 said he had concrete evidence.'

'What sort of evidence?'

'Unfortunately, he didn't say. If 007 had one fault, it was that he liked to keep his cards close to his chest. In that same transmission, he mentioned that he had arranged to meet someone who could tell him exactly what she was up to – but once again, he didn't tell us who it was.' Tanner sighed. 'The meeting took place at the basin of La Joliette and that was where he was killed.'

'He must have left notes – or something. Have we been to his house?'

'He had an apartment in the Rue Foncet and the French police searched it from top to bottom. They found nothing.'

'Perhaps the opposition got there first.'

'It's possible, sir.'

M tamped down his pipe with a thumb that had, over the years, become immune to the heat of the smouldering tobacco. 'You know what surprises me in all this, Chief of Staff? How could 007 allow himself to be shot at close range in the middle of a crowded city? Seven o'clock in the evening, in the summer months . . . it wouldn't even have been dark! And why wasn't he carrying his weapon?'

'I was puzzled by that,' Tanner agreed. 'I can only assume he must have been meeting someone he knew, a friend.'

'Could he have actually met with Madame 16 herself? Or could she have found out about the meeting and intercepted it?'

'Both those thoughts had occurred to me, sir. The CIA have people out there and we've been trying to talk to them. In fact the whole area is crawling with security services of one sort or another. But so far . . . nothing.'

The heavy, sweet smell of Capstan Navy Flake hung in the air. M used the pipe to punctuate his thoughts. The age-old ritual, the lighting and the relighting, gave him time to consider the decisions that had to be made.

'We need someone to look into what happened,' he went on. 'This business with the Corsicans doesn't sound particularly pressing. If there are fewer drugs coming out of France, that's something to be grateful for. But I'm not having one of my best agents put down like a dog. I want to know who did this and why and I want that person removed from the field. And if it turns out that this woman, Sixtine, was responsible, that goes for her too.'

Tanner understood exactly what M was saying. He wanted an eye for an eye. Somebody had to be killed.

'Who do you want me to send? I'm afraid 008 is still out of action.'

'You've spoken to Sir James?'

'Yes, sir.' Sir James Molony was the senior neurologist at St Mary's Hospital, Paddington, and one of the few men who knew M both socially and professionally. Over the years he had treated a number of agents for injuries, including stab wounds and bullet wounds, always with complete insouciance and discretion. 'It's going to be another few weeks.'

'And 0011?'

'In Miami.'

M laid down the pipe and stared at it tetchily. 'Well, then we have no choice. We're just going to bring forward this other chap you've been preparing. It's been on my mind to expand the Double-O Section anyway. Their work is too important and right now we've got one injured, another one dead . . . we need to be prepared. How is he doing?'

'Well, sir, he managed his first kill without any difficulty. It was that Kishida business. The Japanese cipher man.'

'Yes, yes. I read the report. He's certainly a good shot and he kept his nerve. At the same time, though, firing a bullet into the thirty-sixth floor of a New York skyscraper doesn't necessarily prove anything. I'd like to see how he works at closer quarters.'

'We may very well find out,' Tanner replied. 'He's in Stockholm now. If all goes well, he'll be reporting back in the next twenty-four hours. I already have his fitness report, his medical and psychological evaluations. He's come through with flying colours and, for what it's worth, I like him personally.'

'If he gets your recommendation, that's good enough for me, Chief of Staff.' M frowned. 'You didn't tell me his name.'

'It's Bond, sir,' the chief of staff replied. 'James Bond.'

2

Strawberry Moon

Sitting in a corner of Restaurant Cattelin in the medieval district of Stockholm, stabbing at a bad filet mignon accompanied by a worse glass of burgundy, James Bond thought about the man he had come to kill.

Rolf Larsen had definitely had what is called a good war. Starting as the handsome, courageous editor of a clandestine counter-propaganda newspaper, he had escaped from Norway in 1942, reaching England via Sweden. He had joined the famous Kompani Linge, where he had received paramilitary and parachute training, returning to his own country in time to play a key role in Operation Mardonius, an attack on Oslo harbour with limpet mines delivered by canoe. He had become a member of the sabotage group known as the Oslo gang and took part in the destruction of the Korstoll Depot, a repair shop where several German fighter aircraft were destroyed. He had finished the war with a DSO from Great Britain, a War Cross with Sword from the Norwegian government and the admiration of just about everyone who knew him.

Almost immediately, he had moved to Stockholm, taking advantage of the extraordinary financial and social surge that had come from low taxes, a small public sector and a largely unregulated market. He had made millions in 'green gold', exporting sawn timber goods and pulp from Sweden's pine forests. He married Selma Ekman, a Swedish heiress, at once doubling his fortune, and the two of them had two young children. Bond had seen the well-dressed, respectable family the day before as their chauffeur dropped them off at Östermalm's Saluhall, the old food market in central Stockholm. Rolf was in his forties now, his thick hair midway on its journey from blond to silver, his ruddy face and expanding belly the two signposts of a life well lived and a genial acquiescence to middle age.

Except that it was all a lie.

It turned out that Rolf Larsen had been a highly successful double agent, working for the Nazis, taking part in small-scale operations while at the same time keeping his masters informed about the bigger picture. He had been responsible for the deaths of dozens of Norwegian agents, including some who had actually fought at his side. But that wasn't what had signed his death warrant. In 1944, a plan was put forward by the British for an assault on northern Norway, with troops leaving the Shetland Islands on fishing boats, penetrating the fjords under cover of darkness and fog. Two men had been sent ahead to pinpoint a suitable landing position and Larsen had betrayed them both. They had been captured, tortured and killed. The assault had been abandoned.

British intelligence made many mistakes during the war but what the Germans never understood and what a man like Rolf Larsen would never have believed was how doggedly they would work to put things right once it was over. Two men from No. 4 Commando had disappeared after parachuting into enemy territory. But that wasn't to be the end of the story. It was just the beginning. Even before the war ended, the wheels had started turning and slowly, irrevocably the truth had emerged, the investigation closing in on the young hero who was now the wealthy family man. It would be six whole years before the final proof was discovered and by this time there had been several thousand trials and forty executions. A new decade had begun. Dragging a twice-decorated man like Larsen through an exhausted court system would be of benefit to no one. Someone high up had made the decision. This one could be dealt with unofficially.

As he pushed away his plate and called for a coffee, Bond considered what that meant. Nobody in Stockholm knew that he was here: not the police, not the government, not Säpo, the Swedish security service. This had to look like a straightforward murder and to all intents and purposes that was exactly what it was. Larsen was alone. Only that afternoon he had put his wife and children on the train to Uppsala where they were spending the weekend. Bond had watched them kiss goodbye on platform five of the Central Station. Larsen planned to follow them the next day. Right now he was at the Stockholm Opera House, watching a performance of *Tosca*. Bond had always had a loathing of opera; its absurdly large women, its histrionics, its noise. The fact that Larsen was spending his last night there was somehow fitting. He was on his way from one hell to another.

There were to be no guns. Bullets came with a history that stab wounds did not. Bond wondered if this task had been chosen for him deliberately. His first killing had taken place at a distance, on the other end of a telescopic sight. He had been fifty yards away from Kishida when he died. Barely even a witness. In fact, for all Bond knew, the Japanese cipher expert could still have been breathing as his assassin took the lift back down to the ground floor – although this was admittedly unlikely after a bullet had just torn through the back of his throat.

This time it was going to be close quarters. Larsen's family home was spread over the top two floors of a building just round the corner from the restaurant. A room upstairs was occupied by a manservant called Otto who had come out of Säpo and who had the physique and watchful eyes of a professional bodyguard. Otto was a Swede with no criminal record and Bond knew he had to be left alone. The entire house was alarmed, connected to a police station just two blocks away. The kill had to be fast, efficient and, above all, silent.

And what then? Two little girls, aged five and three, would find themselves without a father. A plump, happy wife would become a widow. The newspapers would celebrate the life of a war hero and demand action against the rising crime rate in Stockholm. And, all being well, Bond would be awarded his Double-O number. He would have earned his licence to kill.

It was something that he wanted more than anything in the world – and he had wanted it from the moment he had entered the secret service. Why? Was it a hangover from the war, all those years in the RNVR where killing the enemy had been taken for granted and where any talk of morality or proportionality would have been seen at best as an irrelevance but more likely as a sign of weakness? Or was it the same drive that had taken him climbing in the Aiguilles Rouges and boxing at Fettes, simply the desire to be the best at everything he did? That was it, really. It didn't matter if he was serving his country or his own interests. There were only three Double-O agents in the entire building and they were respected like no others. He was going to be the fourth.

The steak was still sitting, desultorily, on the side of his plate. He gestured at the waiter to take it away, then drew a cigarette, a Du Maurier, out of its signature red packet, already enjoying the comforting flick of his old Ronson lighter. He had been wrong to blame the restaurant for its food. The truth was that he had no appetite, knowing what lay ahead. He glanced at his watch. Five past ten. The fat woman would be poisoning herself or throwing herself off a tower or whatever else it was she did in the last act of Puccini's masterpiece, and soon the audience would be on its way home.

And then . . .

Bond took his time with the cigarette. He had another glass of wine, leaving half the bottle, not wanting the alcohol to dull his senses. Finally, he called for the bill, paid and left.

He found himself in a narrow street, hemmed in on both sides with the great bulk of Stockholm Cathedral rising up at one end. Bond had a sense of being trapped, but that was the trouble with this city: as handsome as it might be, it had been cut into fourteen separate islands with everything bunched together so that to the malefactor it might become nothing more than a series of traps, particularly on a night such as this. He looked up and saw a full moon glowing a deep red in a cloudless sky. A strawberry moon. It was a name from his childhood and brought memories of a life long gone. Now it was a single eye watching him as he walked down the black and empty street, somehow complicit in what he was about to do.

Half an hour later, shortly after eleven o'clock, a light blinked out on the sixth floor of the ornate mansion block that the Larsens occupied. Bond knew his moment had come. He stepped out of the shadows, glanced up and down the empty street, then withdrew a thin strip of plastic from his jacket pocket. The front door, with its Yale-style lock, offered no resistance. Ignoring the lift he climbed six floors to a square hallway with black and white tiles and another door, as ineffective as the first. As Bond eased it open, the blue metal box with the Rely-a-Bell alarm logo mounted high up on the wall blinked but did not sound. The system had been imported from London, and only the day before two men claiming to come from the Wilson Street office had arrived to give it a complete overhaul. They had been carrying the necessary identification papers and seemed to know what they were doing. Nobody had given them a second thought and now the alarm slept peacefully, unaware of the figure slipping past below.

Bond found himself in an expensive, old-fashioned apartment, its furnishings more German than Scandinavian with heavy dark furniture, rugs, chandeliers. He had brought a torch but didn't need it. The curtains were tied back and rose-coloured light was seeping in through double-height windows. He made no sound as he climbed the stairs, past oil paintings brooding in overwrought gold frames. He had studied plans of the building and knew exactly where he was going. He turned a corner and padded down a corridor with an antique mirror at the end. More chandeliers hung overhead, the glass beads forming shadowy cobwebs. The third door opened into the master bedroom. Bond's hand clamped down onto the needlessly elaborate brass handle. Very slowly, deliberately, he squeezed it open.

This was it. He was there.

Rolf Larsen slept in a king-sized nineteenth-century bed with carved headboard, legs and finials, everything white. Without his wife at his side, the amount of space that he occupied was almost obscene. He was a small figure, lying on his back with his head resting on one of five pillows that were grouped around him, as if whispering to him while he slept. It was a warm night. He had thrown off the blanket and was covered by a single white muslin sheet that seemed to stretch out forever, like a ghostly sea. Bond could make out his silver hair, the rise and fall of his chest. He was aware of his own heart beating faster. There was a metallic taste in his mouth. When he had killed Kishida, he had felt less involved. His only concern had been that he shouldn't miss. But this was different. He could smell Larsen. In the all-embracing silence of the room, he could easily make out the sound of his breathing.

Bond reached into the left sleeve of his jacket and pulled out a blade – seven inches long with a Dunlop rubber handle. All the time he had been eating his dinner at Cattelin, the knife had been resting in its leather scabbard, known as the X-sheath because of the way the straps crossed his arm. It was an old-fashioned weapon and one he had last used behind enemy lines. Bond had chosen it in part because it seemed appropriate, but mainly because it would be undetectable until the moment of use, when the quick-release buckle would deliver it neatly into his palm as it had just now. For a moment, he felt the weight of it in his hand. Rolf Larsen stirred in his sleep, some animal instinct screaming at him to wake up. The time had come. Bond acted.

Using the edge of his knife hand he flicked on the bedside light. At the same time he leaned forward, his other hand clamping down on Larsen's mouth before he could call out for help. Larsen's eyes opened, filling almost simultaneously with surprise, understanding and terror. He saw a man aged about thirty, clean-shaven with black hair curving down across his forehead and very straight features; the nose, the mouth and the eyes almost mathematical in their precision.

A three-inch scar on the man's right cheek destroyed the symmetry. The man was wearing a dark suit, a white shirt and a knitted tie. His hand was pressed against his mouth with unusual force, making it almost impossible for him to breathe.

'Larsen?' The man had only spoken a single word but somehow Larsen knew straight away that he was British.

Larsen nodded, his head making a space for itself in the softness of the pillow. The man's hand moved with him, not allowing him the tiniest chance of escape.

'I'm here for Bourne and Calder.'

Bourne and Calder. The two men sent to the northern coast of Norway. The two men Larsen had betrayed. It hadn't been part of Bond's brief to extract any information from the traitor before he killed him, but he had to know for his own peace of mind.

'Do you understand?' he asked.

Larsen hesitated, then nodded very slowly. He didn't need to make any movement. Bond had already seen what he needed in the man's eyes; the acknowledgement of guilt. So be it. Without a second thought, he drove the knife forward, into the neck muscle, slanting it towards Larsen's brain.

He drew back. He had expected death to be instantaneous but in the glow of the bedside lamp he saw that Larsen was very much alive, staring at Bond as if puzzled by what had just happened, his mouth opening and shutting, blood already flecking his lips. He couldn't speak. The blade must have severed his trachea. It had also opened the carotid artery. As Bond sat there, perched on the side of the bed, he saw the most extraordinary sight. Blood was spreading underneath the sheet. There was a perfect circle of it, growing larger and larger. It was like the strawberry moon that

Bond had seen outside, sliding out from behind a white cloud. And still it came. Larsen was staring at it, quite literally transfixed, dying by inches. The moment of death, when it finally arrived, was anticlimactic. His lips were still moving, but more slowly. Then they stopped. His eyes continued to stare. The blood crept another inch, almost touching Bond. Suddenly there was only one person breathing in the room.

Bond removed the knife, wiped it clean and returned it to its sheath. He looked around him, then took Larsen's gold cufflinks, his Rolex Speedking and a wallet containing 300 Swedish krona. It was hardly a reasonable motive for such a violent crime but it would have to do. He glanced one last time at the unmoving pile of flesh that had once been a human being, then turned off the lamp and left. He climbed back down six flights of stairs and let himself out into the street. Crossing the Strömbron Bridge at the northern corner of the island, he dropped the objects he had taken into the water below.

The wallet went first, then the cufflinks and finally the heavy silver watch. It hit the surface and Bond saw the ripples, a series of circles – zeroes, perhaps – closing in on themselves and then vanishing as the evidence of what had taken place sank out of sight.

3
First Day

Breakfast, for James Bond, was the one meal of the day that he considered to be indispensable. Lunch was a pleasure, dinner often a celebration, but breakfast had the seriousness and the solemnity of a ritual, a time when he could sit back and contemplate the day ahead. It was one of the reasons why he was so demanding about the ingredients: the particular brand of jam or marmalade, the unsalted butter, the eggs from French Maran hens boiled for exactly the right amount of time. It wasn't just faddishness. He was giving the meal the respect it deserved.

Although Bond was perfectly comfortable in the kitchen, he made a point of never cooking for himself. He liked to sit down at exactly half past seven in the morning. Sometimes he read the newspaper, but he preferred not to talk and he never listened to the wireless. Whatever horrors the next seven or eight hours might bring, this was a time of quietness and one, it sometimes occurred to him, that hadn't changed throughout his life.

On the day after his return from Stockholm, he came down to the table in his Chelsea home and watched as his elderly Scottish housekeeper, May, came bustling in with a well-laden tray. It was just over a year since she had joined him. He had interviewed three women for the job, explaining that he was a civil servant who worked for an obscure department within the Tourist Office and that this would involve a great deal of travel. The other two had accepted this story but she had looked at him with a glint in her eyes and announced: 'Aye, right! D'ye take me for a numpty, Mr Bond? I'll ask noo questions but ye tell me noo lies!' Bond had been so amused by her response, he had hired her at once.

'Good morning to you's,' she muttered now, that last 's' being as close as she would ever come to 'sir'. 'Did ye have a good trip?'

'Yes. It went very well, thank you, May.'

She continued setting the plates down. 'I don' rightly ken what they're thinking, this business with the Koreans,' she grumbled, handing over that morning's edition of *The Times*. The headlines were full of the American attack on Chinju. 'Ye'd have thought the werld would have had enough o' war.' She sighed. 'It's all the fault of these bawheid communists. I always said ye should never have trusted that Joe Stalin. There's one with a face like a skelped bahoochie. Ah well, what will be will be, I suppose . . .'

She left the room and in the silence that followed Bond enjoyed May's scrambled eggs, which he seriously considered to be the best in the world, alongside hot buttered toast with heather honey from Fortnum & Mason and several cups of double-strength coffee. He smoked two cigarettes and read the news and it was only as he left that he acknowledged that he had been quite deliberately putting all thoughts of Stockholm and Rolf Larsen (the mouth opening and shutting, the eyes staring) out of his mind.

Bond drove to work in a midnight-blue Jaguar XK 120, which he had bought after seeing it at the London Motor

Show and which he had almost instantly regretted. It was the fastest production car in the world, easily capable of reaching the 120 mph that its name suggested, but there was something sluggish about the way it handled and Bond had quickly tired of its angry snarl every time he accelerated away from the lights. He still had the crumpled wreckage of a steel-grey Mark II Continental Bentley tucked away in a storage depot in East London. If he could just find the time to straighten it out and give it a total refit, it might be a worthy replacement.

Bond was aware that his current salary would never have afforded these luxuries: the car, the Regency house close to the King's Road, the full-time housekeeper. His parents had died when he was just eleven years old, leaving behind a trust fund he had inherited when he was eighteen. He sometimes wondered if his life would have turned out differently if they had survived the climbing accident that had taken them. Not having parents, not having the closeness of immediate family, emerging from this emptiness – had all of this in some way moulded the man he had eventually become?

With these thoughts in mind Bond came to a halt on the edge of Regent's Park and continued the last ten minutes to the office on foot. The doorman nodded at him as if he'd barely noticed him, though in fact he had a photographic memory and not only knew the names and the office locations of everyone who worked in the building but – without referring to any written notes – would be able to say exactly when they had entered or left.

Bond turned a corner and walked into the lift. The liftman glanced at him.

'Which floor, sir?'

'The fifth, please.'

There. He had said it, somehow making it a reality.

The liftman pressed the button, then rested the stump of his arm on the control handle, making no comment.

Usually, Bond went to the third floor reserved for 'Communications and Electronics Development', a name that disguised a multitude of clandestine activities. This was where he shared an office with three men and two women, separated by acrylic screens that effectively compartmentalised them, keeping them in their own separate worlds. Bond had spent the past few weeks preparing the logistics for a black frontier crossing into East Germany until Stockholm had come up. That assignment would now have to be handed to someone else.

He stood silently as the doors closed. He knew the liftman – a former gunner who had been wounded at Tobruk – quite well. After all, they had stood together in this little space more than a hundred times. But today everything was different. Could it be that the other man somehow knew about his promotion? That was the trouble with this damned building. Everyone had their own secrets but no secrets were truly their own. Bond felt a certain nervousness in the pit of his stomach, exaggerated perhaps by the sense of rising. Everything about the building looked different. Even the colours – grey, beige, off-white and that drab shade of green beloved by government departments – seemed brighter, more exciting than they had the week before. But of course, it was he who had changed. Barely twenty-four hours had passed since he had taken a second life. In doing so, he had earned his licence to kill, joining an elite force, just four of them in the entire organisation.

Three of them. Bond had heard about the death in the south of France. He was a replacement, not an addition.

The lift doors opened and he stepped out into a corridor much like the one he was familiar with. A group of young women passed him, talking among themselves. Was it his imagination or had they avoided his eye? He knew the number of the office he was looking for and found it, knocked and, to the single invitation of 'Come!', went in.

The single occupant worked silently and efficiently in a blank white box with a picture of the king on one wall and the prime minister on the other. These would have been supplied by the Ministry of Works or perhaps the Government Art Collection, and Bond wouldn't have been surprised if they had been hung at a regulation height. There was a steel filing cabinet in one corner with an aspidistra in a plant pot on top. That might be regulation, too.

'Commander Bond?' The man behind the desk looked up incuriously.

'That's right.'

'Please come in. Take a seat.' There was only one other seat. Bond sat down, facing him.

The man smiled thinly. 'Congratulations on your promotion and welcome to your first day in the Double-O Section. We just have a few formalities to go through. It won't take long.'

Paymaster Captain Troop, RN Retired was the head of administration and well known as a pen pusher par excellence. He lived up to his job description by taking out a pen and laying it on the wooden surface in front of him as if it gave him the power to speak uninterrupted, which he proceeded to do for the next ten minutes, describing Bond's new responsibilities in the driest of tones. He did not pause for questions. He did not expect any and certainly Bond didn't intend to give the display of weakness that would have come

23

from asking them. At the end of his speech, he drew out several sheets of paper from a drawer and tapped them with an authoritative finger. 'Could you sign here, please, Commander Bond? And here?'

Bond did as he was told. His signature was necessarily simple. There were just nine letters in his name and not one of them gave any excuse for a flourish. The first document was a confidentiality agreement that seemed to him to be an unnecessary adjunct to the Official Secrets Act he had already signed when he joined the service. The second provided him with statutory life insurance. The third was shorter and more brutal, giving his employers complete power of attorney over his affairs (and, presumably, the insurance payout) in the event of his being killed in action. Troop waited until he had finished, then swung the papers round with a satisfied nod.

'Thank you, Commander Bond. There is just one last detail to mention, which is that your salary has been raised to £1,500 a year, the same level as a principal officer in the Civil Service. The new figure will show up in your bank statements with immediate effect.' There was a fourth page to sign, agreeing to the financial terms, then Troop took the pen back, screwed it shut and slid it into his pocket. 'I'll show you up to your new office. Your secretary will take over from there.'

Troop was not an unpleasant man although he was cordially disliked by almost everyone in the building. It occurred to Bond that this was part of his job. Every business needs its lightning rod and Troop – small, neat, bland, precise – fulfilled this role admirably. He did not speak as he and Bond took the lift up to the eighth floor and then walked past a series of doors (no numbers here, Bond noticed), stopping at the last one on the right.

'This is where I'll leave you,' Troop said. 'Good luck.' There was nothing more, no handshake. He simply turned and walked back the way he had come.

Bond knocked on the door. It was opened almost at once by a woman who was perhaps a year or two older than him and certainly an inch or two taller. She was dark and slender with the sort of beauty that was all the more alluring because it was so obviously out of bounds. Already, on first meeting, her manner was restrained, her eyes challenging him. But he could see within them the spark of humour that told him they were going to get on.

'Mr Bond?' she asked.

'James.'

She considered the name and smilingly accepted it. 'I'm Loelia Ponsonby. Let me show you to your desk.'

She turned her back on him and he followed her into a small anteroom, enjoying the perfect line of her shoulders and the sway of her hips. She was wearing a cream silk shirt with kimono sleeves and a serious dark-blue skirt. Bond looked for a wedding ring, somehow knowing he would not find it. She walked over to a second door on the other side. This led into a larger room, very square, with three desks and a window looking out onto Regent's Park.

'Loelia,' Bond muttered. 'I can't possibly call you that. Do you mind being Lil?'

She swung round and looked at him coolly. 'As a matter of fact, I do.'

'Well, I'm not going to call you Miss Ponsonby,' he said. 'It makes you sound like a schoolteacher and anyway I had an aunt who used to take me to a village by that name. Ponsonby in Cumbria. I don't suppose you've ever been there?'

'My family's from Kent.'

'Then we already have something in common. That's where I was brought up. It was a place called Pett Bottom, near Canterbury.'

She scowled slightly at the name, wondering if he was making it up. 'I can't say I've heard of it.'

'It's just south of Nackingham.' It hadn't been a good start. Was their entire relationship going to be made up of a vague flirtation based on obscure village names? He went over to the window and glanced out. 'So how does this work?' he asked, more businesslike now. 'I take it I don't have the office to myself.'

'No. There are three of you.' She gestured at one of the empty desks. 'That's Bill's.' She faltered. 'I mean, 008. He only got back to the country last week and he's resting.' The final word had been carefully chosen and Bond recognised the euphemism. '0011 sits here,' she went on briskly. 'But he's away. You probably won't run into each other that often, as a matter of fact. That's the way it works in this section.'

She went over to the third desk. Bond noticed a pile of brown folders had been neatly laid out for his attention, some of them bearing the red star that marked them as top secret. He swung the first of them round and opened it. He found himself looking at a black-and-white photograph of a dead man lying spread out on a quay. He knew at once that the image showed his predecessor, that this man had sat behind the desk that was now his. He closed it again without making any comment.

Loelia Ponsonby was standing by the door. 'We were all

26

devastated by the news,' she said. 'There have been reports and "most secrets" coming in all week. I've put them on your desk with the most important ones on the top. You'd better start with them. M is going to want to see you later this morning and you'll need to be fully briefed.'

Bond sat down in the leather-backed swivel chair. Suddenly he wanted to get this initiation over with. 'All right,' he said. 'I'm going to need some coffee. Black, no sugar. I never drink tea, by the way, so please don't offer it.' He briefly scanned the surface of the desk. 'And I'd like an ashtray.'

'Right.' She turned to leave.

'I'll find out who killed him,' Bond added, speaking more softly. She stopped and looked back. 'I'm sure the two of you knew each other well and I'm sorry it had to happen this way . . . my arrival, I mean. I know it won't be easy, taking his place, but I'll do my best.'

'Thank you.' One last glance and Bond saw the invitation in her eyes. She wanted to be friends. He opened the first of the files. She left.

Bond quickly went through the details of the death in the La Joliette basin, part of the main seaport of Marseilles. He examined the photographs: one of the body floating on the surface of the water and one, taken from a wider angle, showing police cars and an ambulance parked in front of a dilapidated wall. He could make out part of a political slogan painted on the brickwork: —ARITÉ AUX MINEURS. There had been an autopsy. Three shots fired at close range into the stomach and chest. Death instantaneous. Body hurled into the water by the velocity of the 9 mm bullets. Bond made a few notes on a separate sheet and added a question mark in a circle. His initials had been added on the cover, at the bottom of a long list that began with 'M' and 'COS'. He placed a neat tick against them, then moved onto the next file.

This one contained a longer, typewritten memorandum. It was titled: 'A new direction in Marseilles-based criminality?' He began to read.

Background

For all the beauty of its beaches and boulevards, the strip of France known as the Riviera remains a cesspit of corruption and crime with the spoils divided between the Corsican syndicates and the Sicilian Mafia. Torture and murder are quite commonplace with gangland violence erupting at any time and running battles often taking place in the street. What is surprising is that the local populace not only accept this *'grand banditisme'* – as it is known – but seem to admire it. For example, a syndicate boss will often be referred to as *'un vrai monsieur'* while straightforward gangsters such as Paul Carbone and François Spirito have created an almost mythical status around themselves.

There is, of course, a historic folk memory of piracy along this coast which, combined with a strong anti-authoritarian streak, is likely to create unlikely heroes. It is also worth noting that many of these criminals worked closely with the Resistance during the war (or so they like to claim). Although there is evidence that the French authorities have managed to rein in some of the excesses of this criminal fraternity, it is unfortunately true that they continue to receive protection from police and government officials who frequent their bars and enjoy their patronage.

Marseilles has been described as the Chicago of France and it is true that much of the traffic in drugs, prostitution, gambling, money laundering, racketeering and extortion begins here. It has, however, spread rapidly along the coast. Note that Riviera criminality is as opportunistic as it is amoral — the Spanish Civil War, for example, saw a huge spike in arms trafficking and it was at this time that Jean-Paul Scipio (see attached) came to prominence.

Narcotics were, until recently, the number one source of income to the criminal underworld, as well as being the greatest threat to the security of the western world.

Again, Marseilles is the point of entry with supplies coming from Turkey and Indochina to be turned into the highest quality No. 4 heroin by skilled Corsican chemists. Unlike the Mafia, Corsican syndicates tend to be small, less hierarchical and family-based. Laboratories are situated both in Marseilles itself and in the suburbs and surrounding villages and may be extremely rudimentary, contained in basements, unused kitchens and garden sheds. They are highly mobile and can be dismantled and moved to a new location in a matter of hours.

At least three men, all wearing gas masks, are required for the processing, and conditions are extremely hazardous. If the morphine mix is heated beyond 230 degrees Fahrenheit, it is likely to explode. Even so, production has continued uninterrupted and until the end of last year gangs were moving an average of 600 pounds (272 kilos) of heroin each month to the United States, meeting the needs of an estimated 60,000 active users.

However, in the past eighteen months officers from the CRS (the Compagnies Républicaines de Sécurité, which has been leading the fight against the Mafia and the syndicates) have alerted security forces to a strange anomaly. There has been a massive drop in the production of heroin at both local and international levels. The immediate effect has been an outbreak of sporadic violence and murder as dealers/users around Marseilles find their supplies exhausted. There have also been many more hospitalisations and deaths as a result of the dilution of what product remains with flour, chalk, talcum powder and powdered milk. This has been replicated on the streets of New York and London.

There is no good reason why the syndicates should have curtailed their most successful business. Certainly, there has been no significant progress made by the CRS, the SDECE or any other government body which would have led them to retrench. Nor have there been any major vendettas or factional wars in recent times. This leads to the conclusion that the current shutdown must be voluntary and there is speculation that the syndicates may have turned their attention to some other, more lucrative, activity.

There is also a real concern that any interruption to the drug flow may destabilise the political situation in both France and the so-called Golden Triangle of Burma, Thailand and Laos. This could have serious implications for intelligence services in both the USA and Great Britain.

Footnote

(*Comment by C.C.*) It is impossible to examine drug trafficking in the south of France without taking into account the involvement of the CIA – a major error of judgement in the view of this author.

It has long been American policy to support warlords in Burma and other areas close to the Chinese border as these tribal armies have been seen as useful allies in the fight against worldwide communism. There is, however, an unfortunate corollary in that there can be no doubt that these same warlords have taken advantage of US largesse to branch into the cultivation and distribution of heroin.

It is to be regretted that the CIA has also decided to lend tacit support to the crime syndicates in the south of France with exactly the same justification. Here the enemy is seen to be the French Communist Party and the prize, control of the French docks. There can be little doubt that the last two dock strikes in Marseilles were broken by the CIA working hand in hand with the Corsican underworld.

This may have helped the Americans to ensure the smooth running of imports/exports in relation to the Marshall Plan but it has also greatly exacerbated the sense of lawlessness in the area. Worse still, it has allowed the flow of drugs to continue with impunity. In 1945, there was a very good chance that heroin addiction in the United States could have been eliminated in its entirety. This is an opportunity that has been missed simply for short-term gain.

Loelia Ponsonby came into the office carrying a cup of coffee and a heavy glass ashtray. She set both of them down on the desk and left without a word. Bond took a sip of the liquid and grimaced. Well, that was one thing that hadn't changed between floors; every department in the building was served the same vile slop. He made a note to bring in a bag of the Jamaican Blue Mountain coffee supplied to him by a shop at the smart end of New Oxford Street. He took out another cigarette and lit it, then turned to the next page.

Jean-Paul Scipio

Currently, Jean-Paul Scipio is one of the most powerful leaders in the Corsican underworld and certainly the most feared. He is often referred to as the 'Peacemaker' although this is a generic term for high-ranking criminals. He is better known as 'Le Boudin', French slang which can be translated as 'the fat man', a common enough nickname although certainly appropriate in his case as his girth is such that he is unable to fit into a standard car and is said to require a specially strengthened chair when he dines in restaurants.

His size is directly attributable to a vendetta that took place in 1915, ten years after his birth. The vendetta is, of course, a way of life throughout Corsica. At the turn of the century around 900 people a year were being murdered, often for the most trivial reasons – and this out of a population of only 100,000. It is believed that Scipio's father, an olive farmer who may have lived in the Alta Rocca district of southern Corsica, fell out with his neighbour over a land dispute and that the entire family was subsequently attacked and a great many of them killed. The ten-year-old Jean-Paul had his throat cut (it was always the practice to kill the sons to prevent them taking revenge for their dead fathers) and it is a miracle that he survived. However, his lymphatic vessels were ruptured and this was responsible for his subsequent weight gain.

Friends of the family smuggled him out of Corsica and he grew up in Paris where he became an early member of the Bande des Trois Canards, a vicious gang of racketeers who worked out of a nightclub on the Rue de la Rochefoucauld. He became well known for the extreme violence of his methods. He is said to carry a weapon only occasionally, preferring to pulverise his enemies using his own weight and body mass.

He moved to Marseilles at the end of the war and soon became a major player in the narcotics business. He now has control of 80 per cent of the drugs entering the port. Although he enjoys an excessively flamboyant lifestyle, with a prodigious appetite for both food and alcohol, he is unmarried and has no interest in women, leading to speculation that he may be homosexual.

Remarkably, Scipio has never learned English or French and conducts all his business in the Corsican dialect of Pumuntincu. As this is spoken in the southern part of the island – the Corse-du-Sud – it would seem to confirm his place of birth. He is accompanied at all times by a translator.

The printed document was attached to a photograph of a man so enormous that he barely fitted into the frame. At first Bond could not quite believe what he was seeing – Jean-Paul Scipio had enough flesh and muscle for two or perhaps even three human beings. He was wearing a dark, three-piece suit – yards of material – with a tie barely visible beneath the fourth of his undulating chins. His eyes were small, prisoners of his face. His hair was black, cut in the style of Napoleon, although it had the ill-fitting awkwardness of a wig. He was holding a champagne flute, the crystal somehow ridiculous in fingers like party balloons.

Bond slid it to one side and opened the third file, this one marked 'Joanne Brochet, aka Sixtine, aka Madame 16'. He smiled at the extended names, then turned his attention to the photograph that was also attached. This was less useful. Madame Brochet or Sixtine or 16 clearly did not like to have her picture taken. She was wearing dark glasses that covered most of her face, an Édith Piaf beret and a dark raincoat. There had been plenty of photographs taken of her before the war but it was impossible to get any real idea of what she looked like now.

Bond began to read and had just reached the last paragraph when the telephone on his desk rang, announcing itself for the first time. He glanced at it for a moment – as if he didn't quite trust the fact that it was actually his. Then he picked it up.

'James?' The voice at the other end belonged to Bill Tanner, M's chief of staff and a man Bond knew well. 'I hope you've settled in OK.'

'I think I'm finding my feet,' Bond replied.

'Glad to hear it.' There was a short pause followed by the words that Bond was hearing for the first time and which he would hear many times again in the years to come. 'I wonder if you'd mind coming up? M would like to have a word.'

4

Meeting with M

Bill Tanner was waiting for Bond outside the lift on the ninth floor. The two men knew each other well. Theirs was a friendship that had begun in the last years of the war with a chance meeting in the Ardennes, but it had been firmly cemented over sole meunière and a first-rate Chablis at Scott's the day after Bond was recruited to the secret service. It was necessary, but not difficult, to ignore their difference in rank. By the time Bond had joined the offices of 'Universal Exports', Tanner was already working as M's chief of staff.

'Congratulations.' That was Tanner's first word as Bond stepped out onto the thick carpeting that might have been purposefully designed to swallow any sound in this part of the building.

'Thank you, Bill. I'm sure you put in a good word for me.'

'Not at all. You were next in line for promotion and I'm only sorry it had to happen the way it did. How was Stockholm?'

'Bloody.'

'Yes. I read your report. M has it too.' Was there a hint of warning in Tanner's voice? 'Anyway, something's come up. You're not going to find it quite as straightforward as Stockholm – or New York for that matter. But it'll give you a chance to spread your wings, so to speak. I'll take you in and maybe you and I can have lunch later on.'

They had been walking down the corridor as they spoke and now Tanner stopped in front of a green door, opened it and went through. Bond hesitated for a moment before he followed, savouring the moment. He had seen M many times, entering and leaving the building. On occasions they had shared a lift and there had been a brief nod, perhaps a comment on the weather. Bond had attended a couple of general briefings in the conference room on the sixth floor. But this was entirely different. He was entering the inner sanctum. He was actually going to sit opposite M, one to one, for the first time.

And what did Bond know of the man who ruled every aspect of the Secret Intelligence Service, reporting only to senior government ministers who would nonetheless defer to him? Certainly not his name, although his initials were said to be MM. He came from a naval background. That much was obvious from his pipe, his general demeanour, the language he used. He was about sixty years old and tended to wear an old-fashioned three-piece suit unless the weather was unseasonably hot. He was terse but never rude. And there wasn't a single person in the building who would not offer him their unswerving loyalty, even to the cost of their own life.

He stepped into a small outer office, not dissimilar to his own. There was a woman sitting at a typewriter but she had paused with her fingers over the keys. Bond knew Miss Moneypenny by sight and by reputation. He often saw her in the canteen, picking at the salad she usually ordered and she was the undisputed leader of the coterie of young women who worked at the most senior level within the service. He was glad she was M's secretary and not his. She was, quite simply, too damned desirable and he wouldn't have wanted that to get in the way of work.

'I'm James Bond,' he said.

'Yes. I know who you are.' She had sounded severe but her eyes were examining him with interest and he wondered how much she knew. Sitting so close to the lion's den, she must hear every growl that emerged and she would have first sight of the top-secret paperwork that crossed her desk. He found himself thinking that she would make fascinating pillow talk – although at the same time he wondered what sort of man would be brave enough to share the pillow. 'I'm sure we'll get to know each other better,' she went on. 'But not now, I'm afraid. M is waiting.'

'Another time, then.'

'You never know.'

'I'll look forward to it.' He made his way towards the double doors on the other side.

'Good luck,' Miss Moneypenny said, quietly, and went back to her work.

'Thank you.' Bond wondered if he was going to need it.

Tanner had already gone into M's office and as Bond followed him a green light came on high above, signalling that they were not to be disturbed.

M was sitting behind his desk with a report in front of him. His pipe had gone out but there was enough smoke in the room to turn the August sunlight, streaming in over Regent's Park, into shafts. He examined the new arrival with grey eyes that missed nothing. As Bond stood there he was immediately struck by M's authority, his quiet confidence. Decisions would be made in this room that might change the world. Lives would be snuffed out without a second thought. Both the Japanese man, Kishida, and Rolf Larsen would have received their death sentences here. And it would all have been done in a very English way – with a pipe and a cup of tea and the scratch of a fountain pen signing off on the dotted line.

'Come in, Bond,' M said. 'Take a seat.'

Tanner was standing to one side. Bond sat down opposite the man who would now control his destiny.

'So, how did Stockholm go?' M asked.

'I'd say it went very smoothly, sir,' Bond replied.

'Well, the Statspolisen are treating it like a burglary, which is exactly what we wanted. I can't say I'm ever comfortable dealing with the Swedes. You don't know where you are. They were supposedly neutral in the war but that didn't stop them supplying the Germans with iron ore. They lent their railway system to the Wehrmacht too, transporting howitzers, tanks, ammunition and all the rest of it through to Finland. On the other hand, they shared their intelligence with us and we were able to use their air bases in '44. Maybe that's what they mean by neutrality. Playing both sides.'

He tapped the report.

'I understand you spoke to this man, Larsen.'

Bond nodded. He had been thoroughly debriefed when he got back and he had described exactly what had happened. 'Yes, sir.'

'He was awake when you entered the room?'

'No, sir. I woke him up.'

'I'm surprised you thought there was any need. What exactly did you say to him?'

'I mentioned the names Bourne and Calder.'

'And why was that?'

'I suppose I wanted an acknowledgement of guilt, sir. I wanted to be absolutely sure that I was killing the right man.'

It was what M had been expecting. When he spoke again, his voice was brusque and there was a flare of anger in his eyes. 'Do you think I'd have sent you to kill the wrong one? If you're going to work in the Double-O Section, Bond, it might help you to have a little more trust in this organisation. Larsen was guilty. There was no doubt of it. He was responsible for the deaths of at least a dozen people and it was my decision to send an executioner. Not a lawyer.'

Bond accepted the rebuke silently. M might have a point but when the moon had risen and the moment had come, it hadn't been him sitting in the bedroom with the knife. He glanced at Tanner, who was looking away uncomfortably.

'Well, you did a good job,' M went on, more pleasant now. 'And you've certainly earned your promotion. My chief of staff speaks extremely highly of you and I have no doubts at all about your capabilities.' He closed the folder. 'Now, I have an assignment for you. It actually connects with the man you've replaced. I want to know what happened to 007 and what exactly is going on in the south of France, particularly with regard to the Corsican syndicates and the supply of heroin. You might say it's good news that they seem to have stopped producing this muck but 007 was clearly onto something – he said as much in his last transmission – and whatever it was, it got him killed.

'And then there's this woman, Joanne Brochet or whatever she calls herself, to investigate too. We're not sure how she fits into the picture but she's clearly no friend of this country, no matter what our man in the Treasury may think.' Here, he threw a baleful glance in Tanner's direction. 'She's dangerous, unprincipled and it may well be that she was directly or indirectly responsible for his death. She must be in France for a reason and we know for a fact that she has been in contact with the syndicates. More than that, our man was investigating her when he was killed. He went to a meeting to get information and he ended up getting three bullets instead. And finally there's the manner of his death. It happened in a public place in daylight hours and he wasn't carrying his weapon.'

'Yes, I thought about that,' Bond agreed. 'It suggests that he was meeting someone he knew well. The bullets were fired at close range.' He paused. 'It could have been a liaison.'

'Exactly.'

'Do we really have no idea what she's doing in the south of France?'

'No,' Tanner said. 'She's taken up with an American businessman, a multimillionaire called Irwin Wolfe. You may have heard of him or his corporation – Wolfe America.'

'They make film,' Bond said.

'That's right. Film – not films. He started out producing orthochromatic negative stock for the film industry and he was one of the first manufacturers to move into colour. Now he's the third biggest supplier after Eastman and Kodak and he's opened a European plant on the Italian border. He's also branched out into luxury travel. He's got a brand-new cruise ship he's about to launch on its maiden voyage to America.'

'Could he be involved in all this?'

'I very much doubt it. Wolfe is something of a national hero. Before the war, he was an isolationist. He spoke out against America getting involved with the fight against the Nazis. Didn't think it was any of their business. But he had two sons who joined the army and he lost them both on Omaha Beach. They were killed within minutes of each other. The Americans go for stories like that. Losing his two boys. Putting his country ahead of his personal convictions. He's been in and out of the White House many times since then. An adviser to Roosevelt and Truman. He's also getting on a bit. He must be well over seventy and there are rumours that he's unwell.'

'Did 007 mention him?'

Tanner shook his head. 'Not a word.'

'I want you to leave at once,' M cut in. 'Miss Moneypenny will arrange the air ticket for you to Nice. That was where 007 was based and that's where I suggest you start.'

'We sent 007 out under a false name,' Tanner said. 'But there doesn't seem to be any point doing the same for you. After all, it clearly didn't do him any good. He called himself Richard Blakeney, working out of University College. He had an apartment, number twelve in the Rue Foncet. The French police have been in there but it might still be a good idea to have a look around.'

'Station F will provide you with everything you need,' M said. 'But I don't want you to contact the SDECE or any other French departments and I haven't told them you're on your way. I don't like to say this about our friends and allies but we can't be certain they're to be trusted and until we know a little more of what's going on, it might be safer for you to act as an independent agent, so to speak.'

'I agree, sir.'

M reached for his pipe, although he didn't light it. 'There is one more thing. You're going to need a number. You'll be working with 008 and 0011. I don't know why, but 009 sprung to mind. What do you think?'

Bond had been getting to his feet but he sat down again. 'If it's all the same to you, sir, I'd like to take over the 007 designation.'

M raised an eyebrow. 'Really? Why?'

'Well, I suppose there are two reasons. The first is that I

knew ————.' Bond named the man who had died. 'I'd go so far as to say we were friends and I'd like to keep his memory alive, flying the flag, so to speak.'

'And the second?'

'I think it sends out a message. You can take one of us down but it changes nothing. We'll come back the same and as strong as ever.'

M exchanged a glance with his chief of staff, then nodded. 'Well, it makes no difference to me. As long as you're not superstitious. Just make sure you take care of yourself. Good luck.'

The following day, James Bond 007 left for France.

5

'Hold it right there. . .'

The sun has always been a little in love with the south of
France. It beats down, making the sea bluer and the palm
trees greener and the beaches more welcoming than they
have any right to be. As Bond walked along the Promenade
des Anglais, curving round the waterfront at Nice, he found
it almost impossible to imagine the scene in the cloud or the
rain. What would happen to the sun-worshippers, stretched
out on the sand or posing in the shallow water to one side of
him? Or what about the smart set, drifting in and out of the
fashion shops, sitting beneath the canopies with their *grands
café crèmes* on the other? This whole city was a playground
and its children had to be kept in the light.

He had arrived that morning and checked into the Hotel
Negresco. The splendour of the building with its pink dome
and extravagant furnishings had amused him – as had the
fact that he now had a budget that could reach out to afford
it. A licence to kill, it seemed, also came with an almost
unlimited licence to spend. He had quickly unpacked and
now, dressed in a dark-blue Sea Island cotton shirt and white
linen slacks, he looked no different from any of the other
tourists making their way down the famous thoroughfare.

Only the .25 Beretta tucked into his back pocket told a
different story. This was the gun that Bond favoured and he

had tailored it exactly to his needs, removing the grip panels and carefully filing off the front sight above the slide. If he'd been asked why he had made these modifications, he would have hesitated before answering. The main reasons were to make the weapon more effective at close range but the truth of the matter was that it was simply the way he liked it. Feeling the weight of it pressing against his hip reminded Bond why he was here and separated him from the crowd. It was strange, this sense of isolation. As if the sun were shining on everyone except him.

He turned off, leaving the great sweep of the sea behind him. The Rue Foncet was a ten-minute walk away, a long narrow street that ran in a straight line from nowhere in particular to somewhere else. The peace and quiet of the seafront was punctured here by two sweating workmen digging up the road with a jackhammer. Not for them the delights of *la belle saison*. Bond went round them and continued past an old-fashioned tailor's and a flower shop. There were fewer people here and almost no traffic.

The flat Bill Tanner had mentioned – rented by a university lecturer who went by the name of Richard Blakeney – was about halfway along and opposite a funeral parlour, which seemed to Bond unpleasantly prophetic. The main entrance to the building was open. Bond walked in and nodded at a grandmotherly concierge sitting in her vestibule, knitting. She smiled toothlessly back. A flight of concrete stairs led upwards. Bond took them to the fifth floor – which was as high as the building went.

There were two flats here, one at each end of a corridor that had seen better times. The paintwork was flaking and there was dust and debris on the marble floor. Bond quickly examined the door of number twelve, which had been

44

secured with a simple lever tumbler lock. He drew a slim, silver tool from his pocket – a curtain pick – and after listening to make sure there was nobody inside, inserted the pick and manipulated it carefully until he heard the tumbler fall.

He opened the door and found himself in a two-bedroom flat with a high ceiling, wooden shutters and wallpaper with a pattern of faded yellow roses. In the front room a well-worn rug covered a small area of otherwise bare floorboards. There was an assortment of furniture that looked as if it had come from or should be on its way to a flea market. He glanced through a second door and saw a brass bed, unmade, the mattress still holding the shape of the man who had once slept there. There were pictures on the wall – mountains and vineyards, vases of flowers – and old mirrors that threw back reflections speckled with age. Bond could hear a radio playing nearby and the smell of fried onions seeped up from somewhere below. He knew that this was only a temporary address but he wondered why anyone would have chosen to live here. Personally, he preferred the Negresco.

The SDECE had sent back the personal belongings of the dead man but these had amounted to very little: his wallet, silver cufflinks, a Cartier cigarette lighter, a gold-plated Dennison-Omega watch. And yet he had been onto something. He had closed in on an international criminal, the woman who called herself Madame 16, and claimed he had evidence she was in bed with the local underworld. What sort of evidence? Photographs? Letters? And if the French police had already searched the flat and found nothing, why should it be any different for Bond? Never mind . . .

He started in the bedroom. A few clothes hung in the wardrobe: a single-breasted jacket, shirts from Hardy Amies, worsted trousers, three pairs of shoes. They all had a sense of desolation, the knowledge that they would never again be worn by their owner. Bond tapped the pockets, expecting to find them empty. They were. Then he examined the back of the wardrobe, but it was solid wood with no concealed panels. He went into the living room and searched the cupboards, feeling under the shelves. There was a grandfather clock in one corner of the room, a hideous thing. He opened it and rummaged through the workings. He studied every inch of the floor, searching for a board that might come loose. He removed the porcelain lid from the toilet and the panel from the side of the bath. Thirty minutes later, he was certain that apart from dust, damp and general decay, the rooms had nothing to hide.

What else then? A safety deposit box in a local bank? No. If he'd got something, he'd have wanted to keep it close.

Bond went back out into the corridor, looking for any fuse boxes, storage cupboards, even a loose strip of skirting board. He wondered about the old lady downstairs. Could she have been persuaded to look after a package for her nice English tenant? If all else failed, he would try her later.

He went back into the room and took out a cigarette, lit it, then walked over to a glass door that reached from floor to ceiling and opened onto a small terrace overlooking the street. A motorbike had just pulled in on the other side, an Airone Turismo made by the Italian firm, Moto Guzzi. It was painted a firebox red and Bond ran an approving eye over the gleaming aluminium and nineteen-inch wheels. He could imagine the four-stroke, air-cooled engine propelling the rider at 70 mph along the French coast. That was what he would rather be doing, not shuffling about in the shadows of this house of death.

He glanced down and noticed a dark footprint on the wooden floor in front of him. Someone had stepped into an area of black asphalt or tar and they had left a faint imprint of their shoe. But there was something wrong. It took Bond a moment to work out what it was. The footprint was facing into, not out of the room. If it had been the other way round, there would have been no mystery. You come in from the street. You go over to the window and open it. You leave a mark.

But that wasn't what had happened.

Bond turned the handles, pulled open the glass door and stepped onto the terrace. There was a metal table and two chairs. The floor was covered with a latticed metalwork and there was nothing that could account for the footprint. He looked up at the ornamental balustrade that ran the full length of the building just above his head. He had an idea. There was nobody in the street now and, moving quickly, he climbed onto the table, then pulled himself over the balustrade and onto the roof.

All at once, Bond found himself in what might have been the heart of a maze. The blocks of flats in this part of Nice were divided into irregularly shaped quadrangles with inner courtyards, all of them with roofs made out of terracotta tiles. At the bottom of the street, he could see the two men with the jackhammer and beyond them, a park, the trees placed so regularly that they seemed artificial. In the distance was the sea, resolutely blue. The traffic was as solid as ever, cars, buses, bicycles and horse-drawn carriages tangled together in their slow procession along the coast. Next to the road, the restaurants were jammed, tables spilling out onto the pavements with waiters dancing round.

And what of his immediate surroundings? He was in a

strange landscape of chimneys, skylights, washing lines and jutting dormer windows. In front of him, he noticed a white-washed box-like building, about the size of a garden shed and built in the same, haphazard way. It was fastened with a padlock and Bond examined it with growing interest. Although the paintwork was old and flaking, the padlock was brand new. He turned it over in his hands. The lock was a Yale and too narrow for the curtain pick. What then? Bond took out his Beretta and waited for the jackhammer to start up again. As the noise echoed down the street, he fired once. The lock shattered. Bond opened the door.

The shed was floored with black asphalt. It housed some of the machinery that operated the lights and the lift inside the building. There were some old paint pots, tools left behind by workmen, a single bicycle wheel. Bond rummaged around in the shadows without finding anything, then noticed a shelf high above his head. Standing on tiptoe, he ran his hand along it, at first feeling only dust. But then his searching fingers touched something soft, made of paper. It had been placed well back where it couldn't be seen. He took hold of it and dragged it down: a thick envelope, heavy, unsealed, clean. It hadn't been there long.

Back in the daylight, he tipped out the contents and examined them on the ground in front of him: a gun, a wad of 10,000-franc notes (200,000 francs in total), two passports, one of them in the name of Richard Blakeney, an invoice of some sort, printed on a sheet of thin paper, a postcard with a view of the sea and several photographs. Bond glanced through them and knew at once that he had hit the jackpot. Pleased with himself, he slid them back into the envelope. The street was still empty, the bike parked opposite. He swung himself down and went back in through the open door.

He had taken two steps into the room when he felt something cold and unarguably lethal being pressed against his neck, and a voice said, 'Hold it right there.'

Bond froze. Out of the corner of his eye he could see a man wearing a leather motorbike jacket, one arm outstretched, holding a gun, square and silver with a parkerised finish. Inwardly, he cursed himself. He had seen the bike draw up opposite the building but it had never occurred to him that the rider might actually be on his way here.

'I'll have that, if you don't mind,' the man said. He had a gravelly voice and an American drawl.

Bond was holding the envelope that he had found in his right hand. 'And what if I do mind?' he asked pleasantly.

'Just hand it over.'

'Sure.' Bond turned quite naturally, as if passing the envelope across, but he continued the movement, suddenly accelerating, slamming the package into the man's gun hand and at the same time ducking low. The gun blasted out its load but its aim had gone wild, the bullet veering across to the other side of the room, smashing into the face of the grandfather clock. He instantly followed through, slicing upwards, driving his knuckles into the man's throat. It was a sledgehammer punch that almost lifted him off his feet, hurling him into the wall. For a moment he stood there, crowned by yellow roses. Then he slumped to the ground.

Bond stayed where he was, still holding the envelope. He heard the unmistakable sound of a death rattle – but it wasn't the man who had attacked him. It was the internal workings of the grandfather clock. Well, that was one good thing to have come out of the encounter. Bond took the gun – an M1911 Colt Service Ace, much liked by the US government. He emptied it and laid it on a table, then quickly searched the unconscious man. He found coins, keys, a packet of wild cherry chewing gum and an ID card supplied by 2430 East Street in Washington that identified Reade Griffith as a member of the Central Intelligence Agency, helpfully adding that he was six feet tall, weighed 170 pounds, had blue eyes and brown hair. Bond would have added that he was clean-shaven, built like a quarterback and kept himself in shape.

The agent's eyes flickered open. 'That hurt!' he said.

'You shouldn't have pulled a gun on me,' Bond said mildly.

'I'll remember that next time. I don't suppose you could get me a glass of water? My larynx seems to have been crushed.'

'Sure.' Bond went over to the sink and filled a glass. He handed it to the agent.

'You've seen my ID.' Bond had left it next to the gun. 'Did you know it's a felony to assault an agent of the CIA when he's in pursuance of his duty?'

'And it's actually a capital offence to point a gun at a member of the British secret service when he's in pursuance of his.'

'The British secret service? I sort of guessed that when I heard the accent.' Griffith had gulped down some of the water. He got unsteadily to his feet and held out a hand. 'Reade Griffith,' he said.

'James Bond.'

'Nice to meet you, James Bond. And I sincerely apologise for trying to railroad you just now. The trouble with this town is that you never know who you're going to meet – and given what happened to the last occupant of this apartment, I figured it was best to play safe.' Griffith rubbed his throat. The skin had turned a dark mauve. 'When did you get into Nice?'

'This morning.'

'Well, you certainly don't hang around.' He glanced at the envelope. 'Where did you find that?'

'There's a sort of service hut on the roof.'

'That's smart. Smart of him to hide it there, smart of you to find it. So have you finished here then?'

'I would say so. Yes.'

'Then what say the two of us head out of here and get ourselves a drink?'

Bond smiled and handed the CIA man back his gun.

Ten minutes later, they were outside a bar with parasols, wrought-iron tables and haughty-looking waiters in white aprons; the sort of place that could only exist in the south of France. Griffith had made a telephone call before he had sat down, running a background check on Bond while Bond ordered the drinks: a Campari for himself and, for Griffith, a cold beer.

'OK. You and me may have got off on the wrong footing, but it looks as if we're on the same side,' Griffith said. 'Welcome to the south of France. I guess they've sent you to find out what happened to your friend.'

'Did you know him?' Bond asked.

He took out his cigarettes and offered one to Griffith, who shook his head. 'I met him a few times. He was pretending to be some sort of writer but I soon found out who he was and why he was out here . . . the same reason as me, as a matter of fact. It would have turned out better if the two of us had worked together but he preferred to play things solo. Worse luck for him.'

'So what are you doing here?'

'Broadly speaking, my job is to keep an eye on things. I'm sure I don't need to tell you how important the French ports are to our interests – the Marshall Plan and all the rest of it. They're our gateway to Europe and we need to make sure everything is running smoothly. Something bad happens here, it hurts us back home. You can think of me as an American outpost, James, fighting the good fight in my own little way.'

'How long have you been here?'

'About eighteen months. I joined the CIA after the war. Actually, I didn't join them. They came for me. I was with the Marine Corps . . . Tarawa, Saipan, Iwo Jima, working in intelligence. I spoke Japanese and a bit of French. I seem to pick up languages from the girls I've dated. When the war finished, I went back to Harvard to study law but they had other ideas. There was a knock on the door and the next thing I knew, I found myself over here in the Côte d'Azur. Nice place, by the way, if you look out for yourself.'

Bond remembered the report he had read and particularly the comment (by 'C.C.') that the CIA had supported the crime syndicates. 'Looking out for yourself. Does that involve cooperating with Corsican gangsters?'

Griffith laughed. 'That was official policy two years ago but we soon realised it didn't work. These people are animals. Monday they're your best friend. Tuesday they don't trust you. Wednesday, they shoot your head off and no regrets. That's how it goes. In a way, I wish I could get closer to them because right now I've got no idea what they're up to. What I do know is that the supply of heroin seems to have fizzled out and that doesn't make any sense at all. I mean, for the last twenty years that's been their number-one source of income. I've been trying to figure out what's going on around here and when your guy turned up dead, I guessed he must have stumbled onto something. That's why I went round to his place. I wasn't expecting to find anyone there and when you turned up, I automatically assumed you must be up to no good.'

It was a pattern that Bond recognised and which he would have found amusing if it wasn't so dangerous. Two intelligence agencies, operating from different sides of the world, had come to blows in a dingy Riviera flat. That was the trouble with the secret services. They didn't even trust their own allies.

'That was your bike?' he asked. 'The Turismo?'

'Sure,' Griffith said. 'It wasn't easy getting the office to agree to that one but I told them the traffic here stinks. Anyway, I love it. Back home, I drive a Pontiac.' He sipped his beer then set the glass down. 'So in the spirit of transatlantic cooperation, are you going to show me what's in that package?'

The envelope was on the table between them. Bond had barely glanced at the contents and still wasn't sure that he wanted to share them. At the same time, he had taken a liking to Reade Griffith. The CIA man had been outmanoeuvred and he had been badly hurt, but he had taken both with humour and good grace. It was an unusual start to a friendship but Bond felt he had discovered a kindred spirit. He took out the photographs first and laid them down flat.

They showed three people, a woman and two men, meeting over a bottle of wine. They were close together on the crowded terrace of a bar with the old port of Marseilles behind them and, in the distance, a church high up on a hill. Bond recognised the basilica of Notre-Dame de la Garde, which had come through the war unharmed. The name of the bar was printed on the canopy: LA CARAVELLE.

Griffith glanced at the photograph and whistled. 'Well,

you're definitely onto something with this. That's Jean-Paul Scipio. He's not easy to miss. The man with him is his translator.'

The Corsican gangster was instantly recognisable. He was so fat that his shoulders and his head were actually some distance from the table and he would have to reach an almost impossible distance to pick up his glass. He was wearing a three-piece white linen suit, each piece the size of a small sail, and smoking a cigarette. His wig looked completely incongruous, only drawing attention to the fact that its wearer had no hair of his own. The translator, sitting next to him, had made no such effort. He was completely bald, his head a polished dome, and was dressed in a dark suit with round spectacles. The woman facing them was leaning back, a glass of wine in her hand.

Bond examined the long dark hair, the slim body, the folded legs. It was hard to match this photograph with the one he had seen in London, although he was almost certain they showed the same person. 'Sixtine,' he said.

'That's her all right.'

'You've met her?'

'No, I can't say I've had the pleasure, but I've seen the files and I can tell you – she's a piece of work! Last time I looked, she was number three on the CIA Most Wanted List, although we don't arrest her because it's almost impossible to pin anything on her personally. She's too smart for that. She's a go-between, a buyer and a seller, but she always manages to keep her hands clean. At the same time I could tell you a dozen people who've lost everything thanks to her.'

He paused for a moment, then went on.

'You ever hear of Ralph Izzard? A Democratic member of the House of Representatives who was also a member of the

Committee on Military Affairs? He resigned last year after he leaked information about our latest subs that somehow ended up with the Soviets. Or "Big" Bob Harling? He played basketball for the City College of New York until he got caught up in a point-shaving scandal to benefit gamblers in the Mafia. Now he's in jail. Maybe he'll share a cell with Conrad O'Brien, who walked out of his office at IBM one lunchtime, taking with him the top-secret designs for their latest vacuum tube technology. What did all of them have in common? They were clients of Madame 16 and thought maybe she fancied them when in fact she was sucking them dry! And let me tell you, James, that's just the first three who come to mind. There are plenty of others.'

Griffith spun the photograph round. 'So if this little tête-à-tête in a Marseilles café is anything to go by, it looks pretty certain that Madame 16 is in business with the drug syndicates. That's interesting. I wouldn't have said it was quite her style but she goes where the money goes and Scipio's certainly got big pockets. Just look at the size of his suit! What else have you got?'

There were another half-dozen photographs taken at La Caravelle. This sequence showed Sixtine finishing her drink and leaving. Scipio and his translator had stayed behind, ordering a second bottle of wine and several plates of food. The translator didn't eat.

Bond went back to the envelope and drew out the invoice he had noticed earlier. The top of the page was printed with the letterhead and the name of a company – FERRIX CHIMIQUES – with an address in Marseilles. In the right-hand corner, also printed, was the word 'INVOICE' and a number: 82032150. This was the third, or even the fourth carbon copy, stolen perhaps from the bottom of a pile.

The typewriter keys had barely made it through and although Bond could make out a few letters, the rest of it was illegible.

'Ferrix Chimiques,' Bond said. 'Do you know them?'

Griffith shook his head. 'Never heard of them. Chimiques is the French for chemicals and it looks like someone paid quite a lot of cash for whatever it was they bought.' He pointed to the typewritten figure at the bottom of the page. 'There are at least five zeroes. That's 100,000 francs.'

'Presumably they'll have kept the original. We need to pay them a visit. But let's go in quietly.' Bond picked up the invoice and folded it carefully. 'There must be a reason why this was kept hidden.'

'Sure. I'll check them out with my people. See what I can find.'

Finally, Bond took out the postcard. On the front, there was a view of the French coast, possibly Cannes. He turned it over. There was a telephone number on the back and a name: Monique. He showed it to Griffith, who shrugged. 'Why don't you give it a try?' he said.

Bond went into the bar and called the number. A minute later he came back to the table. 'No reply.'

'So what are you going to do next?'

'I don't know. I suppose, all things considered, it might be time to have a word with Sixtine.'

Griffith finished his drink and called for the bill. 'If you like living dangerously, that's probably a good idea. *Cherchez la femme*, as the French say.'

'Any idea where I might find her?'

'Yeah. Sure. You need to head down to the casino at Monte Carlo. She's there most nights, usually on her own. She plays a few hands of blackjack. Then she disappears.'

'Monte Carlo?' Bond couldn't help smiling. He had been there less than a year ago. But for him, the casino would now be a pile of rubble. 'I'll look in tonight.'

'I hope you don't mind if I don't join you.' Griffith touched the side of his neck. 'I might turn in early. I seem to have a sore throat.'

'Let's hope it's not catching,' Bond said.

6

Madame 16

Bond had never been particularly comfortable at the casino of Monte Carlo, even if it was one of the most famous in the world. Of course, it had its own song, 'The Man who Broke the Bank at Monte Carlo', which had become an anthem for all gamblers. There had been the legendary run of luck in 1913 when the colour black had come up twenty-six times in a row at the roulette table. Somewhere in the building was a room still known as 'the morgue', where the bodies of unlucky gamblers had once been stored after they had gone bust and shot themselves at the table. All of this added to its reputation for romance and excitement.

The building continued to dazzle visitors with its old-fashioned opulence, but the architecture put Bond more in mind of a large railway station. And where was the romance? It seemed to him that the wealthiest players – the Italians, the Greeks and the South Americans – were absolutely grim-faced as they took their places at the green baize battlefield, setting their sights only on the business of amassing tax-free capital gains. And there was something unashamedly vulgar about the decor that surrounded them . . . the crimson carpets, the over-theatrical curtains, the inevitable chandeliers. The naiads, painted on the ceiling of the *salon vert*, were actually smoking cigars. It was a small detail but a telling one. For Bond, the casinos at Beaulieu and Le Touquet were less ostentatious and more welcoming. He was comfortable there. At Monte Carlo, he always felt as if he were auditioning for a part in a play he would never actually want to see.

But even as he climbed the steps that led to the grand entrance, dressed now in dinner jacket and black tie, he felt the familiar stirrings of warmth and excitement known to every gambler in the world, the sense that this night would be his night and that even if the casino had carefully stacked the odds against them, he – with lady luck at his side – would bulldoze his way through to victory. And then there was that business to remember from a year ago: the Russian captain and the devastation that might well have followed if Bond hadn't been on the scene. It amused him to reflect that there was still a building for him to walk into.

He didn't intend to take part in any serious gaming tonight but it was against his nature to come here only as a spectator. The moment he arrived, he changed the 200,000 francs he had found at the Rue Foncet into plaques of 50,000. He had no qualms about playing with the funds of a dead man. On the contrary, this would be his memorial to an old friend. If he lost, they would have lost together. If he won, he would donate the winnings to one of the service's favourite charities . . . the British Red Cross perhaps. As he took his place at the roulette table, he breathed in the soft whispers of the room, the murmurs of the crowd, the flutter of turning cards, the rattle of chips as they were swept off the baize, the muttered commands from the croupiers. *'Finale quatre par cinq Louis.' 'A cheval!' 'Carré!'* Bond loved the language of the casino, uttered with all the solemnity and authority of a high priest addressing his congregation, but with more power to change lives.

He reached out and, knowing what he wanted, the *chef de*

partie handed him the card showing the run of the ball since the last session had started. He knew that it gave no indication at all as to what might happen next. The wheel made up its own mind with every spin. It had no interest in the bets, the players, the deserving and the desperate. But there was a habit that Bond had developed over the years that had served him well: he would look for any pattern, any idiosyncrasies in the numbers that had come up and adjust his own game accordingly. He noticed, for example, that zero had shown its ugly face twice in the last hour. It was inconceivable that a casino with the reputation of Monte Carlo would rig the wheel with magnets or any other devices and Bond took comfort from the calculation that the chances of a third appearance might be considered infinitesimal. Two spins later, the zero came up a third time and Bond was down 40,000 francs. He accepted this slap in the face with good grace and ploughed on anyway. After a dozen more *coups*, he had exactly doubled his original stake and left the table with a sense of satisfaction and confidence that the rest of the evening would go his way.

Walking slowly, as if undecided about what to do next, he made his way over to the blackjack tables.

Blackjack – *vingt-et-un* in France, pontoon in Australia – is one of the most popular casino games in the world. It is said that no other card game has earned so much money . . . for the casinos. And that was the problem for Bond. Although there were players who had studied it all their lives, he didn't have the patience to work out the complicated strategies that would supposedly shift the odds back in his favour.

He understood the basics: the distribution of two cards, the draw and the settlement, the attempts by up to seven players, one after another, to reach a total as close as possible to twenty-one (without going over), hopefully beating the dealer. He also knew that the casinos deliberately set out to make it as hard as possible to win a great deal of money. The maximum stakes simply weren't high enough and the only answer was to play for bonuses that came from splitting pairs, doubling down or scoring a blackjack which would pay three to two. He preferred the much simpler drama of the roulette wheel, where the ball tumbling into a single pocket might actually make someone a millionaire.

He saw Sixtine almost at once.

She was sitting on the far side of the furthest table with four other players and she had clearly been winning . . . the plaques were piled up in front of her. No. Sitting wasn't the right word. She was poised, her long and slender legs tucked demurely beneath her and one elbow resting on the table with her arm and hand shaped like a swan's neck, as if she were modelling a cigarette advertisement. Her hair was jet black and hung luxuriously, framing a face that was serious and businesslike. She had very straight eyebrows and a mouth so perfectly in proportion with everything else that it might have been the work of a classical artist. Her eyes were dark brown and although they pretended to be relaxed they were in fact focusing intensely on the game to the exclusion of all else. Bond could see that she had a steely determination not to lose and he could imagine her bringing exactly the same single-mindedness to her business dealings. She was wearing Christian Dior – a black shantung dress with a tightly fitting bodice and a full skirt. It was classic haute couture which could have been made for her and, Bond reflected, probably had been. A gold and diamond *collier cravate* with matching earrings completed the picture. She had lipstick but no other make-up. Nor did she need it.

She was about ten years older than him and, for Bond, that made her at least fifteen years too old to be truly desirable . . . yet he had to admit that she had been – and still was – a beautiful woman. The first lines were making them-selves known at the edges of her eyes and the *café au lait* skin around her chin and down the sides of her elegant neck was beginning to soften. But if she had lost the perfection of youth, she had gained the carelessness and confidence of later age. She was an independent, a woman who had no interest in what the world thought of her. Here I am, she seemed to be saying. Whether you want me or not makes no difference to me. I am the one who will decide.

Quickly, Bond examined the other players. They were exactly the sorts of visitor he would have expected in a casino like this, and it struck him how very different they were from Madame 16 and how appalled they would have been had they known the history of the woman they were playing with. Nearest him was a youngish man in his early thirties, perhaps a schoolteacher or an accountant with his neat hair, his thick glasses and his slightly timid manner. For him, playing cards in the south of France would be a huge adventure, although he would be fighting not to go over his personal limit.

Next came a plump, angry-looking businessman who chewed on his gold signet ring while he played. He was angry because he wasn't getting good cards and in life he was used to having his own way. His wife, reluctant, a little bored, sat beside him. She was more interested in his cards than her own, although she would later blame him for the amount of money they had both lost. On her right – between her and Madame 16 – sat a man who reeked of inherited wealth. He was unshaven, with curly hair, and wore a white dinner jacket while everyone around him was in black. When he made his bets, he slid the plaques as if he expected to lose and didn't really care.

There was one seat free but Bond didn't take it. He preferred to observe his target from a distance.

He watched half a dozen hands, noting at once that, in this version of the game, the hole cards were being dealt face up which might be very much to the players' advantage, giving them a greater knowledge of what remained in the deck. Sixtine was a quiet, confident player who won more often than she lost. She ignored everyone else at the table, her eyes fixed on the cards. Was she playing a system? All the clues were there. She was drinking iced water. Most of the professional card players that Bond knew avoided alcohol. She never spoke, oblivious to everyone around her. When she wanted another card, she tapped a finger impatiently, as if waiting to be proved right. She was playing a game of chance but gave every impression of being in control.

It was on the seventh hand that he worked out what was going on.

Sixtine's hole card was a ten, lying underneath her down card which was carefully hiding its face. She lifted a corner and peeked at it, then immediately turned both cards. They were both tens and she had decided to split them, doubling her bet of 15,000 francs. It was a strange move. Bond knew enough about the rules of *vingt-et-un* to know that you never split tens. Why risk a high score of twenty with two scores that have every chance of being weaker? On this occasion, she was behaving like an amateur and, sure enough, the cards punished her for it. The dealer dealt her a seven on one of her tens and a five on the other. Seventeen and fifteen: two mediocre hands had replaced one good one. Bond waited for her to lose.

The dealer was showing a queen. He turned a card. Bond's eyes narrowed. It was a six. With a score of sixteen, the rules forced him to draw again. The next card was another six. Twenty-two! He was bust!

He saw Sixtine smile as if what he had just seen had been nothing more than she had expected. She had known what was going to happen. There had been no doubt of it. But how? Had she somehow managed to smuggle marked cards into the casino? No. That was as impossible as a rigged roulette wheel. Was she in cahoots with the dealer? Again that was unlikely and it would hardly be worth the risk. But she had split the tens quite deliberately, knowing that the dealer would go bust. There had to be another answer and, with a prickle of excitement, Bond realised what it was.

Vingt-et-un is the exact opposite of roulette in that it is the one casino activity where each game does directly inform the next. The roulette ball has no memory but the cards do.

The deck isn't shuffled until all the cards have been used and it is possible for a player to make assumptions based on what has already happened. So, at its simplest, if all four aces have already appeared, there will be no more 'soft' hands – with the aces counting one or eleven – and no blackjacks. Bond had also noticed that the dealer was using a single deck of cards, which would give the more skilful players a slight edge. More and more casinos – particularly in America – were using two or even three decks to swing the odds back in their favour, which was perhaps why Sixtine had chosen to play here.

But it also means that a player with extraordinary powers of concentration might be able to memorise the whole deck. That same player might also be able to calculate exactly how many cards remain simply by scrutinising the thickness of the deck, the number of cards in the dealer's hands. Bond had attempted this trick himself but he had never quite succeeded, always managing to be at least two or three cards out.

Sixtine had perfected this technique. He was quite sure of it. At the same moment, it struck him that she had also chosen her position at the edge of the table quite deliberately. She was the last to receive her hand, allowing her to use all the cards that had so far been dealt to the other players in her own calculations.

When she had split the tens, she had known almost certainly what cards were remaining in the deck. At the same time, she had worked out – instantly – the odds of the dealer busting himself. She had decided to take the gamble and she had won, in the process making herself 30,000 francs. Even so, Bond wondered, what was the point? This was a woman who made a fortune stealing and selling secrets. Compared to the amounts she was earning, the money she was picking up here would be little more than small change.

The dealer came to the end of the deck, shuffled thoroughly and began again. With a certain fascination, Bond watched the next few hands, standing a little to one side of Sixtine and well out of her line of vision. Never once did she speak. Nor did she lift her head. She won a couple of hands. She lost a couple. And all the time, her gaze remained fixed on the deck of cards, remembering everything that was dealt, measuring how many cards remained, always turning over the odds and waiting for the moment to strike.

Bond saw when that moment arrived. The dealer had reached the last ten or eleven cards. Suddenly, there was a flicker of excitement in Sixtine's eyes and before the dealer had time to collect all the cards and raise the deck for the next hand, she nodded slightly. It was a tiny move, almost imperceptible . . . indeed, Bond wouldn't have noticed it if she hadn't been so still and silent up until then.

At once, the other players left the table. None of them had been looking at her. They didn't seem to know her and now all of them acted differently as they retired. The schoolteacher swept his plaques off the table, as if announcing that he was quitting while he was ahead. The plump businessman's wife muttered something to him and with a little sigh and a shrug of his shoulders he slid off his chair and walked away with her. The curly-haired man also decided, quite suddenly, that he needed a drink and, with a slight yawn, sauntered over to the bar.

What was going on? The dealer was as surprised as Bond but since there was now only one player remaining, he had more than enough cards to go ahead. He glanced questioningly at the lady in front of him. She smiled. She was ready for the next hand.

The five players were a syndicate! Bond was sure of it. The dealer might not have noticed but the entire group was working in concert and their departure from the table had been carefully rehearsed. The idea was to leave Sixtine on her own at a specific moment. There could only be one reason why. She knew the values of the remaining cards in the deck and had worked out exactly when it would work to her advantage to go head to head with the dealer. Right now, the odds must be stacked in her favour and she was preparing to make one last maximum bet.

The dealer leaned forward but before he could begin the next deal, Bond had taken three quick steps and placed himself on the empty seat at the far end of the table, opposite Sixtine. He knew that his being there would change all the odds and nullify everything she had calculated and he was amused to see a slight narrowing of her eyes and a darkening of her cheeks as she acknowledged his presence. Bond took out a plaque for 50,000 francs, the maximum bid, and laid it on the green baize. Sixtine glanced at him for a moment with just the hint of a frown. Then she did the same.

The cards were dealt. Bond had the eight of hearts. Sixtine had the seven of clubs. The dealer also had a seven – in spades. Bond's hole card was yet another eight, this one in diamonds. Sweet sixteen! It seemed appropriate. He wasn't at all surprised by so many identical values. Sixtine must have known that there were sevens and eights clustered together at the bottom of the deck and worked out her strategy accordingly. So what would she do in his position? Bond displayed both his cards, splitting them and placing another 50,000 francs on the table. The dealer dealt him two more cards. They weren't good: a nine of clubs and a five. Bond now had seventeen in one hand and thirteen in the other. Should he stand – or try to improve the lesser of the two hands? He glanced at Sixtine. She had deliberately engineered this situation. She knew the values of all the remaining cards. She had worked things out so that she would win. Yes, of course. Bond waved a hand. He was going to stand.

Now it was Sixtine's turn. Whatever she had, it wasn't a pair. She took one last peek at her concealed card and threw another 50,000 plaque onto the table, doubling down. This allowed her just one more card. The dealer turned it. The card was a queen of clubs. Bond knew at once that it was bad news. Scowling, Sixtine turned over her hole card. It was the five of hearts. With the queen and her original seven she now had twenty-two. She was bust.

And what of the dealer? He left his seven of spades lying

on the table and turned over its ugly sister, the eight of spades. This was just about the worst possible combination for him. He had fifteen and according to the rules he had to draw again. He did so. An ace! It still wasn't enough. He drew again, an ignominious knave of clubs, which busted him. Bond had four cards making up two indifferent hands but they had still managed to win him 100,000 francs.

The miniature drama was over. The cards lay there, irrelevant after their moment of glory. Then Sixtine twisted in her seat like a cork being drawn out of a wine bottle and walked away without saying a word. Looking at the wreckage of what she had left behind, Bond could see why she was angry. If he hadn't imposed himself on the game, the distribution of the cards would have been very different. Sixtine would have had the matching pair – the eight of diamonds and the eight of hearts. If she had split, she would have been given the two sevens, giving her a total in each hand of fifteen. Bond had no doubt she would have stood at that point. The dealer would have had the five of hearts as his hole card and the eight of hearts face up. A total of thirteen. He would have been forced to draw and would have received Bond's nine of clubs, busting him.

The 100,000 francs that Bond had won should have been Sixtine's. Scooping up his plaques, he nodded his thanks to the dealer, then followed her out of the room.

7

Russian Roulette

She hadn't ordered yet. Bond found her in the Bar Salle Blanche which, with its palm trees and full-length mirrors, its dazzling turquoise and gold mosaics and chandeliers, took wealth and extravagance to places even they might never have imagined they would go. She was waiting for the barman when Bond walked over.

'I think I owe you a drink,' he said.

She turned and her dark eyes settled on him in a way that he found both challenging and seductive. Briefly she examined him as if she had never seen him before. 'You don't owe me anything,' she said.

'I brought you bad luck.'

'I don't believe in luck.'

'Bad timing, then.'

'That may be true.' She considered. 'I don't see why I should refuse a share of your winnings. What do you propose?'

'A glass of champagne, perhaps? I can recommend the Taittinger Blanc de Blancs Brut '43.'

'I'm not in the mood for champagne.'

'A dry martini then.' She nodded and Bond turned to the barman. 'I'd like two martinis,' he said. 'Three measures of Gordon's, one of vodka, half a measure of Kina Lillet. It needs to be served ice cold with a slice of lemon peel. All right?'

'Of course, monsieur.' The barman smiled and nodded.

'Wait a minute.' Sixtine had stopped him before he'd turned away. 'I'd like mine shaken, not stirred,' she said.

The barman was about to argue but then he fluttered his eyelids. 'Whatever madame desires.'

As he hurried away, Bond turned to her quizzically. 'Does it really make a difference?' he asked.

'Oh yes.' She was quite serious. 'My late husband used to say that if you shake a cocktail, you bruise the alcohol. Also, you melt more of the ice. Stirred not shaken was one of his mantras. He was very specific about things like that.' She drew out a cigarette and allowed Bond to light it. 'Ever since he died, I've made it a point of principle to do everything the opposite of what he told me.' She glanced at the cigarette in her hand. 'He didn't like me smoking, either.'

'When did he die?' Bond asked.

'Not soon enough.' She picked up her handbag and went over to a table. Slightly bemused, Bond followed her. Even in this short encounter, he had decided that she was not like any woman he had ever met. For one thing, she was impossible to read. She didn't seem to care if he stayed or went.

He sat down next to her. 'Do you often play here?' he asked.

'I prefer the casino at Estoril, in Portugal. It's more majestic. And I play at Crockford's when I'm in London.'

'Always on your own?'

'What makes you think I'm on my own?'

Was this a tacit admission of the syndicate that had been playing alongside her? Bond wondered where the three men and the woman had gone. Were they watching her now?

And where had she found them in the first place? 'You knew every card in the deck,' he said.

'No. But the more cards that have been discarded, the easier it is to predict the odds. That's why I enjoy *vingt-et-un*. I saw you playing roulette earlier. That seems to me to be a complete waste of time. Why should you pursue any activity over which you have no control?'

'Why gamble at all, then?' Bond asked.

'My husband was a gambler. He lost everything. I've made it my personal crusade to take a little back.'

The drinks arrived at their table and with them a short, bald man in black tie, bristling with excitement. With a sinking heart, Bond recognised Émile Tournier, the general manager of the casino. The two of them had met before and the smaller man could not contain his delight. 'Monsieur Bond! What a pleasure to see you again!' he exclaimed in heavily accented English. 'You should have informed us that you were coming. You will please accept these drinks on the house. And if you and madame would care to have dinner, the restaurant is open to you and there is no question of a bill.'

'Thank you.' Bond gave him a thin smile. In other circumstances, the very mention of his name might have been a death sentence. As it was, the intrusion was annoying enough.

'It is my pleasure. It is the pleasure of the Casino of Monte Carlo. When I think what might have happened if it had not been for you. *Formidable!* Please let me know if there is anything that I can do for you and I wish you both a most pleasant evening.'

Bowing, he backed away. Bond and Sixtine were left with the drinks. 'So now you know my name,' Bond said.

'Oh – I knew it already,' Sixtine replied with a shrug of

indifference. 'You are James Bond of the secret service. You were recently elevated to the Double-O Section, which means you have a licence to kill. It makes me wonder who in this building has made themselves your target. Me, perhaps? I hope not. I enjoy my life and I don't think I've done anything recently that would put me on your assassination list.'

So she had known about him all along. How was that possible? There were only a handful of people who knew about the Double-O Section, let alone his promotion to it. Bond was impressed. Sixtine had to be incredibly well informed. Her connections might stretch as far as the offices in Regent's Park. He would remember to tell Bill Tanner that their security procedures needed a thorough overhaul once he got back.

'In that case, you must know why I'm here,' he said.

'No. Are you going to tell me?' She was very direct, looking straight into his eyes as if she could read what lay behind them. Her English was perfect, although Bond had picked up the faintest traces of a French accent, which lent it an added sophistication.

He picked up his glass. The liquid was slightly cloudy, a result of the treatment it had received, but when he sipped it he could discern no difference in the taste. 'A friend of mine was killed,' he said. 'You might have known him as Richard Blakeney.'

'I didn't know him at all.' She sounded bored. 'Was it an accident?'

'He was shot three times at close range.'

'Then he was careless.'

'You say you didn't know him but he certainly knew you.'

'A lot of people claim to know me.' She searched for an ashtray. Bond slid it towards her. 'I never met Richard Blakeney or anyone else from British intelligence,' she went on. 'I assume he was one of yours? How are things in Regent's Park, by the way? It's been quite a while since I had any dealings with your people. It's a shame, really. You're so much more polite than SMERSH.'

'I'd be interested to know what you're doing here in the south of France.'

'I'm sure you would. But I can't imagine why you'd think I'd have any interest in telling you.'

Bond smiled. 'Can I at least ask if it's business or pleasure?'

'My business *is* my pleasure. If it wasn't, I wouldn't continue.' Her eyes levelled on his. 'Do you take pleasure in killing people?'

Bond was completely thrown by the question. He didn't even know why she had asked it. He ignored her. 'Why did you meet Jean-Paul Scipio?'

She shook her head. 'That's not how it works, James. You know who I am. You know how I make my living. Any information that I have is for sale or for exchange. Nothing is free. I'm interested to know what it feels like to be a young man with so much power. Who else can choose between life and death with no fear of retaliation? Only a secret agent or a psychopath.'

It was her use of his first name that struck him. She was speaking to him as if, in some way, she already owned him.

'I certainly don't feel like a psychopath,' he said. 'And I have less power than you think. I merely do what I'm told. As to the rest of your question, I don't need to answer it. We've both been through a war. There are heroes and there are villains. You just have to decide which side you're on and you go where that takes you.'

It was enough – for the moment. 'I have no interest at all

in Jean-Paul Scipio,' she said. 'He's a drug dealer. His business and mine have nothing in common.' She shrugged. 'Why would I want to meet him?'

'That's what I'm asking.' Bond took one of the photographs out of his pocket and laid it on the table. The dark eyes glanced down briefly then flickered away. 'This was taken at La Caravelle bar in Marseilles,' he said. 'Why do we have to play games with each other? You might find it easier to tell me the truth.'

'I didn't say I hadn't met him. I said I wouldn't want to – and that's absolutely true. For a start, he's repulsively fat. He has no manners.'

'When was this taken?'

'How many people have you killed?'

Bond hesitated. 'Two.'

'In France?'

'One in New York. One in Sweden.'

'I was at La Caravelle just over a week ago. It was a Tuesday, I think. Scipio invited me and it seemed sensible to accept.'

'What did he want?'

'My turn, James. How did you know I would be here this evening?'

'I didn't know. But I heard you came here sometimes and I hoped to meet you.'

She looked at him coldly. 'You could have waited until I'd finished the game and introduced yourself then.'

'On the contrary, I enjoyed playing cards with you. In fact, watching you was an experience in itself. I imagine it must help a great deal if you surround yourself with friends.'

She didn't deny the accusation. 'What did that man mean

just now? The little man with the moustache? What was it that would have happened if it wasn't for you?'

Bond made a gesture with one hand. 'It was nothing.'

'Why don't you let me be the judge of that?' Now it was her turn to smile. 'It seems to me that we may have common interests. You're in the south of France because you want to know what Scipio is doing. And what Scipio is doing might just possibly make a difference to the reason I'm here too. Right now I could stand up and walk out of here and you might never see me again. Or we could keep talking and see where that takes us. Of course, if you find my company boring . . .'

She was sitting, more relaxed, her elbow resting on the back of the banquette. Bond liked the way she looked – her bare arms, the curve of her neck and the glittering gold choker with its single diamond nestling in the cavern of her throat. The black silk seemed to flow around her hips and breasts. She was wearing classic stilettos, black satin decorated with rhinestones. He felt disconcerted. Somehow, from the moment they'd started speaking, she'd had the upper hand. He decided to tell her what she wanted to know. Why not? She already knew who he was. There was no way she could use the information. And it might be worth winning her trust.

'I don't find you at all boring,' Bond said. 'On the contrary, I was simply thinking that the story wouldn't be of any interest to you. But if you want to hear it, let me order a couple more cocktails . . . shaken, not stirred. It may take a while.'

He signalled to the waiter, then began.

'It happened last year and concerns a ship, a Soviet cruiser called the *Aleksandr Kolchak*, making a propaganda trip, showing the flag around the Mediterranean. Its first port of call was here in Monte Carlo and I was sent down to take a closer look.'

'A look? Is that all?'

Bond lit a cigarette for himself. 'Well, actually we'd been trying to intercept the signals it was sending back to Kronstadt, but we hadn't been successful because we didn't know what wave bands it was using and we didn't have the schedules. So far we'd been unable to pick up any transmissions and I was here to see if there was any way round that.

'It soon became clear that there wasn't very much I could do. The *Aleksandr Kolchak* was moored about half a mile out. It was a Chapayev-class cruiser, a 600-footer with double shaft-geared steam turbines and the usual range of guns. It was sitting there decked out with flags and it had aroused quite a bit of interest and favourable comments in the town. It looked gay enough. The Soviet sailors had also made a good impression . . . they were all excellently behaved.

'The trouble was, of course, that no visitors were allowed anywhere near and even using scuba in the middle of the night seemed like a waste of time. I nosed around a bit without much success and tried to speak to some of the crew, but they'd been warned off talking to anyone. I was beginning to think I was in trouble but then I had a stroke of luck. One evening I happened to see a fifty-year-old man, grey-haired, obviously Russian, coming into the casino quite reluctantly with a rather attractive French tart. It was clear straight away that she was having to cajole him to go with her. And the thing is, I knew at once who he was – none other than Captain Nikolai Stolypin, the man in charge of the *Kolchak*.

'I followed them in. Of course, the captain was completely bowled over by the casino. I'm sure he'd never seen anything like it in Moscow or Odessa or wherever he came from. He'd soon cracked open his first bottle of champagne and after a couple of glasses, when he was feeling more relaxed, the girl led him over to the roulette table and showed him how it worked. He took to it like a duck to water, playing red or black at first but soon trying out more interesting combinations. Russians are all gamblers at heart and it wasn't long before Stolypin was placing bets with the best of them. He was winning, too . . . getting more and more excited, ordering more champagne, having a wonderful time. In fact everything went terrifically until, inevitably, it didn't. Quite suddenly he began to lose. He'd managed to stack up a good pile of plaques but over the next few hours I saw them dwindle and finally disappear. He was bust. There was no doubt of it. At the same time, I knew it wouldn't stop him coming back.'

'You're right about the Russians. They're like children, really. They have no self-control. It comes from always being told what to do.'

'You've had many dealings with them?'

'Don't change the subject. I want to hear more.' Sixtine was clearly absorbed by the story. She could see it all: the foreigner, out of his depth, drawn into a world he could never completely understand, the heat of the moment, the flowing champagne.

The second drinks arrived. Bond stayed silent until the waiter had gone.

'Stolypin came back the next night,' he continued. 'And the night after that. I made sure I was there for the whole of it. The *Kolchak* was due to leave in a week and he seemed determined to make the most of his time. Somehow it didn't surprise me that he continued to lose. That's often the way it goes with roulette. It's almost as if the wheel can scent weakness and actually takes pleasure in spinning against you. Anyway, every night he'd play until his pockets were empty, but the following evening he'd still come in for more. I didn't see the girl again. He no longer had any interest in her. By the end of the week he was obviously a desperate man, his eyes fixed on the wheel, gambling fiercely and even insanely. The other players were watching him with bated breath. I'd say they were rather frightened of him.

'The last time, he played until five o'clock in the morning. I noticed that he'd been looking at his watch from time to time and exactly on the hour he hurled his chair back and got up. I knew this was the critical moment. All his money was gone. He called for the manager – that was the man you saw just now – and the two of them went into his office with an anxious group of casino officials. As it happened, I'd already met Monsieur Tournier, and he had an idea that I was a policeman of some sort. He let me tag along, which was how I became a witness of what happened next.

'The Russian made an impassioned speech in pretty execrable French. He was sweating profusely and there was no doubt he was in a bad way. He said that he had lost all his own money. Worse than that, he'd raided the cabin of the ship's paymaster and stolen more cash from the safe. The bottom line was that he was down 1 million francs. And then he announced his masterstroke. He was ruined, he said, but in revenge he was going to destroy the casino.

'Stolypin pointed out of the window. It was all very theatrical. "I gave orders that if I was not back on board at a quarter past five, my cruiser's main armament was to be trained on this casino," he exclaimed. "I have ordered my gun crews to fire at six o'clock whether you return the money to me or not. I shall die but I shall have the satisfaction of knowing that this monstrous, capitalist enterprise will have been razed to the earth!"

'Well, you can imagine how that went down. Tournier and the other officials rushed over to the window. I followed them and the sight that greeted us in the first light of the morning was pretty dramatic. The *Kolchak* had twelve six-inch B-38 guns mounted in Mark 5 triple turrets and they were slowly swinging round. In about thirty seconds they were all aimed broadside. We watched them being slightly elevated and converged. At the same time, the pennants were being stripped from the masts . . . a nice touch, that. I turned round and looked at Captain Stolypin. There was a wild, dedicated gleam in his eyes. He'd struck what he must have imagined to be a heroic pose, like one of those ghastly monuments to the October Revolution. The streak of madness that is in all Russians had most definitely come to the surface.

'There was a large clock on the wall and it ticked off the minutes while the officials tried to argue with the captain, falling over themselves in their desperation. In the end, Tournier ran to a safe in the wall. He opened it and pulled out several packets of 100,000-franc notes which he threw onto the table. But by now, Stolypin had decided it was all over for him. He sat there stubbornly, furiously shaking his head.

'It was half past five. Only thirty minutes remained until the balloon went up. Finally, the officials remembered that there were still a few people playing in the casino and decided it might be an idea to evacuate them. In the meantime, I had a quiet word with Tournier and persuaded him to leave the room with all the others. He agreed. By now, he was ready to quit the entire building. So off they all went and the two of us were left alone.'

Sixtine sipped her drink, leaving a red crescent moon on the side of her glass. There was the rattle of a ball, silence and then a cry of triumph accompanied by a smattering of applause from the salon next door.

'Stolypin spoke better English than French,' Bond continued. 'I had very little time to persuade him so I laid it on pretty thick. The casino would pay him back his money – there it was, right now, in front of him – and no one needed to be any the wiser. If the guns actually opened fire, it might be the start of a world war. His entire crew would be massacred. The captain had to think of his wife and family in Russia and what would become of them. I asked him his wife's name.

'For a moment he stayed silent, then he broke down and burst into tears. "Irma . . ." It was the first word he had spoken since we were alone together. I put an arm round his shoulder and said to him, very quietly: "Irma is waiting for you now. Go home to her. Let's forget about this."

'He nodded and got to his feet, tears streaming down his face. At the same time, he began to scoop up huge wads of cash, stuffing them into his tunic. They obviously meant as much to him as his absent wife. But at the last moment, I grabbed hold of him, pinning down his arm. He looked at me, alarmed. "There is just one other thing," I said. "If I'm going to let you walk out of here, I'm going to need the answer to one question. Give it to me and you will be back on board your ship – with the money – in just a few minutes. You'll be having breakfast with your officers and all will be forgotten and forgiven. Otherwise, the casino will be evacuated. I'll report to London and they'll warn Washington. Whether war comes or not, you will have disgraced the Soviet navy."

'A minute later, Stolypin walked straight out of the room, past the officials standing on the other side of the door, avoiding their eyes, trying as best he could to hold onto what little dignity remained. He didn't look back until he had left the casino.

'And that's why Monsieur Tournier was so kindly disposed to me just now. They all came rushing in and I explained that I'd managed to persuade the captain to change his mind. And it was true. Looking out of the window, we saw Stolypin standing up in a two-masted pinnace, frantically waving to his crew as he shot out from the shore. He reached the ship and at the same time we saw the guns slowly swing round fore and aft again, settling back in their mountings. It was a close thing, mind you. The clock was showing 5.59.'

'That was certainly worth a couple of free martinis,' Sixtine said. She thought back. 'But what was the question that you asked him?'

Bond finished his drink. 'The frequencies and times of transmission of his ship's radio, of course,' he replied. 'That was all I wanted and, to be honest, if he hadn't given it to me, the casino and Captain Stolypin could have gone to blazes.'

Sixtine laughed out loud. It had an extraordinary effect on her features. Suddenly, warmly, she had come to life and Bond seized the moment to press home his advantage. 'You were going to tell me about your business with Scipio,' he said.

'Was I?' She sounded surprised.

'Did he want to talk to you about Ferrix Chimiques?' It was a long shot. But the invoice and the photographs had been in the same envelope. There had to be some connection.

'I don't even know what that is.' Her smile had faded and Bond regretted his direct questions. He knew that she was

81

disappointed in him. 'Scipio wanted me to have a drink with him for the same reason as you. He wanted to know what I was doing here and he tried to intimidate me. He didn't succeed. That's all there is to it.'

Bond didn't know if she was telling the truth. 'All right,' he said. 'But it seems to me that I've told you a great deal more about myself than you've told me about you. Why don't we meet again somewhere a little less formal? There's a restaurant I know in Beaulieu . . .'

She thought for a moment and some of the humour returned to her eyes. 'I'm not sure I'd trust myself alone in a restaurant with a British spy. But there's no reason why we shouldn't see each other again. I'm staying with a friend. His name is Irwin Wolfe.'

'I know who he is,' Bond said.

'He's having a party tomorrow night. He has a villa called Shame Lady above Cap Ferrat. Why don't you come along? I'm sure he'd love to meet you.' She stood up. 'Thank you for the drinks. But as you didn't actually pay for them, you still owe me 100,000 francs.' She looked at him curiously. 'I may find a way to extract it from you.'

'I might enjoy that.'

'I wonder.'

As she walked away, he called after her. 'Shame Lady?'

She turned. 'It grows in the garden. It's a plant.' She paused. 'I hope you weren't thinking it referred to me.'

He watched her disappear into the crowd.

8

Not So Joliette

The basin of La Joliette stretched out, sullen and sweltering in the August heat. There wasn't a breath of wind and the black water beside the jetties had the thick, noxious quality of melting tar. James Bond gazed around him at what should have been Europe's busiest port but the midday sun was beating down on empty quays with piles of sacks, pallets and oil drums left haphazardly, the shacks and walkways abandoned, railway lines glinting uselessly in the sunlight with no sign of any trains. In the distance, a collection of freighters, tankers and luxury cruise ships, some of them shrouded in scaffolding, lay in their berthing stations ignored by the gantries and cranes that rose up around them. Even the seagulls seemed too exhausted and dispirited to fly, hunched on the walls and the telephone wires in morose silence.

'Where is everyone?' Bond asked.

Reade Griffith laughed. 'It's midday, James. You don't separate a French dock worker from his lunch, not unless you want the unions coming down on you like a ton of bricks. They'll be somewhere inside having a three-course meal – and don't forget a decent red wine and a selection of half a dozen of the best cheeses.'

Bond had hired a Citroën Cabriolet-Roadster in Nice, resisting the attempts by the agent to steer him towards the new

Deux Chevaux-Vapeur proudly on display. It was named after its air-cooled front engine but Bond wasn't impressed. 'That's not a real car. It's an oilcan on wheels.' He and the CIA agent had made the three-hour journey together along the coast. During that time, Griffith had brought Bond up to date.

'I've had it checked out and as far as I can see Ferrix Chimiques is completely legit. It imports chemicals from all over the world and supplies a whole load of different industries in France. I've arranged an appointment for us this afternoon with the managing director, a man called Andria Mariani.'

'Andria? That's a Corsican name, isn't it?'

'It might be – although the company is registered here in Marseilles. You're going to be Mr Howard from Universal Export, looking for a European partner. I'm Bill Plover from Polygon Agrochemical Supplies, your international representative.'

'I'm going to have to get into their accounts or wherever they keep their invoices.'

'You got any idea how you're going to do that?'

'I'll find a way.' Bond thought for a moment. 'Before that, I want to take a look at La Joliette . . . where the shooting happened.'

'Yeah. I'd like to see that too.' Griffith glanced over his shoulder as he changed gear. 'I never asked you. How did you get on with Mata Hari?'

'She's certainly an interesting character.'

'Did she tell you anything?'

'We're meeting again tonight.'

Griffith raised an eyebrow. 'You've certainly made an impression, James. But I'd take care if I were you.'

The section of the dock where the body had been pulled out of the water was closed off to the public with red-painted signs reading PRIVÉ and ENTRÉE INTERDITE. These seemed to have been ignored by two people fishing – perhaps a father and son – at the far end of the otherwise empty quay. A young stocky French-African man with suspicious eyes and a weather-beaten face was sitting on a three-legged stool beside a wooden shack that served as a security office with a barrier that rose and fell to let cars in to the dock. He was wearing a uniform that he'd unbuttoned against the heat and there was a walkie-talkie clipped to his belt. He was listening to Mistinguett on an ancient wireless. 'C'est mon gangster, / De lui rien ne m'étonne . . .'

As the Citroën pulled up, he lowered himself off the stool, barely glanced at Griffith, then walked round to examine Bond. 'Vos papiers, monsieur,' he demanded. Bond had his passport with him and flashed it through the window. The man examined it for what seemed like a long time, then returned the document as if it had been of no interest to him in the first place. Satisfied, he lifted the barrier, allowing them to drive through.

'That's strange,' Bond muttered as they continued forward.

'What?'

'He asks to see ID but he doesn't ask us what we're doing here.'

Griffith considered. 'Maybe he doesn't care.'

'Maybe he already knows.'

The man hadn't, however, returned to his stool. Instead he went into the shack, moving now with greater speed and purpose. He snatched up his walkie-talkie and pressed the button to transmit. There was a hiss of static before he was connected but nobody answered.

'It's them,' he said. He spoke French with an Italian accent. 'One of them is the American. The other is James Bond.

They've just driven through.' The man lowered the walkie-talkie and went back to his music. He didn't even know who he'd been talking to. He'd just done what he'd been told.

Meanwhile, the Citroën continued its progress across the empty harbour, driving along a flat, concrete surface that was a road, then a storage yard, then a jetty; it was impossible to say where one ended and the next began. It stopped in front of a low brick wall. Bond and Griffith got out.

'Is this the place?' Griffith asked.

'Yes,' Bond said. 'This is the place.'

He had seen it at once: the graffiti on the wall that had been present in the photograph. Now he could make it out in full. SOLIDARITÉ AUX MINEURS. There was something hopeless about the message, as if it was left over from a battle that had already been lost. The letters, written in red ink, had begun to fade. Even the brickwork was crumbling, hammered into submission by the blazing Marseilles sun. Bond looked around him. The two fishermen – or rather, the fisherman and the boy – were about twenty feet away at the end of the jetty. The boy was wearing a string vest and a cap. He had a face that was blackened with oil and dirt and arms almost as thin as the rod he was holding. As Bond and Griffith walked forward, he turned to look at them. Meanwhile, his father stared straight ahead, his eyes fixed on the unmoving water. He was bearded, dressed in a blue chore jacket and shapeless trousers. They had caught a couple of fish which lay, bright silver with mauve streaks that were turning rapidly grey, in the dust. Bond saw the boy staring but knew there was no chance of their being overheard.

He walked over to the water's edge and looked down.

This was where the dead man had been found. Bond remembered the photographs: the splayed arms, the three bullet holes, the flesh already bloated after its time in the sea. He tried to imagine that last embrace with the dark, unsmiling water. Had his eyes been closed as he hit the surface or had that been his last sight on this earth, the window shattering as he entered oblivion? It was very likely, Bond knew, that he too would die violently. It had to happen: the one mistake, the single moment when he lowered his guard. The thought didn't worry him. It could have happened already, while he was working for the secret service, or a dozen times during the war. He had grown used to the idea and had deliberately chosen to go through life with the same carelessness as the little ivory ball that span around a roulette wheel, blithely ignoring the certainty that it must one day drop into double zero.

There was, of course, a difference. Ever since Bond had been given his new status, the rules had changed. Death was now his business. It was he who span the wheel. He wondered if it somehow made him complicit in what had happened here in the Joliette basin. After all, there was no real difference between him and whoever had pulled the trigger three times, ending the life of the man he had now replaced. He remembered M growling at him at that first meeting. 'It was my decision to send an executioner. Not a lawyer.' That was what he had allowed himself to become.

He found himself thinking again of Larsen in his bed in the Stockholm flat. What would the man have felt as the knife sliced into his neck? There would have been pain, of course, but not so very much of it because true pain only comes with recovery. You have to live beyond an injury to feel it. So what then? It might have been sadness that he would never see his wife and children again, remorse for what he had done during the war or simply anger that this executioner from London had forced his way into a private home bringing with him not justice but murder.

The moment of death. Bond would encounter it one day and learn all its secrets, but now, staring into the water, he saw only the reflection of himself.

'He knew the person who killed him,' he said.

'How can you be sure?'

'He came here for a meeting. There's no other possible reason. There's nothing here.' Bond pointed in the direction of the two distant figures. The boy had turned to the older man and was whispering something in his ear. 'Look around you. If anyone had approached, he'd have seen them. If he'd thought he was in danger, he'd have tried something. At the very least, he'd have turned and run. But he was shot in the chest and at close range. He just stood here and let them do it.'

'You're right, James. But there is one other thing that might have brought him here.' Griffith pointed towards a building on the other side of the water. It was an office, very square and flat with three storeys and three sets of windows identically spaced. Because of the shape of the basin, it would take them ten minutes or more to walk round. Bond saw two large silver letters spelling out 'FC' above the door. The metal had tarnished, making them less visible. It was why he hadn't noticed them before. 'Ferrix Chimiques,' Bond said.

'Exactly. We're right on their doorstep. I don't think that's a coincidence.'

'What time did you say we were coming?'

'Twelve forty.' Griffith looked at his watch. 'We ought to move – unless there's anything else you want to see.'

'No. There's nothing here.'

They walked back to the car and got in.

As they drove away, the fisherman and his son got to their

feet. The two of them were Corsican but the boy's mother had been English. She had run away from her genteel life in Buckinghamshire to work in one of the *caboulots*, or 'hostess bars' in Ajaccio. She was dead now. Aged six, the boy had been struck down by meningitis, which had caused him to go deaf but which had left him with an unusual gift.

He could lip-read in three languages.

Now he repeated everything that Bond had said. The father nodded, patted his son on the head and walked over to a telephone box, set back from the quay. He dialled a number, making sure that he inserted his finger into the correct slot, then pressed in a coin. Like the French-African guard, he had no idea who he was talking to.

'His name is Jems. He is a friend of the Englishman who was killed. There are two of them and they are going to the chemical company, Ferrix.'

There was no word of thanks at the other end but nor had the man expected it. Just silence, then a click. The father hung up, then put his arm around his son. *'Ben battu, Paulu.'* Well done.

'Ti rigraziu o bà.'

They walked off together, leaving the fishing rod and the two dead fish behind.

9

Called to Accounts

'This way please.'

The girl who had come down to the waiting room to collect them was slim and pretty, Bond thought. He liked her shy smile and the way the brightly coloured chambray of her pencil skirt wrapped itself around her, emphasising the curve of her bottom. How old was she? Probably in her late twenties, although her china-blue eyes and straw-coloured hair made her look much younger. He could imagine her waking up in the morning and getting ready for work. She would probably have a two-bedroom flat, which she shared with another girl somewhere on the edge of Marseilles, and she would take it very seriously, the wardrobe, the make-up, the choice of jewellery. But actually it was all play-acting. What she needed was a strong man who would pluck her away from all this and take her to the bright lights of Paris or Amsterdam perhaps. She might pretend to be the meek little secretary. Bond would have liked to have shown her she could be something more.

But that wasn't going to happen today. He followed her through a door and into an office that ran the full length of the building with desks spaced out, like the windows, at precise intervals, the lights uniform and exactly placed, young men and women bent over typewriters and folders. Nobody looked up as they passed, he noticed. Nobody spoke. It may have been a company importing and distributing chemicals, but there was an almost military atmosphere in the place.

They emerged on the other side and took an uncarpeted staircase up to the second floor. Both Bond and Reade Griffith, walking beside him, were wearing suits despite the heat of the day. He hoped that he looked like a middle-ranking executive from a reasonably successful British company. Once before, Bond had hidden behind the facade of Universal Export, a bland, almost meaningless name which managed to be both respectable and ambiguous. There was even a dedicated phone line within the Regent's Park office of the secret service where an efficient young woman would field queries from anyone who called and might offer to put you through to 'Mr Protheroe in sales' – although it was an offer that was rarely taken up.

The girl led them down a corridor and into a wide office where two windows framed an olive-skinned man who was sitting at a desk. To begin with, Bond ignored him, looking over his shoulders and out through the windows to the extensive loading bay beyond. There was a lot of activity. Men in overalls were shifting crates and oil drums, helped by forklift trucks that carried their loads into the open warehouses that surrounded them on three sides. More warehouses stretched out behind. Bond saw printed warning signs which echoed those on the quay. AVERTISSEMENT – PERSONNEL AUTORISÉ SEULEMENT. DANGER! Unlike the docks, there was clearly no stop for lunch with wine and cheeses here.

He turned his attention to the man who had stood up to welcome them. Andria Mariani, the managing director of Ferrix Chimiques, was smiling pleasantly although the dark hair swept back over his forehead, the narrow eyes and aquiline nose had the effect of making him look both distant and disdainful. His grey suit provided an unappealing background for a burgundy tie stamped with a chintzy diamond motif. As he moved forward, there was something oily about his motion. His handshake was weak, unenthusiastic.

'Good morning, Mr Plover. And Mr Howard, I believe. Please, will you be taking a seat. Coffee?' He had a delicate voice that still succeeded in doing violence to the English language. His accent was both French and Italian, somewhere between the two.

Bond and Griffith sat down. 'No thank you, Mr Mariani,' Griffith said.

'That's good then, Monique. You can go, please.'

So the girl's name was Monique! Bond remembered the name he had seen on the back of the postcard at the Rue Foncet. Suddenly everything was coming together and he wished he had examined her more closely, or at least more professionally, when she had greeted them. But she had already disappeared, gliding through the door and closing it behind her.

He forced his attention back onto the man sitting opposite him. 'It's a pleasure to meet you, Mr Mariani,' he said. 'As I'm sure my agent, Mr Plover here, will have informed you, I represent a corporation in London that has recently moved into the field of agronomy. We have acquired extensive farmland in the West Country, Wales and Ireland – mainly fruit and vegetables, some dairy – and we need to buy large quantities of fertiliser and insecticide. I take it these are areas in which you operate.'

'Mr Howard, we operate at every area. Feedstock, fertiliser, medicine, pharmaceutical products.' He announced each word as if he had just found it in the dictionary. 'Whatever you want, we can find it for you.'

'Do you import from America?'

'From China, Korea, India, Vietnam . . . many of our chemical product are from Asia. But also from America. Yes. Sometime.'

'DDT?'

'DDT, sure. But you know, Mr Howard, there are better chemical now. Cheaper and more effective. You hear of toxaphene? Or maybe dieldrin.' He was suddenly suspicious. 'You know these product?'

'Of course,' Bond replied, smoothly. 'Dieldrin is an organic chloride. It's developed in Denver, in America, I believe.' He sighed apologetically. 'And that's the problem, Mr Mariani. Like everyone else in Great Britain, we have to deal with import quotas.' He glanced at Griffith as if seeking his approval. 'It might be very helpful to us, actually, if we were able to disguise or, shall we say, obscure the country of origin.'

Mariani's dark eyes flared. 'Mr Howard. This is a legitimate company. Nothing we do in this company against the regulation. Everything in white and black.'

'My friend wasn't suggesting otherwise,' Griffith cut in. 'Please don't get the wrong idea, Mr Mariani. As a matter of fact, the paperwork is very important to us . . .'

'That's right.' Bond picked up the cue. 'My chairman is actually a stickler for detail.'

'Stickler?'

'He likes everything written down. I'd be interested in looking at your accounts department and your billing systems. I presume that all happens here.'

Mariani didn't appear to have understood everything Bond

had said but he gestured vaguely. 'Accounts on the floor underneath.'

'Do you have many clients in London?'

Bond had changed the subject quickly, as if he weren't actually interested in the layout of the building right now. Griffith took over, going into details about quantities, costs, timings, export licences and the logistics of moving merchandise from Marseilles to different parts of Britain. The conversation was so ordinary – so businesslike – that Bond had to ask himself why he was being so careful. The invoice that he had found in the Rue Foncet was in his jacket pocket. Why didn't he just bring it out and show it to the managing director? Wouldn't Mariani simply tell him what he wanted to know?

And yet Ferrix Chimiques was involved in some way with organised crime in the south of France. The faded copy of the invoice must have been stolen for a reason and the man who had stolen it had been killed just five minutes away from where they were sitting, on the other side of the basin. With his looks and his broken English, Mariani might be nothing more than the small-time business executive he appeared to be, but Bond wasn't going to give him the benefit of the doubt. He had been told where the invoice department could be found. There were other ways to get the information he needed.

They finished. Mariani pressed a button on his telephone, then stood up and shook hands with both men. At the same time, the door opened and a second girl came in to escort them downstairs. Bond was annoyed that it wasn't Monique. Of course, it was a common enough name but he would have been prepared to bet that it was the same Monique who had appeared on the postcard and he had hoped for a chance to speak to her. He wondered if the telephone number he had found connected with the office here. Well, he would have plenty of time to find out later.

He followed Griffith out of the room and back down two flights of stairs, noticing once again the orderliness of all the activity around him. They reached the main entrance with two glass doors holding the sunlight at bay.

Bond stopped suddenly and patted the sides of his jacket. 'How very stupid of me,' he said. 'I've left my spectacles in Mr Mariani's office.'

'I will call up for you,' the woman said. She was about the same age as Monique but more severe, with a studied lack of empathy. This was the first time she had spoken.

'No need. I'll just run back up.'

'We'll wait for you here.' Griffith understood what he was doing. He stepped in front of the girl to prevent her moving and at the same time, before she could protest, Bond hurried back through the office and up the stairs.

He was moving quickly and, although he passed a few people, nobody had the time or the presence of mind to stop him and ask where he was going. He reached the first floor and found himself looking down a long corridor with vinyl flooring, panels of frosted glass windows and about half a dozen blank doorways facing each other on both sides. He noticed a red button – a fire alarm – set into the wall beside him and without a moment's hesitation stabbed out with the heel of his hand. At once, a bell began to jangle hysterically throughout the building. There was a brief, frozen pause. Then, all along the corridor people appeared, streaming out of the doorways and making their way towards him. They did not speak. Nor did they seem particularly concerned. Bond stood there as they brushed past him and down the stairs.

He waited until the corridor was empty, then hurried forward, going in the opposite direction to everyone else.

Nobody seemed to have noticed him and yet the girl downstairs knew that he had gone and might guess what had happened. All too soon someone would realise that it had been a false alarm. Security might be on their way up already. How long did Bond have? A couple of minutes at most.

He passed one empty room, then another. Everywhere he looked, he saw the same furniture, the same equipment – swivelling chairs and plain wooden desks, Remington 'Quiet-Riter' typewriters, anglepoise lamps, wire-framed In and Out trays – all of them statements to the deadening routine of office life. He heard the bang of a drawer and a young man in a white short-sleeved shirt came rushing out carrying a sheaf of papers that he must have thought worth saving from the flames. Bond decided to take a risk and grabbed his arm.

'*Le département des comptes. C'est où?*'

The man pointed vaguely with his elbow, in a hurry to be away. The alarm was still echoing. Bond found the door that had been indicated and went in. He knew at once that he had come to the right place. Three of the walls were lined with filing cabinets – at least sixty of them in battleship grey, each one with three solid drawers. There were two rows of desks stretching from one end to the other but they had all been abandoned with files left open and sheets of paper scattered everywhere. Bond picked one up at random. It had the same shape and format as the carbon copy, with an eight-digit number printed in the right-hand corner. Bond drew the copy out of his pocket and memorised its number. 82032150. All he had to do was find the original.

He tried the nearest drawer. It was locked. Surely the staff hadn't had time to secure the room in the thirty seconds since the alarm had started? He tried another and this one slid open to reveal several hundred documents, bunched together, hanging vertically in cardboard files. Ignoring the written details – what had been ordered, when and how much had been paid – he examined the numbers, relieved to see that they had been filed in numerical order rather than by company name. This batch ran from 00120206 to 00135555. He glanced at the dates and saw that they were four years old. That made sense. The carbon copy belonged to a much more recent transaction.

He hurried across the room and pulled open several more drawers before he found what he wanted. There was a clump of invoices, about seven or eight of them, which had all been drawn up at the same time and which related to a single customer. The company hadn't been named but had the initials 'W.E.' It had purchased a number of different chemicals, including potassium iodine, nitric acid, sodium bisulfate and gelatin. He glanced over his shoulder. He was alone in the room. Quickly, he thumbed through the pages until he found the one he wanted. He pulled it out. The invoice had been issued to W.E. on a date nine weeks before, following the delivery of thirty gallons of a substance called acetic anhydride (all the chemicals, Bond noticed, were listed in English). He folded the sheet and slid it into his pocket. With so many thousands of invoices in the room, it was extremely unlikely that anyone would notice it had gone and it hardly mattered if they did. They could put it down to an administrative error. Nobody would know he had been here.

He slid the drawer shut and at exactly that moment, the bells stopped. The silence, after the hammering of the alarm, was dramatic, and the office, without its workers, felt alien, abandoned. Bond straightened up and turned to see a woman standing in the doorway, staring at him. She could have been the mother of the girl who had taken him back downstairs; a typical French matron with bad skin, her hair tied back in a tight bun, mountainous breasts and even horn-rimmed spectacles with a narrow chain dangling under her chin. She was dressed entirely in black and was looking at him with disgust, as if she were the authoritarian headmistress of a private school and he a boy who had just broken into the tuck shop.

'What are you doing in here?' she asked.

'I was looking for Mr Mariani's office,' Bond said innocently. 'I think I left my reading glasses there.'

'This is not an office. This is the accounts department.'

'I know. I can see that. I was just about to leave.' Bond smiled at her. 'I hope there isn't a fire or something. What was that all about?'

'It was a malfunction. I will show you to the exit.'

'Thank you. We can call up to Mr Mariani from the reception desk. It was very clumsy of me. I can't imagine how I forgot them.'

'Please, will you come with me.'

She led him out of the room. The staff hadn't begun to return yet and the building was quite empty. Bond followed the woman without saying anything more, his eyes fixed on the thick black stockings that covered legs which reminded him of a grand piano.

'Through here,' she said. They had come to a set of double doors.

And that was when three thoughts came to Bond at the same moment. The first was that this was not the way he had come. The woman had led him further into the back of the building, away from the staircase. The second was that he had dismissed her because she was stout and elderly. She couldn't possibly be a threat to him. But although the two of them had never met and he had not spoken a word to her, she had addressed him in English, not French. She knew where he came from, which quite probably meant that she also knew who he was.

They were no longer alone. The third thought arrived too late for Bond to take action. A man had stepped out of a doorway behind him. He heard a footstep on the wooden floor and began to turn just as something flashed down in the corner of his vision. He felt it hit him, hard, on the back of the head, propelling him towards the woman, the black fabric of her jacket and dress stretching out to become an entire world of blackness into which Bond folded himself, leaving consciousness far behind.

10

The Acid Test

When Bond came to, he found himself seated with his mouth gagged and his head slumped forward. His hands were securely tied behind him, not with cord but with some sort of metal wire that was cutting into his flesh. There was no possibility of movement. His fingers were already numb. His ankles were also secured to the legs of the solid, wooden chair on which he had been placed. His head was throbbing and he could taste blood but as far as he could tell, he hadn't been seriously hurt. Whoever had attacked him must have used a leather billy club or perhaps a sap, a weapon still carried by the police in some parts of America. Worse damage had been done to his self-esteem. He had allowed himself to be led into an obvious trap and now he was helpless, tied up and alone.

No. Reade Griffith was still in the compound and would come looking for him eventually. He couldn't have been unconscious for more than a few minutes so the CIA agent had to be somewhere near. The question was, would he arrive soon enough?

Bond hadn't moved or opened his eyes. There might be something to learn, some advantage to be gained if he pretended he was still unconscious. He waited a few more seconds until he was certain that he was alone. Then, slowly, he lifted his head and looked around him.

He must have been taken to one of the warehouses he had seen from the office – somewhere on the edge of the main complex, away from any witnesses. There were shelves on both sides of the room with dozens of glass flagons, cartons and different-shaped packages neatly arranged in long lines. He could not see any doors or windows and assumed that the only way in must be behind him. A row of bare light bulbs dangling overhead threw a dim, yellow light across the concrete floor. Bond tried to find some purchase in the wire but moving his wrists only caused him unnecessary, self-inflicted pain. He examined the products that surrounded him. The bottles had labels that identified the contents only by their chemical formulae: HNO_3, H_2SO_4, Al_2S_3 and so on. It was obvious that this part of the compound wasn't in day-to-day use. The writing on the boxes had faded. Everything was covered in dust.

He heard a loud grinding, the sound of metal against metal and, somewhere out of his field of vision, a door slid open. It was followed by footsteps on concrete. The door slammed shut again with an echoing crash and he looked round to see four men walking towards him, in no hurry, taking their time. They knew he was helpless and that very thought sent a tendril of fear twisting through his stomach. He fought back, reminding himself that he was in one of the world's busiest industrial ports and that this was the middle of the day! There were at least a hundred people working for Ferrix Chimiques and quite a few of them must have seen him being brought here. They were ordinary Frenchmen and women and no matter how scared they were of Mariani or whoever was behind him, they might still talk. It would be an extraordinary man who would rely, absolutely, on their silence.

That man stood in front of him.

Bond recognised Jean-Paul Scipio from the photographs he had seen both in London and in Nice. How could he fail to? Scipio must have been one of the most recognisable men in France. The photograph that Bond had seen didn't do him justice. The actual physicality of the man – the amount of space he occupied – was breathtaking. It seemed incredible that he could move, that somewhere inside this explosion of flesh there was an actual, working skeleton. He was dressed in the same three-piece suit that he had worn at La Caravelle but it now seemed to Bond that the heavily buttoned waistcoat and belt had a secondary purpose: they were holding all the monstrous parts together. He had taken his time as he crossed the warehouse, wheezing with the effort and using a shooting stick to support himself. When he was facing Bond, he unfolded it and sat down, the leather seat vanishing into the soft, obscene curves of his buttocks. He rested his hands on his stomach and Bond saw that he was wearing an assortment of rings, some gold, some silver, some set with precious stones; one on almost every finger. As he perched there with his legs apart he looked for all the world like a cannibal king, perhaps one who had just eaten his entire court.

Bond found himself staring into a face that had a strange, babyish quality. It was utterly hairless apart from two faint commas that were his eyebrows. Scipio was almost certainly bald. At close quarters, the wig looked even less convincing than it had in the pictures, black and shiny, sitting lopsidedly on his skull as if it had been put on in the dark. He had very small, pale blue eyes that were straining to see past the bulging cushions of his cheeks and a pursed, circular mouth with thick lips. As he moved the great football of his head from side to side, Bond noticed a dark mauve line buried inside one of the folds of flesh, stretching all the way round his neck. This must be the scar that he had been left with when his throat was cut at the age of ten.

A second man stood just behind him and again Bond recognised him from the photograph that had been taken at the Caravelle bar. This was Scipio's translator. He was a slender man, also bald but unafraid to show it, with a head that looked as if it had been carved out of white marble and then polished. His face was dominated by eyeglasses that were two glittering round discs held together by wire. His nose was slender, his mouth downturned, as if endlessly expressing disapproval. He was wearing a suit with a narrow tie and highly polished shoes. It was impossible to tell if he was older or younger than Scipio: the age of both men was indeterminate. He was completely expressionless, looking at Bond but hardly seeming to notice him, as if he had trained himself not to become too involved with whatever circumstance was presented to him.

And the other two men? They were dressed in black jackets and jerseys. One had a broken nose, disfiguring a face that had been ugly to begin with. Bond had seen their type before. They purposefully wore the blank faces and bored eyes of hired hands and he suspected that it must have been one of them who had wielded the club. They could hurt him, kill him or simply cut the wires and let him go. It made no difference to them. They would do what they were told. One of them stepped forward and removed the gag from Bond's mouth. Bond breathed in gratefully but did not speak.

'*Bon dopu mezziornu, Mr Bond,*' Scipio said.

'Good afternoon, Mr Bond,' the translator began.

'*Sò quale vo site è perche site qui.*'

'I know who you are and why you are here.'

Bond watched the double act with a certain fascination. Scipio's voice was hoarse and high-pitched, another result perhaps of his childhood injury. It was quite possible that his vocal cords had also been damaged by the knife that had slashed his lymphatic vessels. There was something forced and extravagant about the way he spoke. This was a man who had grown up in a world of vendettas and high drama and he had come to enjoy acting the part, particularly when he had, in every sense, a captive audience.

But it was all to no purpose. The translator was just doing his job and communicated in a way that was bland, matter-of-fact. Scipio might threaten his enemies with torture and death but the translator would relay the words as if they were a weather report. The two spoke at almost exactly the same time, in competition with each other. But whether he intended to or not, the translator was undermining his master. His was the voice of reason. He did not threaten. He simply explained.

'You are James Bond 007 of the British secret service,' the translator continued. His English was perfect but he had to adjust his sentences continually to keep up with the man who was speaking, occasionally backtracking as he struggled to find the right word. 'It was a mistake . . . a great mistake for you to come here to the south of France. A friend of yours also came here and attempted to impose himself on my . . . Mr Scipio's . . . business affairs. He paid the price. Do your employers not understand . . . have they not understood . . . by now that you have no place here? I have no interest in your country. It has never entered my mind even for one second. But that is the arrogance of the British. You are a tiny island with bad weather and bad food also but you still think you rule the world. You will not wake up to the fact that you are becoming irrelevant and were it not for your geographical location and your friendship . . . kinship with Europe, you would be irrelevant already.'

Scipio paused and ran a tongue between his lips. Bond watched the obscene, moist thing run from one side to the other. The translator was staring at him, the glass moons of his spectacles glinting dully in the soft electric light. '*Perchè vanu mandatu qui?*'

'Why did they send you here? Have I not made it clear that I have all . . . that I have total control here in Marseilles – the port, the city, the police, the justice system? It is all mine!' He spread his hands as if to emphasise his point. 'I believe your presence here to be an impertinence. You are playing with the big boys, Mr Bond, and you have not been invited. I am busy. There are many other things I could be doing with my time but it seems that I must send a second message to London, warning them to stay out of my way. And this time I am going to make sure they listen.

'You will be the carrier . . . you will carry that message. I could kill you here . . . right now in one of many ways. I have only to give the order. But sometimes, Mr Bond, there are worse things than death. This is . . . this is what you are about to discover.'

Even speaking was an exertion for Scipio and he stopped to recover his breath. Bond wondered how his heart could possibly cope, constantly straining underneath all that weight, pumping blood down arteries that must no longer be fit for purpose.

He chose that moment to answer back. 'We know who you are, Mr Scipio,' he said. 'We know about your business here in Marseilles but you may be surprised to learn that we aren't interested in you. For all your bluster, you're just a low-level crook. I'm here for other reasons. And I should warn you that anything you do to me will be paid back tenfold. You would be more sensible to let me go and pretend we never met. In fact I would recommend that you run away and hide while you still can, although, looking at the size of you, I would imagine that might not be so easy.

'As for your remarks about my country, you wouldn't be the first psychopath to underestimate us. The last one ended up blowing his brains out in a Berlin bunker. We hanged all his associates. You are a very large man but you are small by comparison. I'd get out now, while you have the chance.'

The translator had been taken by surprise but had quickly begun converting the words into Corsican, expressing them in the same dull monotone so that by the time they arrived in Scipio's ears they had been stripped of their venom and their contempt.

Scipio waited until he had finished, then began again.

'Bravely spoken, Mr Bond. I have respect for you. In my country . . . in my original country, we expect our enemies to be courageous. Courage, as much as hatred, is the fuel of the vendetta. Well, we are about to . . . we will now put all that to the test. I am going to send you back to your masters a different man to the one who is sitting before me now. I am going to teach you a lesson you will not forget. You are a young man and, as I understand it, you have only recently been elevated to the Double-O Section. Perhaps you will consider, after this, that you have chosen the wrong vocation. Carlo, Simone . . . *Appruntà ellu!*'

These last words were spoken not to Bond but to the two men who had been standing silently throughout the exchange. At once they began to move. Automatically, Bond tensed himself, his hands straining at the wires. It was useless. He could only watch helplessly as one of the men went over to the shelves and drew on a pair of thick, rubber gloves. Once they were secure, he reached up and grabbed hold of a heavy glass container, almost barrel-shaped, with a transparent liquid inside. Meanwhile, his colleague had leaned over Bond and pulled his jacket back over his shoulders. Then, reaching out with both hands, he tore Bond's shirt open, exposing his chest and stomach. Bond watched with queasy fascination as the first man walked over to Scipio, carrying the bottle.

'Hydrochloric acid.' Scipio spoke the two words in English and the translator repeated them before they continued in their separate languages. 'It is also known as spirits of salt. One of the wonders of the human body is that we produce much . . . many quantities of hydrochloric acid in our gut even though it has the ability to do us great harm. How much harm, you are about to discover, Mr Bond. I would like, first, to show you . . . to give you a demonstration.'

He nodded and the man with the rubber gloves set the container down and opened it, being careful not to breathe in the fumes. The second man dragged a metal table across the floor, placing it a short distance in front of Bond. Then he went over to the shelves, chose an empty glass vial and carefully positioned it in the middle of the table. Very carefully, controlling the flow, the first man filled it with at least two pints of the liquid from the container. Even from where he was sitting, Bond could smell the chemical and his eyes began to sting. When the vial was full, he screwed the lid back onto the container and carried it away. Bond had a very good idea what was being planned. He could feel his body rebelling as his animal instincts took over, fear feeding his imagination and both tearing through his entire being.

'Show him!' Scipio instructed.

The man with the rubber gloves tilted the vial so that some of the liquid spilled out onto the table. As it came into contact with the silver surface, there was an angry hissing and white smoke rose into the air. The metal bubbled and changed colour, eaten away by the acid. Bond choked. For a moment he was blinded but he could still hear the acid doing its work. Scipio and the translator watched in silence. Finally, the demonstration was over. The top of the table was pitted with holes, the metal contorted into ugly grooves. Some of the acid had dripped through to the floor below and that was burning too. The chemical stink was in Bond's nose and throat. He was not crying but involuntary tears were streaming from his eyes. He tried to block out thoughts of what was to come, but inside he was screaming.

'I am certain you are a man with imagination,' Scipio said. 'You are not going to die today, Mr Bond, but I want you to imagine that you return to London blind and disfigured. Your friends and colleagues will no longer be able to recognise you. You will have no hair. Your lips and nose . . . they will have been eaten away. It will be impossible for you to continue in your current occupation. Indeed, there will be no work for you anywhere in secret intelligence. How can you be secret when you have the appearance of a freak? You will retire and spend the rest of your days in some sort of home although I understand . . . I am told that the pain will never go away. In truth, it makes me sad to do this to you. You are a very handsome man. I admire good looks, especially in the masculine form. But, as I have explained . . . as I have already explained, I must send a message. Remember what I have said. This is my domain and you and your people must learn to stay away.'

Scipio stood up. He folded his shooting stick away.

'Wait!' Bond rasped.

Scipio made no reply. He simply nodded.

The henchman, protected by the rubber gloves, threw the entire contents of the vial into Bond's face.

Bond screamed. He felt the hideous liquid, ice cold with its first touch, splash into his hair, his face, his eyes, his bared shoulders and chest. At the same time, he jerked backwards, overturning the chair and crashing down to the ground. The acid was burning into him, taking away his hair, his skin, the flesh beneath. His chest and his stomach were on fire. Some of the liquid had soaked into his trousers and was already attacking his groin. He was blind. He could feel his eyes shrivelling in their sockets. He was still screaming. He was being consumed, on fire. He was . . .

. . . alone.

Scipio had gone. His men had gone with him. Bond was lying on his back with his arms trapped by his own weight and the bulk of the chair, his legs bent above him. He was covered in the liquid and there was a puddle of it around his shoulders but the pain he was feeling had concentrated itself in the back of his head where it had struck the floor. And nowhere else. He was soaking wet, half out of his mind with the horror of it all, but he wasn't burning. His vision had cleared and once again he could see.

It wasn't hydrochloric acid.

Bond had been through the worst agony he could possibly imagine but he understood now, just as Scipio had told him, it had only been his imagination. At some stage during the presentation, perhaps when he had been overcome by the fumes, they had switched the vial and it was chilled water that had been thrown into his face. The rest of it Bond had inflicted on himself and even now, knowing the truth, he could still feel his system recoiling in shock, his heart beating at twice its normal speed. The sudden trauma might have killed an older man.

It had been a brilliantly conceived lesson in terror and absolute power.

Later, much later, he heard the door grind open a second time and a man come hurrying in. Bond was still lying with his arms pinned behind him, his feet above his head.

'James?' It was Reade Griffith. The CIA man rushed over to him. 'Jesus! What happened to you? I've been looking for you all over this joint. They told me you'd left another way but of course I wasn't buying any of that. What have they done to you? Are you OK?'

'Scipio . . .' To his surprise, Bond was barely able to talk. His breath was catching in his chest. It was as if his entire body had voluntarily shut down.

'He was here?' Griffith picked up the back of the chair, carrying Bond with it, tilting it back onto its legs. Bond's shirt hung open, the buttons torn. 'I'm going to have to find some wire cutters. Your wrists are bleeding. Hang in there. I'll be back in a minute.'

Bond closed his eyes and tried to force himself to relax. He knew he'd had a close escape. For some reason, Scipio had decided to give him no more than a warning. But what a warning! Bond found himself contemplating the sheer, cold-blooded brilliance of it. It had been a display of total confidence. And what was that business about good looks 'in the masculine form'? Bond put it out of his mind. He knew that in the new world to which he belonged, it was absolutely vital to have the edge over his adversaries. If he didn't believe that he was stronger than them, he would never defeat them.

That edge had just been ruthlessly torn away. Sitting there, dripping wet, exhausted, Bond wondered how he would ever get it back.

11

Shame Lady

Later that evening, coming out of a scalding hot shower with a glass of Haig & Haig whisky inside him, Bond felt a lot better. His wrists were still hurting and he had thought about treating the cuts with a tube of Smith's Cream that he carried in his washbag. But he didn't want to walk out smelling like a pharmacy counter. Instead, he'd dried himself, got dressed, then wound a bandage around both wrists, concealing them beneath the cuffs of his ivory-white silk shirt. That would have to do. He still had a vague, throbbing headache but the whisky would help settle that. As he left the bedroom, he caught a glimpse of himself in the mirror and stopped to examine the blue-grey eyes, the lines of his jaw, the scar on his right cheek which he had come to accept as an integral part of who he was. Just a few hours ago, it could all have been taken from him.

Standing there, he considered his reflection as it might have been if Scipio had followed through with his threat and it occurred to him that although he had often thought about life or death, he tried to avoid dwelling on the myriad possibilities in between. Which would he prefer? To die instantly or to spend the next thirty years with pain and disfigurement? He'd had the same thought once or twice during the war. The bravest men had not necessarily been the ones who had been killed but those who had been left to struggle through the rest of their lives with however much of them remained.

He flicked the light off and went down to the Royal Lounge, where Reade Griffith was waiting for him, gazing up at the spectacular chandelier that had supposedly been commissioned by Tsar Nicholas II but delivered, too late, after the start of the Russian Revolution. 'I see they put you up in style,' he said, as Bond took a seat opposite him. 'I ordered bourbon on the rocks. I hope that's OK.'

'Bourbon will be fine,' Bond said.

A waiter brought the drinks over and Bond lit a cigarette. On the other side of the room, a man in black tie was playing 'Some Enchanted Evening' on a grand piano. It was typical hotel music, filling the space without actually entertaining anyone.

'So how are you feeling?'

Bond nodded. 'OK.'

'Still going to the party?'

There was no need to ask. As well as the silk shirt, Bond was wearing a midnight blue, single-breasted suit with turn-back cuffs, a charcoal grenadine tie and black moccasin shoes. He looked completely relaxed, one leg crossed over the other. He lifted his glass and the two men drank.

Although it had been left unsaid, they were both disappointed by the results of their visit to Ferrix Chimiques. W.E., the initials on the invoice, stood for Wolfe Europe, a subsidiary of Wolfe America, the company that Bond had heard about when he was in London. On the face of it, this was a significant development. The chemical import/export business was clearly connected to Jean-Paul Scipio and the Corsican syndicate. He might even own it. It seemed that Bond had found a connection to Irwin Wolfe.

But Reade Griffith had checked out the chemical compound Wolfe Europe had purchased and there was a perfectly simple explanation for it. Acetic anhydride was used to convert cellulose to cellulose acetate – the main component of photographic film. 'I don't get it,' he sighed. 'Your guy went to all the trouble to get the invoice. He stashed it away on the roof. But it's meaningless! Wolfe has to buy his chemicals someplace so he buys them from Ferrix Chimiques. What's the big deal?'

'The invoice could have been falsified.'

'There were hundreds . . . thousands of invoices in that place, James. You think they were all fake?' He thought for a moment. 'Maybe you should talk to Monique.'

'I'll see her tomorrow.'

'And Madame 16 tonight?'

'I don't see why not.'

'I'll tell you why not, my friend.' Griffith lowered his voice. 'Scipio knew who you were. He called you by your name and your number. There was only one person who could have given him that information. Her!'

Bond nodded, suddenly recognising that there was a large part of him that wanted to believe in Sixtine, and that – despite everything – he had taken a liking to her when they met in the casino. But all the evidence was against her. 'They knew we were coming,' he said gloomily. 'They were expecting us. And for what it's worth, when I met her, I actually mentioned Ferrix Chimiques. I asked her about it.'

'That wasn't too smart. She probably telephoned them the moment she left you.'

'It does look that way.'

Griffith jiggled the ice in his glass. He looked rueful. 'I warned you about her, James. She's the spider in the web.

She's living with Wolfe. She's met with Scipio. And now she's got you in her sights. Maybe I should tag along and hold your hand.'

Bond smiled. 'I think I can manage.'

'Well, OK. But take care. I'd have said we've had enough scares for one day . . . and I'm telling you, that lady scares me. Quite seriously.'

Bond thought about the CIA agent's words as he drove the short distance past Villefranche and round the bay to the peninsula which – though barely one square mile in size – had become the most elegant location in the world. Bond had never been particularly impressed by the trappings of money and success – he had met too many wealthy people whose wealth was all that defined them. But there was something unassailable about the glamour of Cap Ferrat: the gardens and the walkways and the fabulous villas along with the artists, writers and international statesmen who had once occupied them. At night, with the stars thrown carelessly across a black velvet sky and the scent of pine and eucalyptus still heavy in the warm air, with the waves lapping and the luxury cruisers tugging at their anchors, it was hard to imagine anywhere more perfect. It might be a millionaire's playground but it was the one place in the world where even the most fleeting of visitors would feel like a millionaire.

Shame Lady was a brand-new construction built plainly, obviously to impress. It sat in the wooded hills above the little port, rising up on white, concrete legs like an attack dog about to spring. Huge, square windows gave the occupants spectacular views of the coastline. High walls and one-way glass made sure that nobody passing could return the favour. It was embraced by the gentle curves of multiple terraces planted with olive trees, rose bushes and tumbling ivy, but the main building was itself angular and hard; a case of modern architecture at war with nature. A flight of white marble steps led up to the front door, marked out by flames burning in silver chalices. Two burly attendants with clip-boards guarded the way. Bond was on the list. He was admitted.

The party was already in full swing. There was a jazz band playing, white-jacketed waiters somehow finding a way through the guests. Bond was offered and accepted a glass of champagne as he made his way up and sipped it approvingly, recognising the delicate flavour and quiet effervescence of a 1934 Pol Roger. The house had been designed so that the windows slid completely out of the way, removing any defi-nition of what was inside and what was out. One moment, Bond felt grass beneath his feet. The next he was on carpet, surrounded by artworks hung and lit with the sort of care that suggested the multimillion-pound auction houses from where they had undoubtedly come. The furniture was aggres-sively modern. The guests seemed to have been selected for their fashion sense, their looks and their youth. This was a crowd of people for whom appearance was everything. They glittered a little too self-consciously as they stood and chat-ted in French and English, at the same time plucking caviar on blinis, lobster tails and smoked salmon from silver trays.

And yet for all its extravagance, Bond found himself with the uncomfortable feeling of being alone in a crowd. From the snatches of conversation that he overheard, these people were bankers, investors, stockbrokers with their wives, girl-friends and mistresses. None of them had any connection to him or to anyone he would want to know. Many of the girls – Bond knew the type well – were over made-up, feverishly eyeing each other, already competing for the men who would take them to bed. Standing next to him, a man in a blazer and cravat brayed with laughter and threw back half a glass of champagne, barely tasting it as it passed down his throat. Everyone else was behaving in a similar way. Already Bond was wishing that he had taken Reade Griffith up on his offer and brought him along. He could have used the company.

But then he saw Sixtine entering the room from the garden, looking sophisticated and gorgeous in another Dior creation, this one the very palest pink, strapless, with a wasp waist, decorated with intricate beading and pearlescent sequins. She had a simple diamond necklace around her throat and matching earrings. There was a silver clutch bag tucked under her arm.

She was holding onto the arm of a man in a velvet dinner jacket and white evening shirt but no tie. Bond knew at once that this was Irwin Wolfe. He somehow made it clear that all of this – the house, the champagne, the guests – belonged to him and that the party could continue only under his sufferance. He was not a large man but he exuded confidence and control. He had a yachtsman's face, chiselled by the wind and blessed by the sun with that hallmark of the very rich: an all-year tan. In his early seventies, he moved into the room with the ease of a much younger man. His eyes were a pale blue but they had a bright, slightly glazed quality that suggested to Bond that he might be taking medication. He still had a full head of hair, a silvery white, swept up extravagantly in a bouffant style. When he smiled, he displayed perfect teeth.

Together, the two of them had entered like film stars or minor royalty. They were gay and they were welcoming but still there was something forbidding about them and Bond noticed the guests stepping back to allow them to pass.

Nobody spoke to them unless they were spoken to first. And when there were a few words – a greeting, a pleasantry – there was a sense of benediction, an honour received.

Sixtine saw Bond and immediately led Wolfe over to him. Even as they came towards him, Bond noticed how close they were to each other, moving like dance partners, and a small part of him recoiled. Was he jealous? Why would he possibly be? He had no time to answer the question. Suddenly they were in front of him.

'Irwin,' Sixtine said. 'This is the man I was talking to you about, the one I met at the casino. His name is James Bond and he owes me 100,000 francs.'

Wolfe smiled and held out a hand. 'Nice to meet you, Mr Bond.' He had a solid American accent, one that had no shyness and liked to make itself known. 'What brings you to the Côte d'Azur?'

'Business,' Bond replied, non-committally. Wolfe was still clutching his hand with a surprisingly strong grip. 'Import and export,' he added, hoping that would be enough.

'Oh really? What exactly?' The man was refusing to let go in any sense.

'Agro-chemicals.' Bond fell back on the same cover he had used at Ferrix Chimiques. 'I represent a company that owns farmland in Great Britain.'

'That's interesting.' Finally, Wolfe released him. 'So you met my baby girl in Monte Carlo?' He leaned over and kissed her awkwardly on the naked curve between her shoulder and her neck. She didn't try to push him away and seemed to enjoy his advances. 'And I hear you gave her a good spanking!'

'Irwin – I don't know what you're talking about.' Now she was coquettish.

'At cards, baby. At cards!'

'We were playing *vingt-et-un*.'

'As long as it wasn't *soixante-neuf*!' He laughed loudly at his own joke and Bond felt a sense of revulsion that was somehow at odds with everything he had heard about the man he was meeting. But then Wolfe turned to him, suddenly serious. 'So when did you get down here, Jim?' he asked.

'A couple of days ago.' Bond felt the need to be polite and looked around him, trying to find something to say. 'I have to congratulate you. You have a magnificent home.'

'Oh – this little place isn't my home. I live in Los Angeles. I had this house built by a guy from Paris when I expanded my business into Europe. It took me two years to get the permission to build. Would you believe that? There was a little church up here, a run-down chapel that nobody used. It had been here for centuries and that's about how long it took me to persuade them to let me knock it down. It was the same at Menton. I have a plant about twenty miles from here and I said to the local authorities – the mayor or whoever – you don't get round to giving me what I want, maybe I'll close down and take my business elsewhere.' He rested his hand just above Sixtine's waist and jerked her closer towards him, as if he needed her to be on his side. 'That quickly changed their minds.'

'Irwin is in the film business,' Sixtine explained.

'I make the stuff. I don't shoot it. Sixtine here is fascinated by my work. She's always asking me about it. I can't understand why. I've never yet met a woman who understood technology.' He lowered his hand to cup the curve of her bottom and Bond was astonished that Sixtine didn't seem to mind. 'That's the way I prefer it,' he went on. 'My first wife was good for three things. Boys. She gave me two sons. Boats. She was crazy about cruising. And bed.' It was a formula he had used before. He challenged Bond not to be amused by it.

But Bond wasn't playing. 'Are your sons here tonight?' he asked innocently. He knew the answer. He was needling Wolfe quite deliberately.

A flash of something ugly glimmered briefly in the man's eyes. 'No, Mr Bond. Both my sons are dead. They fell on the battlefield. In fact, they were taken from me on the same day.'

'Oh. I'm so sorry.'

'Don't be. A great many Americans made sacrifices and some of them may well have asked if it was worth it. After all, it was the Jews' war. It was nothing to do with us. But our president – Frank Roosevelt, I knew him well – decided that we had to come in and save the world and that was what we goddamn did. I'd like to think where you Limeys would be right now if it hadn't been for us! It may have cost us dear and in my view it will continue to cost us for years to come. But I'm proud to have played my part.'

It seemed to Bond that Wolfe had uttered this last sentence with difficulty. As for the rest of his little speech, he had heard it all before and dismissed it.

Sixtine sensed the atmosphere between the two men and cut in, trying to make light of it. 'You mentioned boats,' she said. 'You should tell James about the *Mirabelle*.'

'The *Mirabelle*!' Wolfe visibly softened. 'She's named after my first wife and it won't come as any surprise to you when I say she's a beauty. Are you interested in cruise liners?'

'Very much so.'

'The *Mirabelle* was built in your country in a place called Birkenhead – but I brought her down here to be fitted out. You Brits are good mechanics but you know damn all about design. 24,250 tons. 680 feet in length. Fully equipped with all the latest technology from the anti-roll stabilisers to some sort of new-fangled funnel that stops smuts falling on the upper deck. She's set to make her maiden voyage and all I can say is, Moore-McCormack and the Grace Line had better start looking over their shoulders because our package makes their fleets look like a bunch of rusting tubs.'

'I'd like to see her.'

'Then you should get your ass on board. But you'd better make it soon, Jim. We're weighing anchor Tuesday morning, 8 a.m. We're allowing three weeks for the crossing. We could do it in half the time but we're going to be dealing with any last-minute kinks, spending the first week just a mile off the French coast. It's a shame I can't invite you to make the trip with us. The mayor's going to meet us when we dock at the New York harbour. The vice president's hoping to fly in. We're going to have a party on board like you wouldn't believe. I've spent $1,000 on the fireworks alone!'

Tuesday was four days away. 'I'm sure I could look in before then,' Bond said.

'Then why don't you arrange a time with Sixtine? She's going to be with me on the crossing. It wouldn't be a maiden voyage without a maiden and it should be fun – just the two of us with no passengers and 550 cabins to choose from.'

'Maybe you could come along tomorrow?' Sixtine suggested.

'Sure. Tomorrow afternoon. How about teatime? You Brits like your tea don't you! Let's say four o'clock.'

'Four o'clock will be fine,' Bond said. 'Is she berthed in Marseilles?'

Wolfe shook his head. 'No. She's here in Nice. Sixtine will make the arrangements.' His hand was still resting on her obscenely. It looked like a dead crab. 'Come on, honey. There are some people I want you to meet.' He steered her away.

Bond stood where he was for a minute, surrounded by the young crowd. He was still holding half a glass of the Pol Roger but suddenly he had no appetite for it. In fact he didn't want to stay here a moment longer. He wondered why he had come. Someone shuffled up to him and tried to make conversation but after a few brief words he twisted round and made his way out.

He was halfway down the marble steps when a voice called out his name. He turned and saw that Sixtine had come out of one of the side windows. She must have made her excuses and separated from Irwin Wolfe almost at once. Bond walked up to her. 'Yes?' he asked coldly.

She looked at him curiously. 'Why are you leaving?' she asked.

'Why should I stay?'

'You've only just arrived.'

'It's been a long day and I'm not really in the mood.'

He might have left right then but she held him with her eyes and made the decision for both of them. 'I want to talk to you. Come with me.'

Without waiting for a reply, she turned her back on him and walked into the shadows of the garden, leaving the party behind. Bond watched her for a moment, then followed. He liked women and felt comfortable with them. He had always thought he understood them. But everything about Sixtine – even her name – was disconcerting and it seemed to him that in the short time he had known her he had been presented with at least three different personae. At the casino in Monte Carlo, he had thought her intriguing, a little lonely but entirely in control. To Reade Griffith she had been

121

dangerous: a spider in a web, a Mata Hari. It was an opinion shared by M. But just now, inside the house, she had allowed herself to be fondled and petted by a man at least thirty years older than her. She was clearly no fortune hunter so what was she doing here? And, for that matter, what was he doing following her meekly across the lawn? He should have just told her to get lost.

They came to a swimming pool surrounded by strange little plants with flowers that looked like pink dandelions. These were the shame ladies that Sixtine had described. Bond had seen them once in Jamaica and remembered being told that the leaves shrank when they were touched. That was why the name had been given to them. Sixtine continued walking towards a Japanese-style pavilion constructed at the far end of the pool. Inside, there were wicker chairs and cushions with heavy, floral covers. She threw herself down with her arms folded behind her and her body spread out, the sequins on her dress catching the light of the moon. She glanced up as Bond arrived but she had never doubted that he would come. 'Do you have a cigarette?' she asked.

Bond took out a packet of Du Maurier and handed her one. She looked at it disdainfully. 'Canadian cigarettes named after a minor British actor. There's a place I go to in London. Morlands. You should give them a try. If you're going to pursue such a filthy habit, you might as well do it with style.'

'To hell with you, Sixtine,' Bond said. He lit her cigarette and one for himself. 'Why exactly did you invite me here? What do you want?'

She raised an eyebrow. 'You're in a bad mood.'

'You could say I've had a bad day.'

'Have you? Do you want to talk about it?'

'I have a feeling you already know.'

She didn't deny it. Instead, she blew out smoke and said: 'You were looking for Scipio. Did you find him?'

'Yes.'

'And?' Bond didn't answer so she added: 'I'm genuinely interested.'

Bond turned on her. The moon was behind him and there were dark shadows over his eyes. 'I know who you are,' he said. 'I've seen your file. I know about the Kosovo papers. I know about some of the people who have been your victims.'

'I prefer to call them clients.'

'I'm sure you do. This may all be a game to you but a friend of mine was killed . . .'

'You already told me.'

' . . . and I've been sent to find out who was responsible. Right now, I'd say you're the most likely suspect.'

'I told you. I never even met him. Why should I want to get involved with the British secret service? I have my own reasons to be here, James, and although it might hurt your ego, you really ought to consider the possibility that they have nothing whatsoever to do with you.'

'Maybe you should let me make up my own mind about that.'

'Maybe I don't care what you think.'

'Then stop wasting my time.' He was about to leave, but paused and looked at her coldly. 'Are you sleeping with Irwin Wolfe?'

If Bond had meant to insult her, he had succeeded. Her eyes flared. She threw down the cigarette and ground it out with a twist of her foot, then stood up so that she was facing him, eye to eye, and they were just a few inches apart. 'What damned business is it of yours?'

'Are you?'

'What do you think?'

Bond couldn't help himself. He grabbed hold of her and pressed his lips against hers, his hand clamped on the flesh of her upper arm, holding her tight. He didn't know how she would respond. At that moment, he didn't care.

Finally, he released her. She took a step back. Her dark hair had tumbled across her eyes, which glinted with anger but also amusement. 'Well, well, well,' she exclaimed. 'The British spy can't get what he wants by consent so he has to try force.' She touched her hand to her lip. 'Is this how you treat your women? Given a choice, I think I prefer Irwin Wolfe.'

For a moment neither of them spoke. The swimming pool stretched out behind them, the long strip of water glowing in the darkness. The jazz band had struck up another tune. It sounded a long way away.

'I invited you here because I like you and I'm interested in you,' Sixtine said. 'But you're going to have to take it one step at a time, James, and I want to make it clear that you are never to touch me again without asking. Come to the *Mirabelle* tomorrow and afterwards we'll have cocktails and see if we can come to a business arrangement that satisfies us both.'

'Is that all it is with you?' Bond asked. 'Business?'

'Why else are we here?'

She brushed past him and he watched her return to the house. Irwin Wolfe had stepped onto the terrace and was looking for her. Bond saw the two of them meet. The older man put his arm around her shoulders and swept her indoors. She took one look back as if trying to find Bond in the darkness and then she was gone.

12

Le Grand Banditisme

Bond had been wrong about Monique de Troyes, the girl who worked at Ferrix Chimiques and whose first name and telephone number he had found on the back of a postcard. She did not live in a two-bedroom flat on the edge of Marseilles, but in a two-storey house, with her parents, in the neighbouring town of Aubagne. Every morning she took the train to Marseilles and then a bus to the port area and every evening she did the same in reverse. But he'd been right about her age. She was twenty-seven. And she was pretty.

It had been easy enough to trace her address through the telephone number and Bond was sitting in his car outside the house at eight o'clock the next day. It was a Saturday so she would not be at work and he hoped she had not gone away for the weekend. Aubagne was a pretty enough town, baking in the August sun but cooled, at least, by the breezes from the mountains that surrounded it. Parts of it dated back to the Middle Ages and those were where the streets were at their narrowest, the buildings at their most charming. A church steeple and a clock tower jealously fought for attention but they were largely wasting their time as few tourists ever found their way here. It was typical of so many French towns and villages set back from the sea, existing in its own little world. Dogs would bark and cats would stretch out in the street. Old ladies would sit outside their homes wrapped up in their own thoughts and in clothes too warm for the weather. Everyone would know everything about each other but at the end of the day there wouldn't be all that much to know.

Monique's father was a butcher, a lifelong communist who had only ever visited Paris once. He had travelled there to fight the fascists in the riots of 1934. It didn't bother him that his daughter didn't share his views. In his opinion, women shouldn't interest themselves in politics. A small, round-shouldered man with a heavy moustache, he had a home that exactly suited him, stuck on the corner, as if it had always been there, with its back to the village and the traffic rumbling past. It was a deep red with three white shutters and a narrow front door. There were two bedrooms side by side on the top floor with a kitchen and a bathroom below. The house had no garden apart from a small concrete space at the front, which was so ill-defined that it was often mistaken for the pavement and, sipping his Ricard before dinner, Monsieur de Troyes would find himself in serious conversation with anyone who happened to pass.

Bond had been waiting an hour when Monique finally appeared – alone, fortunately. She had discarded her smart office clothes for a simple skirt and blouse and carried a basket, obviously on her way to the morning market that had opened just after dawn in the street named after Maréchal Foch. Bond got out of the car, closing the door behind him, and the sound of it slamming shut must have attracted her attention because she glanced across the road and then, without hesitating, swerved away and began to walk quickly uphill. She had recognised him. Bond smiled to himself and quickened his pace. He caught up with her outside a dusty chapel with two angels looking down on him, palms held up as if warning him to stay away.

There was nobody else in sight. Monique was making no secret of the fact that she had been hurrying to separate herself from him and not because she needed to be somewhere else, but suddenly she stopped and swung round. With her sandy hair tied back and her blue eyes staring, she looked even younger than he remembered from the office. She was angry or perhaps afraid. Or both.

'What do you want?' she demanded, speaking in French.

'I need to talk to you,' Bond said.

'I don't want to talk to you. Go away.'

'I can't do that, Monique. I'm sorry. I don't want to upset you but you knew a friend of mine and I have to talk to you about him.'

'Is this about Richard Blakeney?' She spoke with an accent that split the surname into three syllables and it took Bond a moment to remember that this was the alias the dead man had used.

'Yes,' he said.

'I don't want to talk about him. There is nothing I can tell you.'

'You remember me.'

'Of course. You came to Ferrix. You shouldn't have gone there.' She clutched her basket as if she could use it for self-defence. 'Please, monsieur. My parents have sent me to the market. I will get into trouble if I don't do as they say.'

'Let me come with you . . .'

'No!' She blurted out the word and it occurred to Bond that being seen with a strange man in a small, closed community might cause her all sorts of problems.

'All right. I don't want to make any trouble for you.'

'Then go away! If I am seen talking to you, they will kill me. If they even knew you had come here, they would kill me.'

'Nobody knows I'm here and nobody is going to hurt you.'

She looked up and down the street as if challenging him. But they were still alone apart from the stone angels. She seemed to notice them for the first time and drew strength from them as if they were watching over her. Perhaps this foreigner was right. Monique was a simple-minded girl who went to church every Sunday and lit candles to the memory of her grandparents. She had been brought up to believe that the world was a bad place but that she would be protected from it, living in a provincial town with her parents. Getting a job fifteen miles away had been the one adventure of her life and it had taken all her mother's powers of persuasion to get her father to allow her to go.

She made her decision. 'I have to go to the market but I will meet you afterwards. There is a café near the station. It's called Le Papet. You can wait for me there.'

'Monique – it won't do you any good hiding from me.'

'I have said I will come.' Now there was anger in her voice. 'I will be there in one hour.' She turned and walked away.

The railway station at Aubagne is almost absurdly handsome. Painted a royal yellow with arched windows, ornate canopies and palm trees, it could at a glance be the home of a retired ambassador or perhaps a small casino. It is careful to keep its distance from the wide, busy road which skirts the town and stretches on towards the mountains. Cars and buses, it seems to suggest, belong to a more vulgar, modern age. It was built by an architect who believed in train travel, at a time when travellers enjoyed champagne and caviar on the Orient Express or listened to chamber orchestras playing Tchaikovsky on the Golden Eagle across Russia.

James Bond was sitting at a table just opposite with a view of the station clock that both told him how much time had passed and taunted him with the suggestion that Monique might not, after all, show up. The inside of the bar was a small, unassuming room, packed with tables and, on this Saturday morning, with customers. However, it had spread itself out with a canopy that stole a large stretch of the pavement and this area was quieter. Bond had ordered *une noisette* – two shots of espresso with a drop of hot milk – and a croissant that he didn't really want. He had spent the last hour pulling it apart but had eaten very little of it. He had also smoked two Du Mauriers although they had reminded him of Sixtine's jibe. He thought of their meeting in the garden, his lips crushing hers. He was a little disgusted with himself. Why couldn't he get her out of his head?

The clock was showing twenty past ten when Monique finally appeared, crossing the road without the shopping basket she had been carrying earlier. There was a brisk determination about the way she walked, as if she were on her way to an appointment with the dentist and thought that it would hurt less if she got it over with as soon as possible. She saw Bond and sat down opposite him. Even before she spoke, her eyes were challenging him. You forced me to come here, they seemed to say. What do I have to do to persuade you to let me go?

'Can I get you a drink?' Bond asked.

'No, thank you.'

'Don't be ridiculous. It's a hot day and you've been shopping.' He called to the waiter. 'I'll have an Americano,' he said. 'With plenty of ice.'

'And for madame?'

She hesitated, then relented. '*Un orange pressé.*'

The waiter swivelled round and left. He hadn't recognised Monique but most of his customers were probably commuters, never staying long.

'I don't know what you want,' Monique began. 'But I can't help you.'

'You can start by telling me why you're so afraid.'

'I already told you that.' She looked left and right. All the other tables were unoccupied but even so she leaned forward, keeping her voice low. 'You wouldn't understand. You don't live here. But in Marseilles you have to be careful who you talk to and what you say—'

'Please, Monique. Don't waste any more of my time.' Bond went in hard. 'I know you were friends with Richard Blakeney. Maybe more than friends.'

Her eyes filled with tears. But they were tears of indignation. 'I didn't sleep with him! You are a pig to suggest that.'

'But you were fond of him.'

'I liked him.'

'How did you meet him?'

She drew a breath, gathering her thoughts. Bond could see that the girl had a steely edge and he admired her for it. 'I don't even know who you are,' she said. 'You called yourself Mr Howard when you came to the office. Is that your real name?'

'Does it really matter?'

'I suppose not. And maybe Richard also lied to me. I can see that the two of you are the same. Give me a cigarette!'

Bond held out the packet. She took one. He lit it for her.

'I met Richard about a month ago. He was at the station at Marseilles and he said he couldn't find the right platform.'

Bond almost smiled at the obvious pick-up line. It wasn't one he would have used himself.

130

'He was also travelling to Aubagne. It is only a short journey but we chatted. He seemed a nice man. He told me that he was working for an insurance company and when we arrived he asked me if I would like to have a drink with him. We came here. We sat at that table.'

She pointed.

'He started asking me about Ferrix Chimiques and of course I knew then that there was nothing accidental about our meeting and that he had chosen me deliberately. I should have told him to go away right then. It would have been better for me if I had. It would have been better for both of us. But he was charming. He made me smile.'

'What did he want to know?'

'He was interested in one of our clients, a company called Wolfe Europe. He wanted to know what chemicals they had been buying from us. Of course, what he was asking was impossible. We have hundreds of clients and we sell thousands of chemicals. How could I possibly have that information? So he asked me to look at the accounts and to bring him copies of any transactions that had taken place in the last six months.'

Bond took out the carbon copy of the invoice that he had found in the Rue Foncet and unfolded it on the table. 'You took this?' he asked.

She examined it briefly and nodded. 'I took fifty different invoices. I had to be very careful. I took four or five each time. Nothing ever seemed to satisfy him. He returned them all to me. Except this one.'

'But what's the significance of this chemical, acetic anhydride? Wolfe Europe makes photographic film. It's part of the process.'

'I don't know.' She shrugged. 'He didn't tell me.'

131

The waiter arrived with the drinks. Bond's Americano – a mixture of Campari, sweet vermouth and soda – was the right colour but he took out the twist of lemon peel and set it aside. It was too early in the day for such fancies. Monique had ordered fresh orange juice but seemed uninterested in it.

'What did he tell you about himself?' Bond asked.

'He didn't tell me anything and anyway anything he did say would have been untrue. He said he was working for an insurance company but that was a lie, wasn't it? He's the same as you. You are both handsome Englishmen with cold eyes. You both want information. That's all. You don't care what happens to me.'

'I do care what happens to you, Monique,' Bond said and meant it. 'That's why I drove all the way to Aubagne. Nobody knows I'm here and after I'm gone we won't see each other again.'

'They know everything!' Monique said. 'I warned Richard when he asked me to steal the papers. This is Marseilles. It is the city, you know, of *le grand banditisme*. You learn to keep quiet, never to step out of line. I warned him but he didn't listen and they killed him. When I discovered that a body had been found at La Joliette, I knew it was him, even before he had been identified.' She paused. 'He said he was going to take me to Paris and to London. I've never left the south of France. But it was all lies. If he hadn't been killed, he would have gone away and forgotten me. Just like you.'

They sat looking at each other. She hadn't touched her drink.

'Do you know who he went to meet, the day he died?'

'No. He never told me anything.' She stood up. 'I have nothing more to say to you, Mr Howard, and now I have to go back to my family. Please, leave me alone.'

'Thank you, Monique. I'm sorry about Richard. You may not believe it, but I'm sure he cared for you. And for what it's worth, he was my friend.'

'Do people like you have friends, Mr Howard? I wonder.'

She walked away from the table and crossed the road, heading towards the station and the centre of the town which lay just behind it. Bond waved for the bill. At the same time, he heard a car approaching. He knew at once that it was going too fast and even as he registered the roar of the engine, he twisted round, dreading what he was going to see.

Monique was halfway across the road. She had stopped, freezing as she saw the black, four-door Peugeot 202 Berline hurtling towards her. It was a true gangster's car with its fat, rounded mud guards, its windows set far back and the bonnet and long, slanting nose that made it look so aggressive. There were two men inside but they were gone in a blur. Bond saw the car make contact. It had aimed for Monique quite deliberately. There could be no doubt of it. She was scooped up, twisting in the air. By the time she hit the tarmac, the car had travelled beneath her and was well on its way out of the town. Somebody screamed. Suddenly there were people on the pavement, coming out of the station, coming out of the bar, closing in on the horror of what had just occurred.

Bond was already up and running. He saw the car disappear round a corner in the far distance and heard the scream of the tyres. His own car was still outside Monique's house. There was no way he could follow them.

He reached the girl and knew at once there was nothing he could do. Her dress was torn and there was blood on her arms and legs, more blood streaming from her head. It was impossible to see how many of her bones were broken. He had never seen anyone look more pitiful in death and he had to fight back a sense of rising anger and sickness. She had been just twenty-seven years old.

How had they known? Bond had asked Sixtine about Ferrix Chimiques but he had never mentioned Monique and he hadn't told anyone that he was coming here today. More than that, he had been careful driving out of Nice, making sure he hadn't been followed: an elementary precaution. Someone – the two men in the car – must have been watching the girl as she left her house, met Bond, went about her shopping and then came here. They knew about the stolen carbon copy. The decision to kill her had already been made. It had just been a coincidence of timing that Bond had been there to see it happen.

And what now? A police car had drawn up. Two uniformed men got out. A small crowd gathered. Bond stood up and backed away, not drawing attention to himself. If anyone asked, he was just a tourist. He didn't know her and he had nothing to do with her. He had just been passing by.

13

Love in a Warm Climate

'It's great to see you, Jim. Welcome aboard.'

The words grated in Bond's ears even as he took his last step off the gangplank and surrendered himself to the streamlined beauty and extravagance of the *Mirabelle*, its two gold-plated funnels towering over him and the promenade deck with its pristine honey-coloured wood stretching into the distance. Irwin Wolfe had been there to greet him, dressed improbably in naval whites complete with cap and the name of the ship – and his dead wife – emblazoned on his chest. Once again, Bond noticed the strange gleam in the man's pale blue eyes and wondered whether it was pain or fanaticism. For this was his creation, this floating world.

The *Mirabelle* was 676 feet long (Wolfe had rounded the number up) and eighty-five feet wide with two propellers, each weighing twenty-eight tons and turning at two revolutions per second. The geared steam turbines had been built by Vickers-Armstrongs in Barrow-in-Furness and would deliver steam at 400 lb per square inch at temperatures of 700°F. The two funnels were the creation of Thornycrofts of Southampton and had been equipped with a newly patented device to keep smoke from the upper decks. The ship had three decks open to the elements: the sports deck, the sun deck and the promenade deck. It was on the last of these that

Bond was standing, with frenetic, last-minute activity continuing all around him.

Men were on their knees polishing the handrails and swabbing the decks. More men dangled over the side, cleaning portholes, tightening rivets, touching up the paintwork. An endless stream of supplies was being carried on board – furniture, linen, crates of wine, frozen food, lamps, vases – while a uniformed purser holding a clipboard shouted out instructions. 'Midships, A deck 10. Forward, B deck 8, Forward, Baggage Room, R deck aft . . . and be careful with those!' This last command was directed at a team of black workers carrying large cardboard boxes marked 'FEUX D'ARTIFICE', and Bond was reminded of the party Wolfe planned to throw once he arrived in New York.

There was no party atmosphere now. Instead, Bond was aware of a deadly seriousness, a sense of acolytes coming together in the brilliant cathedral that the best engineers – all of them British – had constructed. And in just three days, the turbines would hum into life, the propellers would turn and the 25,000-ton vessel would slip its moorings and head out to sea at a stately fifteen knots.

'So, what do you think?' Wolfe demanded. He waited, his eyes hungry for Bond's response.

'She's beautiful,' Bond said grudgingly.

'The most beautiful ship on the seven seas!' Wolfe exclaimed. 'She may not be as big as the *Queen Mary* or as fast as the SS *United States* – but hell, they can keep their Blue Ribands. What we've got here is simply the most luxurious way a human being will ever cross the Atlantic.'

Before he knew it, Bond had Wolfe's hand on his shoulder and the two of them were walking towards the bridge as if they were old friends.

'We have just 200 first-class and 320 second-class cabins, although I could have fitted in twice that number if I'd really wanted. But you travel on the *Mirabelle*, you get more space, your own private terrace, a separate bathroom and proper beds. Why, if you book into one of our diamond suites we'll throw in a Bechstein grand piano, a fireplace, a bar and a personal butler to look after you. You'll also find real masterpieces hanging on the wall. We've got works by Cézanne, Picasso, Toulouse-Lautrec . . . I've had people searching the auction houses all over Europe to buy the right art.

'We've got three restaurants and five kitchens, two of them working round the clock for snacks and cabin service. I stole our top chef from the Ledoyen in Paris. You tell me where else you'll find three Michelin stars in the middle of the sea! Oysters, caviar, prime fillet steak, fresh lobster . . . every single meal is going to be memorable and the wine cellar would make you weep. There's a café grill on the upper deck that converts into a cinema and a nightclub and we're going to host symphony orchestras in the main dining saloon. We've got two swimming pools, a library, a beauty salon, dog kennels, parking for a dozen cars – there's even a synagogue on the lower deck. Well, the Jews are the ones with all the money so we've got to look after them and we'll be carrying our own floating rabbi. Everything here is the latest. Our telephone system will connect you with anywhere in the world. And you wait until you see the engine room!'

It was late afternoon but the sun was blazing down. Bond could feel it on the back of his neck. Wolfe was still holding onto his shoulder. He found it hard to focus on what the millionaire was saying and there was something about his voice – unctuous, self-satisfied – that he found almost repellent. The death of Monique de Troyes was still in his mind.

To have gone from that to this in the space of just a few hours made him ashamed. He forced himself to look interested, to pretend that he was impressed. He had to remind himself he was doing his job.

'I thought Sixtine was going to show me round,' he said.

'Sixtine wouldn't be able to find her way round!' Wolfe tightened his grip. 'I thought this was the beautiful lady you'd come to see. The *Mirabelle*! If you want a word of advice, you'll leave that other little lady alone.'

'I didn't realise the two of you were so close.'

'Close? Between you and me, Jim, I may have found me the next Mrs Wolfe. I haven't popped the question yet but give a woman a diamond the size of a ball bearing and you can be pretty sure of the answer. I'm going to leave it for the night we reach New York. Shame you won't be around.'

Was there something vindictive in this last statement? Wolfe let go of Bond and walked up to a man who had been waiting for them at the entrance to the first-class drawing room. He was also dressed in whites, which contrasted with his dark mahogany skin and jet-black hair.

'I'd love to give you the complete tour, Jim, but as you can imagine I'm a little busy right now. And anyway, it would take you the rest of the weekend to see everything. This is Dr Borghetti. He's the ship's medic and the only person on board right now who's on full salary but with nothing to do.' It seemed an unnecessary jibe and one that clearly irritated the doctor. 'He'll take you into some of the main rooms and give you an idea of what we've created here. Then we can have that cup of tea you were so keen on and maybe Sixtine will join us.' He turned to the doctor. 'Take Mr Bond into the main state rooms and show him a couple of the cabins. Then bring him to the Wolfe bar. OK?'

'Right, Mr Wolfe.'

'I'll catch up with you later, Jim. Enjoy yourself!'

Wolfe left, walking back in the direction he had come from. Bond examined the doctor. He was, Bond thought, surprisingly ugly with an overly fussy little moustache decorating an otherwise bland and uninteresting face. The colour of his skin couldn't quite disguise the acne that had disfigured him as a child and left its mark around his neck and chin. If Bond fell ill on a ship like this, he wouldn't expect to be treated by someone who looked permanently diseased himself. Borghetti forced himself to smile as he began the tour. He spoke English badly.

'This way, please.' The doctor opened the door and for the next forty minutes, Bond explored the sumptuous interior of the *Mirabelle*. He was in no mood to enjoy it, not after what had happened in Aubagne that morning. And the truth was that he would never have been drawn to what the steam cruiser represented. He had no argument with extreme wealth and overindulgence – on the contrary, he felt completely at home in casinos and first-class hotels. What was missing here was an exit door. To be trapped at sea with only the idle rich for company would have all too quickly become suffocating. He'd have ended up drinking too much and bedding the cabin girls.

They began on the upper decks: the dining saloon, the smoking room, the library, the lounges. Wolfe had been true to his word: Bond had never seen so much shining chrome and Lalique glass, so many fine Persian rugs and onyx tables. The windows and ceiling lanterns had been carefully designed to allow as much light as possible to flood in, fighting against the claustrophobia that is endemic to even the largest cruise ships. There were chandeliers, too, and art deco lamps – hundreds and hundreds of them. And yet without laughter and dance music, without women in long dresses and men in black tie, in the all-pervading silence and the emptiness, the *Mirabelle* had about as much allure as a furniture showroom. Its very newness was unwelcoming.

As they continued, Bond became aware of one peculiarity. The ship was equipped with an extraordinary number of fire extinguishers. In normal circumstances, he might not have noticed but everything else was so exquisite – mosaics, murals, silk hangings and so on – that the ugly red cylinders really stood out, particularly as there were so many of them. Perhaps they might be less conspicuous once the crowds arrived but Bond was surprised that the designers had been so careless. And why remind the passengers, so overtly, of the dangers of a fire?

He might have mentioned this to Borghetti but the doctor was less than friendly as he guided Bond from area to area. From the passenger decks, they passed through a service door and down a series of staircases to the engine rooms. This was a completely different world of snaking pipes and cables, gantries and narrow spaces. Everything was hard and metallic, every inch of space taken up with the complicated equipment that would somehow connect in order to power and direct this huge ship. There were more people working here, too. A fifty-strong crew was going through a series of last-minute checks, clambering up and down ladders that passed through submarine-style hatches, calibrating the brand-new machinery. Bond saw trimmers, coal passers and firemen even though the boilers were not yet alight. Everyone was busy. Bond could easily imagine the organised chaos that would follow when the ship was actually underway.

Eventually the doctor took him back to a bar that seemed

to have been modelled on the Savoy in London – all dark wood and plush – and which the ship's owner had named after himself. Bond was relieved to see that the promised tea had not been served. Also, Sixtine had arrived. She was sitting in a double-sized velvet armchair, smoking a cigarette, looking as if she would rather be somewhere else. It struck Bond that, outside the casino, she had the sort of face that found it hard to disguise what she was thinking. But then again, perhaps it was more the case of having a temperament that didn't care anyway.

'So, what do you think?' Wolfe demanded.

It was the sort of question that could only have one answer and Bond had no choice but to provide it. 'She's magnificent,' he said. Then he added, as an afterthought: 'You seem quite nervous about her.'

'Nervous?'

Bond had been impressed by the ship's engineering. But there was still a part of him that resented having to admit it to Irwin Wolfe and he had deliberately chosen to prick at the man's self-importance. 'I've never seen so many fire extinguishers,' he explained. 'I suppose you must be worried about a short circuit in the wiring or something.'

Wolfe smiled but without humour. 'I'm not worried about anything, Jim. Every last detail on this boat has been thought out and we've got the sea trials starting in three days to pick up any issues.' He jabbed with a finger, making his point. 'But when you've spent over $2 million on a project, it makes sense to protect your investment. I guess you wouldn't understand these things. But that's how it is.'

'I quite understand,' Bond said affably.

'Irwin has bad news,' Sixtine said, in a voice that didn't sound too sorry at all. 'He's cancelling tea.'

'That's right.' Wolfe nodded. 'I'm heading out to the plant at Menton. I have some last-minute business that needs taking care of.'

'I'll come with you!' Sixtine spoke casually, as if the thought had only just occurred to her, but Bond got the feeling that somehow it mattered to her.

'That's not a good idea, honey. You'd only get in the way. I'll see you tomorrow.'

'But you promised you'd take me out there, Irwin. You know I'm keen to learn about your work. And this is my last chance if you're leaving on Tuesday.'

'I'm sorry.' Wolfe was adamant. He gave her a thin smile. 'It won't work for me right now and anyway, I've already told you, there's nothing out there that would interest you. You really want to learn about film production, you can visit my plant in Massachusetts.'

'But I'm here right now.'

'Honey, let's not argue about it, OK?'

There was no point continuing. Sixtine stubbed out her cigarette and stood up. 'All right, then. I'll go home and have an early night. The south of France isn't any fun without you.'

She was acting. Bond was sure of it. But Wolfe was satisfied. He grabbed hold of her and pulled her towards him, kissing her on the side of the cheek as if he were nervous of the fullness of her lips. 'You mind showing my guest off the ship?' he asked.

'Of course,' she said. 'And don't worry. I'll make sure he doesn't set fire to anything on the way.'

'Good to see you again, Jim.' Another handshake. 'Next time you come to America, you know how to get there.'

'I certainly do.'

Bond and Sixtine left together, taking the gangplank

down to the quayside of the port of Nice. This was where the *Mirabelle* had been berthed for its final checks before it headed out to sea, surrounded by cranes that stood like courtiers, bowing their heads to an undoubted queen. Bond had walked over from the Negresco but Sixtine had driven. A bright red two-seater MG TD was waiting cheerfully for them on the forecourt with its hood folded back and Bond knew at once that it was hers. Sure enough, she took a key ring out of her bag and twirled it around her finger as they walked across.

'Come with me,' she said without looking at him, perhaps not caring if he came or not. She opened the door of the little car and climbed in.

'Where to?' Bond asked, climbing in beside her. 'Are you going back to Shame Lady?'

She shook her head. 'No. I don't like being there on my own.'

'Isn't Wolfe going to turn up later?'

'I like it even less when he's with me.'

'Then where?'

She reached into the glove compartment and took out a pair of sunglasses, then turned the key in the ignition and Bond listened appreciatively to the throaty growl of the tiny 1,250 cc engine which had been perfectly tuned. 'Let's make it a mystery tour,' she shouted. 'It's not very far and it's going to be a beautiful evening.'

She was right. The sun was already setting as they roared out of Nice, following the coastal road towards Cannes with the Mediterranean a deepening scarlet on their left. They passed the airport and the new developments – offices and apartments – that were already springing up beside the sea, threatening to overwhelm the area and, one day for sure, to destroy its casual charm.

Bond had always believed that even the best women drivers had a reticence, a lack of confidence behind the wheel. They would interrogate corners before they attacked them and the more powerful the car, the less they would seem to be in control. But Sixtine handled the MG like an expert, smiling carelessly as she pushed the engine above sixty, her dark hair streaming in the wind, the sunglasses masking her eyes. The traffic was heavy but she cut in and out of the other cars, sometimes with inches to spare, smiling at the blasts of their horns and changing through the four gears with the incisiveness of a surgeon.

They came off the main road at Antibes and dropped down the Boulevard du Cap until it reached the end of the headland. Here, a narrow lane continued steeply downhill with pine trees on both sides. Bond saw a glimpse of water – a secluded bay ahead of them – but before they reached it Sixtine span the wheel and drove through the open gate of a small, old-style house with pink walls, tumbling bougainvillea and a roughly paved courtyard planted with lemon trees and olives. A balcony with stone columns stretched out over the front door and presumably offered a sea view. It was a jewel box and, once again without asking, Bond knew it was hers.

The house wasn't locked. Sixtine led him into a living room with French windows that opened onto a small, private garden with a swimming pool running its full length to one side. A high wall, thickly covered in ivy, separated the house from its neighbours. There wasn't a breath of wind. With the warm, velvet touch of the evening, everything smelled of pine and eucalyptus. A thousand cicadas were sawing away as they welcomed a darkness punctured only by a slither of silver moonlight.

'Will you have a glass of Dom Pérignon?' she asked.

'I'll join you.'

'Of course.'

She put on a record. It was an Édith Piaf album, *Chansons Parisiennes*. Then she went into the kitchen, leaving Bond to admire the furniture – antique but comfortable – and the brightly coloured modern art. Sixtine liked to read. There were two shelves of books in English and French, a lot of classical fiction, some history and politics. The house was a bolthole but it had been furnished with care. It had a distinctly feminine touch in the choice of the duck-egg wallpaper, the ornate mirrors and the thick Turkish rugs. The quiet piano music suited it.

A moment later she was back, holding a bottle and two glasses. 'I've always liked Antibes,' she said. 'Nice and Cannes are already spoiled and overcrowded. In a few years' time they'll be impossible. But when I'm here I feel like I'm hiding from the world.'

'I can't imagine you hiding from anyone.'

'You'd be surprised.'

'So why have you brought me here?'

'Why did you come?'

She looked at him and he saw the amusement in her eyes. At the same time, he felt the desire that had taken hold of him the night before at the swimming pool. He caught hold of himself. 'I've had enough of this. Why do you have to treat everything like a game?'

'Because it is a game. Haven't you noticed?'

'For you, maybe. Not for me.' He turned on her. 'What are you doing in this country? You don't love Irwin Wolfe, so why are you with him? He's talking about marrying you, for God's sake!'

She threw her head back and laughed when she heard that. 'Maybe I'll get a boat named after me. Can you see me as the next Mrs Wolfe? The first one killed herself, you know. She threw herself out of the ninth floor of a building rather than spend another night with Irwin. He says she fell. But even he doesn't believe it.'

She poured the champagne but Bond shook his head. 'Not for me, thank you. You asked me why I came here. Well, it wasn't to drink champagne with you. I want information.'

'You're becoming tiresome, James. That's what you said the first time we met. And I told you then: I don't give anything away for nothing.'

He took a step towards her. 'This time it's going to be different. You're going to tell me what I want to know.'

'Oh yes? And how do you propose to get it out of me?'

It was all the invitation he needed. In fact, he hadn't wanted to be invited. He had already decided to take what he wanted and to hell with the consequences.

He grabbed hold of her and drew her against him, pressing his mouth onto hers and forcing his tongue between her lips. He could feel her breasts, large and warm, against his chest and swept his arms around her, drawing her close. He didn't expect her to resist and was surprised to find both his wrists suddenly clamped in her hands. For a moment he stared at her, puzzled. Had he misread the signals? But then, with a mischievous smile, she lowered herself onto her knees, pulling him down onto the rug with her. Still she held him, not allowing him to come close. Bond could feel the passion rising in him but he got the message. If this was going to continue, it would be on her terms.

It was a new experience for Bond. Sixtine was older than him. She'd been married. She might even have a child. All of this put her in a different place, a world apart from the many girls he had slept with, often only once. Kneeling on the rug, locked in her arms, which were still warning him to keep his distance, Bond examined the deep brown eyes, the lips, the voluminous black hair. The years had done her no harm at all; in fact they had elevated her, giving her an aura of experience and confidence that he found strangely attractive. The first woman he had ever slept with had been six years older than him – he'd been still in his teens – and he remembered how much greater the age difference had seemed at the time. He felt that same sense of daring now. Bond wanted Sixtine but he knew that he had to wait for her to give her assent and part of him cursed the fact that even now, in this intimate moment, she insisted on playing games.

Slowly, she nodded. The music had changed. He could hear 'La Vie en Rose' whispering around him.

Bond pulled her towards him.

Afterwards, when they had finished, she stood up and walked out of the room, leaving Bond on his own. It was dark outside but there was a Tiffany light glowing on a table. Bond got dressed and threw back his champagne, then helped himself to some more. When Sixtine returned, she was wearing a satin dressing gown fastened at the waist and nothing else. Her hair was wet. She had been in the shower.

'Well, if that's your interview technique, I have to say I like it,' she said. She noticed his glass. 'I see you've helped yourself.'

'I hope you don't mind.'

'Of course not.' She found a packet of cigarettes and lit one. 'I have some fresh fish and salad in the refrigerator. I'm not a good cook. I don't do sauces or special recipes. If it takes more than five minutes to prepare, I'm not interested.

But there's also the champagne and I have a decent bottle of Puligny-Montrachet. Will you stay for dinner?'

'I'd like that,' Bond said.

'You can lay the table – the one in the garden.' She pointed. 'The plates are in the cupboard.'

She went back into the kitchen. Bond opened the cupboard and found plates and sets of cutlery . . . but only two of each. Sixtine lived here alone and obviously didn't encourage too many guests. He carried what was needed outside, thinking it had been years since anyone had asked him to lay a table.

A few minutes later she joined him, holding the wine, which she held out for him to open. It was good to feel the chill of the bottle in his hands. 'I bought the house just after the war,' she said. 'I like to have as many properties as possible. I never know where I'm going to be.'

'There are a lot of things I want to know about you,' Bond replied. 'But to be honest, I don't give a damn when you got this house.' He felt a wave of tiredness. Suddenly he was disgusted with himself . . . this play-acting . . . happy families. 'For God's sake, Sixtine. A friend of mine, a good friend, was shot in Marseilles. And this morning a pretty girl who had never done anyone any harm was run over and killed in front of my eyes, simply because she'd met the wrong man. You have a beautiful house and this is a beautiful part of the world but it's all been poisoned. Scipio and his men, Ferrix Chimiques, Irwin Wolfe . . . there's something very ugly going on and whatever may have happened between you and me, that's the only reason why I'm here.'

She stopped and looked at him and he saw that he had hurt her.

'You're right,' she said. 'I understand exactly what sort

of man you are, James, and I know why you're here. But we have this moment together so why don't we enjoy it? Let's have dinner together like two people who have found each other and who have just made love.' She paused, allowing her words to sink in. 'And then I'll tell you everything you want to know.'

14

Secrets and Lies

They had dinner in the garden with the swimming pool shimmering behind them and the stars crowding out the night sky. Everything was silent. The cicadas had decided enough was enough. True to her word, Sixtine had prepared the simplest of meals: grilled fish, salad, cheese she had picked up from the Marché de la Libération in Nice, fresh bread. They sat next to each other at the table and for a while they didn't speak. There was a part of Bond that was uneasy, at war with himself. As much as he now saw that it was inevitable they should have become lovers, he was worried that he had confused the situation and that he might come to regret it. Put bluntly, it was still quite possible that she was his enemy.

As if sensing what was on his mind, she levelled her eyes on him and said, without emotion: 'Do you still want information?'

'Yes.'

'I thought we might enjoy the evening together.'

'I'll enjoy learning more about you.'

She considered. 'What do you want to know, James? Was I responsible for the death of your friend? No. Or the girl this morning? I don't even know who she was. You asked me what I was doing here in the south of France. Why should

I tell you? You know nothing about me and unless it's connected to your work, you care even less.'

'You're wrong.' Bond lifted his wine glass and swirled the
honey-coloured liquid in the palm of his hand. Puligny-
Montrachet is one of the few wines that can trace its origins
back to Roman times and he enjoyed it as much for its age
and antiquity as its taste. 'I want to know everything about
you. Not just what you're doing here in France. You're obviously quite an operator. My office in London has a healthy
respect for you and I can see that you've enjoyed putting me
in my place. But why don't we leave the games behind us
now? Why don't you tell me about yourself?' He put his hand
on his chest. 'I cross my heart it'll go no further than where
we are now. If we're both on the same side, it seems crazy to
have secrets from each other.'

'If we're both on the same side . . .' She let the words hang
in the air. 'All right.' She held out her glass and Bond refilled
it. 'But if you betray me, if you make any move against me, I
will never forgive you, James. More than that, I will make
sure you regret it. Just because I've given myself to you
tonight, don't think I belong to you. The opposite is true.
Because of tonight, part of you belongs to me.'

Bond said nothing. He waited for her to begin.

'You may be surprised but I was born in New Zealand. I
don't even remember the place, really. My father was from
France. He was an engineer and he'd been invited down
there to work on the main trunk line from Auckland to Wel-
lington. My mother made dresses. I was there for the first
five years of my life and I remember almost nothing about
that time except that I felt bored and trapped. There were
only about a million people living in the entire country and
everything was very ordinary, very safe. It was all beige. Nice

little houses with nice little gardens but I don't think I was a nice little girl. I was glad when the work finished and my father announced that we would have to move back to Paris. I can still remember the excitement I felt as I packed my suitcase. Paris – even the word – was like something out of a fairy story. It was the secret door that was going to take me to a new life. How could I have known that we were going to arrive just in time for the outbreak of a world war?

'It's hard for me to describe my feelings about the city a month after we got there. On the one hand, there was the glamour: the Eiffel Tower, the Seine, the boulevards, the shops with their huge windows that made Auckland look like the nowhere it had always been. But at the same time, there were guns everywhere. People were afraid. The Germans were getting closer and closer – at one stage they were just fifteen miles away and hundreds of taxis turned up to carry French soldiers to the front. I actually saw them leave and thought how ridiculous it was, that all these young men should get into taxis to take them to their death.

'By now, my mother was working in a defence factory. My father had got a job helping to build the railway from Montparnasse to Porte de Vanves. I didn't see either of them very much. I was looked after by a neighbour, an old lady who smelled of sour milk and who talked to her cats. I think I was a very angry child. After the first excitement, Paris was a disappointment to me. I was trapped in a small flat in Montrouge, which isn't even part of the city. It's a suburb in the south. I'd learned to speak French from my father but I didn't have any friends. I went to a school that was run by nuns and they were vicious. The food was horrible. In a way, those were the days that made me what I am because if there was one thing I learned it was to be self-sufficient. I had to find the strength to look after myself.'

She fell briefly silent, looking into her wine glass as if it could provide some window into her past life. The robe she was wearing was unfastened at the collar and Bond found himself examining the line of her throat and the valley below. Her hair was still damp from the shower and it suited her, making her look more wild and unpredictable. The moon was behind her and the shadows wrapped themselves around her.

Eventually, she went on.

'Every day, I prayed that things would change and they finally did, though not in the way that I had hoped. On 30 August 1914, my mother was killed by a German bomb that fell onto the Rue des Vinaigriers when she was on her way home from work. It was a completely random event. A German pilot was flying a Taube. That's the German word for "dove". He dropped three bombs by hand. One of the bombs fell into the chimney of a building and blew up a flat. It was the third bomb that killed my mother . . . as far as I know she was the first civilian ever to be killed in an air raid. In fact, there were three other casualties although nobody else was killed. It was completely hushed up at the time. The French were worried about morale. My father only told me what had really happened a few weeks before the war ended.

'By that time, everything was over for him. He hadn't been able to cope after my mother died. I've always believed that women are much stronger than men. We take the cards that life has dealt us and get on with it. Without our support, men just crumple and give up. That was how it was with him. He was drinking heavily . . . and I don't even know how he managed it because alcohol wasn't so easy to find. Sometimes he didn't seem to know who I was. I can still see him now. He had been a handsome man but he didn't eat and he didn't look after himself. He had eyes that stared at me as if he was

153

wondering how I had got there. It was like he was collapsing into himself and I wasn't at all surprised when I came home from school one day to find the neighbour sitting in our empty flat. She told me he was dead. She said he died of a broken heart but it's more likely that he killed himself. I never found out. What difference did it make to me? Either way, I was alone.

'When the war ended, I was sent to England. It turned out that I had an aunt who lived in London, in Pimlico, and she agreed to take me in. I don't need to tell you very much about the next few years. I grew up. I went to school. People talk about "the roaring twenties" but they never really roared for me. There were jazz clubs and cocktail bars all over London. Women were beginning to break out. They were smoking cigarettes and driving cars, wearing the clothes they wanted to wear. People talked about "flappers". You would still have been in short trousers, James. I'm sure it means nothing to you. It hardly meant anything to me, either. I was growing up with my aunt Lucy and she did everything she could to protect me from the world outside. Or maybe she was trying to protect the world from me.

'It's funny to think how ordinary everything was for me and how quickly I settled into what might have become my new life. I went to secretarial college and started working for an insurance company in Knightsbridge with radiators that were turned on full and plants on the windowsills and a tea trolley that came round every day at eleven o'clock in the morning and four in the afternoon. Aunt Lucy made me sandwiches and I would go out when the sun was shining and eat them in the park. There were other girls there and we got on well enough. They used to talk about the boys they were seeing and I wondered how much longer I was going to be alone. One of the underwriters took a liking to me and he drove me to Clacton in his Austin Seven and that was about as glamorous as it got.

'And then everything changed when I met Danny.'

She hadn't been eating her food, chasing it around the plate with her fork instead, and now she gave up altogether. She reached for her cigarettes. She smoked Morlands, the brand she had mentioned. Her cigarette was slim and elegant with a single silver band. She lit it. The flame leapt up briefly, reflecting in her eyes.

'Danny Salgado – that was what he called himself,' she went on. 'We bumped into each other outside Knightsbridge station, quite literally, and he invited me for a drink. He was dark-haired, a few years older than me, expensively dressed. He wore a hat. Now that I think about it, he looked a bit like you but maybe a little more worldly. He had an extraordinary charm. That was the thing about him. The way he smiled at people, they sort of fell in love with him without a second thought and he knew it. He could turn it on with waiters, with police officers, with anyone he fancied. I saw him do it. It was like a technique. I'd never met anyone like him but you have to remember that I was still in my twenties and I'd been living half my life with a spinster aunt. I didn't know much about anything.

'Danny told me that he was a business adviser. I wasn't even sure what that meant but from the very start he made it clear that he didn't like talking about his work. All I knew was that he worked with a lot of very important people. He was always travelling and he always went first class. Later on, I discovered he had three passports. I found out a lot of things about Danny but only when it was too late. Anyway, he took me for dinner that night – to Kettner's in Soho. I had never been anywhere like it but everyone seemed to know him. He bought champagne and when it was time to pay, he scattered five-pound notes like they were meaningless to him. The bill was almost a week's salary for me. "Plenty more where that came from, Jojo," he would say. Jojo was what he called me and he was always saying cheesy things like that but somehow he made them sound all right. He loved jokes. He was the sort of man who could start a party just by walk-ing into the room.

'I didn't sleep with him that night. In fact, it was a long time before I let him take me. He was the first man I'd ever been to bed with and I wanted to know him as a friend before I took him as a lover.' She smiled wistfully, smoke trickling between her fingers. 'It was easy to become friends with Danny. He had a suite of rooms at the Dorchester and that's where he made a dishonest woman of me. When I woke up the next morning, he'd already gone but he left a note for me and a few minutes later there was a knock at the door and a bellboy came in with a huge bunch of flowers, champagne and breakfast on a trolley. We saw each other again a few days later and already he was urging me to give up work and move in with him – even though I didn't actually know where he lived.

'Danny and I got married three months later at Chelsea registry office. Aunt Lucy came to the service and I can still see her sitting there, trying to be happy for me when actually she disapproved. She was scared for me, I think. She must have known intuitively what sort of man Danny was but she never spoke a word against him. She didn't believe it was her business even though she was sure it wouldn't end happily and she was right. She's dead now. She died quite young and I miss her terribly. She was the only close friend I ever had.

'I was very happy for the first couple of years. Danny had bought a flat in Heddon Street, close to Piccadilly. At first I assumed it was for both of us although actually it was just for me. He gave me an allowance and he was generous. We travelled together – to Cannes, to Vienna, to Rome and to Malta. We stayed in the best hotels and went to wonderful restaurants. Danny was a gambler and he took me with him to the casinos. He was the one who introduced me to *vingt-et-un*. He always said it was the one casino game where you could actually beat the house, which was ironic in view of what happened. He taught me how to memorise the order of an entire pack of cards. I can still do it to this day. And he also showed me how to work out exactly how many cards the dealer was holding just by glancing at his hands. I spent hours and hours learning that, not because I thought it would be useful but because I wanted to please him.'

Bond had also stopped eating. He poured himself some more wine and settled back in his chair. He wondered why Sixtine was telling him all this. Perhaps it was because, although she would never admit it, she was lonely. He had thought that when he saw her for the first time at the casino. Who she was and what she did had set her apart from the rest of the world, and perhaps what she craved more than anything else was intimacy in every sense. Again, for someone who traded in information, freely opening herself up to him was the most effective way of lowering the barriers between them. She really did want him to believe that they were on the same side.

'My love affair with Danny ended pretty much the day I got pregnant,' Sixtine said. 'Although I didn't see it at the time. He was so happy when I told him. There were more flowers. Dinner at the Ritz. An expensive doctor in Cavendish

Square. But at the same time, it was as if a switch had been thrown and he no longer felt comfortable with me. I knew it at once when he was in bed with me a few days after I'd told him and it was as if he wasn't there. His whole manner towards me changed. He'd always made me feel special but now his eyes would flicker over me as if I'd become part of the furniture. He used to be someone I could talk to but now it was just a few sentences and he would be gone as soon as he could.' She sighed. 'I'm making it sound melodramatic but actually it was very ordinary. Isn't that how marriage works? The days go by and you settle into a routine and piece by piece everything is taken away from you until there are two complete strangers sitting in the same room.

'Suddenly, he was travelling more. He'd often been away for days at a time but after the baby was born – it was a boy – it became weeks. Danny loved being a father. He was so proud. But maybe there was a side of him that was afraid of responsibility, who didn't want to be tied down. I never complained. I tried to make things easy for him. That's how much of a fool I was. I had been married to him for five years before I discovered the truth.

'I should have known from the start. Perhaps I had known and all along I'd just been pretending that I didn't. There were the three passports, for a start, the different names. There had been telephone calls in the middle of the night, strange men who never announced their names arriving at the flat. And the money! Envelopes full of banknotes with no real explanation about where it was all coming from. I'd never met his parents or any of his relatives and the friends that he introduced me to seemed to change from season to season so that there was never anyone who was actually close. You know the mistake I'd made, James? I made Danny my whole world. I'll never do that again with another man.

'He wasn't a business adviser. He was a crook – plain and simple. I learned the truth from a Scotland Yard detective called Jack Travers who came looking for him and who took pity on me. Or maybe he wanted to use me to hurt Danny. I don't know. Anyway, Danny had started his career as a confidence trickster. No surprises there. He was what was called "the roper" for a well-organised gang who worked in London and sometimes on transatlantic crossings. The roper is the one who pulls in the mark, which was exactly what he had done with me. All it takes is a lot of charm and plausibility. They had a series of scams with fanciful names: the Huge Duke, the Last Turn, the Hot Seat, the Tear-up . . . you wouldn't believe how much practice went into it all. There were half a dozen of them pretending they didn't know each other when in fact they were working together. I'd met some of them but I never knew their real names.

'Recently, he'd branched out. He'd set up a racket forging National Health and Unemployment stamps. They were being printed in Poland and he was selling them through gangs that he was meeting in different parts of London . . . the Hoxton Mob and the Elephant Boys. He was a familiar figure, hanging out at clubs and racecourses. It seems that everyone knew him. Except me.

'And I suppose it goes without saying that I wasn't the only woman in his life. Far from it. DI Travers made sure I got all the details. Danny had girlfriends all over London. I got the impression that he must have been laughing about me when he was with them because I was the only one who didn't know the truth. I'd constructed this little dream of being a wife and a mother when actually I was just a convenience. I'm not even sure why he married me, although later on I found out that Salgado wasn't his real name so it didn't matter anyway because the whole marriage was null and void, part of the pretence.'

The evening air was getting cooler. Sixtine drew the robe closer around her. Bond lit another cigarette.

'Don't worry,' she said. 'I'm not going to talk all night. You said you wanted to know everything about me. Well, I'll spare you that. This is the edited version. Do you want me to go on?'

'You can talk as long as you like,' Bond said. 'I'm not going anywhere.'

'I hope not, James. At least, I hope not tonight.'

She drank the rest of her wine and pushed the glass away.

'I left Danny. We never had a row. We didn't have any confrontation. I simply took my son and went back to Aunt Lucy. She'd been expecting me. My old room was ready for me and there was another room up in the attic for Julian. I'll say one thing for Danny. He still sent me money every week. I don't know whether it was for me, for his son or just for his conscience but I didn't have to go back to work. I never saw him again. The truth is, in a way, we really had loved each other and we didn't want to see each other now that everything had changed. It was better just to live with the memories.

'When the money stopped, I knew it could only mean one thing. Danny had disappeared and nobody would give me any information about him so I went back to Travers and he told me exactly what I expected to hear. Danny had been shot dead by one of his gangster friends. It turned out that in the last few years of his life, despite everything he'd said, he'd allowed gambling to consume him – not just cards but craps and roulette – and in just a short time he'd been cleaned out by the casinos. It was all gone: the flat in Piccadilly, the cars, the nice clothes. I wondered how he'd found the money to send to me. Travers smiled when I asked him that. It seems he'd been dipping his hand in the till, stealing from his associates. That was what got him killed. I would have liked to have taken Julian to visit his grave but that wasn't going to happen. Danny was probably weighed down at the bottom of the Thames. He didn't leave anything behind. Not even a memory.'

Sixtine shivered.

'Let's go back inside. I'm getting cold.'

They went into the living room. Sixtine sat on the sofa with her legs drawn up beneath her. Bond sat opposite, waiting to hear the end of the story.

'Another war was on the way and part of me was glad,' she said. 'Isn't that terrible? But I needed my life to be shaken up. I wanted a new world to explore. I was thirty years old when war was finally declared and I thought about joining the Women's Land Army or the ATS, but Aunt Lucy had a friend who taught at Imperial College and, knowing that I spoke fluent French, he suggested I apply for a job at somewhere called Bletchley Park. It was all top secret and I shouldn't be talking to you about it even now. I went for an interview at a little office near Green Park and the next thing I knew, I'd signed the Official Secrets Act and I was on my way to Buckinghamshire with a job that would pay me thirty-six shillings a week – although I'd have to lose a guinea out of that for digs. Julian stayed in London with Aunt Lucy.

'I was at Bletchley for most of the war. I started in the indexing hut . . . naval intelligence. My job was to look out for any words or phrases in French and German that might be of interest and put them down on cards for cross-referencing. It was a rather grim place with terrible food and I worked long hours, six days a week, but I was very happy there. I had a lot of friends, even though most of the girls were younger than me. We had to be close to each other because we weren't allowed to talk about anything to anyone else. I remember swimming in the local reservoir during the summer, dances at Woburn Abbey, the Odeon at Fenny Stratford. I used to meet RAF pilots from Cranfield at a pub on the Grand Union Canal and there was a Polish airman I was close to for a time. In a way, I was protected, in a sort of cocoon. The work I was doing was important. We all knew that. I didn't have to think about the rest of my life, about Danny, about any of it.

'And then, in the summer of 1943, the same professor who had recommended me to Bletchley came calling a second time – only now he wanted me to join an organisation I'd never heard of and which, he said, would put my life in great danger. I knew at once that he wanted me to become a spy and I was right. He was talking about the SOE.'

Sixtine shivered again but this time Bond knew it wasn't because of the cold.

'I was recruited and sent to Scotland for training in field craft, weapons, demolition, night-and-day navigation and all the rest of it. I was thirty-four by then and I found it completely exhausting. Then it was off to Beaulieu for cryptography, weapons, escape and evasion techniques, Morse . . . I know you were in naval intelligence, James, so this is all probably very familiar to you.'

'How do you know?' Bond interrupted. 'When we first met, you knew my name and everything about me. How did you get that information?'

She looked him in the eyes. 'You think I've been spying on you?'

'It's what I assumed.'

'Well, you're wrong.' She paused. 'Irwin Wolfe told me about you. He even showed me your photograph and warned me to keep away from you.'

Bond considered what she had said. He still wasn't sure if he should believe her. 'That's very interesting. But you were telling me about your work with the SOE . . .'

'Actually, I don't want to talk about it very much. It ended badly, very badly.'

'You're still alive.'

'They used to say that a wireless operator with the SOE had a life expectancy of six weeks, so I suppose I was lucky.' She took the cigarette that Bond was smoking, used it to light her own, then handed it back. 'I was given the code name of Sixtine and I was sent out for the first time at the end of 1943. My job was to join the Stockbroker Circuit as a courier, relaying messages in and out. There was a strange irony. Stockbroker had launched a successful attack on the railway workshop at Fives-Lille and they'd also developed an interesting method of sabotage which they called "Phantom Train". They'd hijack a locomotive and send it rushing down the tracks. Eventually it would crash into another locomotive or a building without any need of explosives. I was with them for three months and it always struck me as funny. When I was a little girl, my father had been creating the French railway system and here I was with the people who were destroying it. It made me wonder what he would have thought.

'I was sent into France three times and on the third time my luck ran out. I'm not going to tell you what happened. I never talk about it. I don't even think about it. I was arrested by the Gestapo one day after I parachuted into northern France and a week before D-Day. Of course, I'd been betrayed. They knew I was coming.'

Bond could see the memories tearing through her and reached out to hold onto her – but she shrugged him away.

'I'm all right. A lot of people were hurt in the war and I was just one of them. But there was something that hurt a lot more, although I only found out about it later and maybe it will explain to you everything you want to know.' She took a deep breath. 'I say that I was betrayed and it was true. When I parachuted into France that third time, the Germans knew I was on my way and they were waiting for me. I fell right into their arms. But it was only later I discovered that the SOE had been aware of this all along. They knew that I would be arrested, interrogated and probably killed. There were whole networks – Stockbroker, Prosper and many others – that had been infiltrated by the Germans. But the SOE were playing a double game. They didn't want the Germans to know that they knew. They wanted to distract their attention from the Normandy landings and if that meant sacrificing people like me, then so be it. And believe me, I wasn't the only one.

'Yes, James, I'm still alive. But when I got back to England from Ravensbrück, which is where I had been kept prisoner, and when I understood what had been done to me, how I had been manipulated, a large part of me died. It's still dead now.'

She didn't want to smoke any more of her cigarette and stubbed it out, the sparks rising around her fingertips.

'That was when I decided I would never allow a man to tell me what to do again,' she went on. 'I would have no allegiance to anyone – and not to any country. I would go into business for myself. I would get rich and I wouldn't care how I did it. I kept the name, Sixtine, because it was also a number and it seemed right that I should deliberately set aside part of my humanity. It's something you and I have in common. They call you 007 because they know it will make it easier for you to kill brutally and without remorse. It matters to them that you should be a double zero. They have taken part of your humanity too.'

Bond didn't believe what Sixtine was saying. He knew there had been double agents within the Special Operations Executive. He himself had spoken to Henri Déricourt, who had controlled air operations and who had been prosecuted for treason fourteen months after the end of the trial. Bond had taken a dislike to the French pilot but in the end Déricourt had been acquitted. He couldn't believe that there had been some sort of conspiracy running through the upper echelons of the organisation and he was tempted to argue with Sixtine.

He decided to stay silent. He still needed information from her. He had to see this through to the end.

'I don't think of myself as a number,' he said. 'I've already told you why I choose to do the work that I do. But there are two things I want to ask you. The first is – what happened to your son, Julian? You haven't mentioned him.'

She made a vague gesture with one hand. 'He's in the Bahamas. I have a house there and he's happier away from me. It's easier for both of us that way.'

'And you still haven't told me what you're doing in the south of France. What about Irwin Wolfe? I know you don't love him. I imagine you don't even like him. So what do you want from him?'

Bond waited. In a way the entire conversation had been leading up to this.

'I'll tell you,' she said. 'Because I don't want there to be any secrets between us and it may be that we can even help each other. I would have thought you'd have guessed anyway.' She paused. 'The first thing you should know is that Irwin is a sick man. I think he's dying. He takes about a dozen pills every day but they're not helping him any more. The strange thing is, his illness only makes him more determined. It's driving him on. He's developed a new product which could make him another fortune – even if it's one he'll never get to spend.' She paused. 'Do you know anything about Technicolor film?'

'I know a little. I don't often go to the cinema. I've always found more interesting things to do in the dark.'

She nodded. 'I'm sure. Well, the basic process of Technicolor is very simple. The colours are divided into three basic components: red, green and blue. The trouble is, it demands three separate negatives and that causes complications.'

She was businesslike now, unemotional, as if everything she had been saying for the last hour had been forgotten. Bond observed her with a sense of admiration he had rarely felt for a woman. Child, orphan, wife, mother, widow, secret agent, prisoner and self-confessed criminal, she had managed to break down her life into separate compartments with a ruthlessness that had ensured not just her survival but her success. He remembered Reade Griffith, almost in awe of her. 'I can tell you – she's a piece of work!' It was true. Bond had never met anyone quite like her.

'Multiply the negatives and you divide the light,' she went on. 'So you have to use a lot more lighting when you're shooting the film. And that makes it much more expensive.

'But Irwin, or the people working for him, has invented a type of 35 mm colour negative stock that has a much wider latitude. It's good for indoor and outdoor photography. He calls it G-Vision and it's going to put Technicolor and all the rest of them out of business. Which is where I come in. There are certain people I know who want the formula. They've paid me a considerable amount of money to steal it.'

So that was it: industrial espionage, as simple as that. Bond couldn't help smiling. At the same time, he wondered who the people were behind Sixtine and knew she wouldn't tell him. 'He produces this new film stock at his plant in Menton,' he said.

'That's right. Or at least, that's what I believe. I've been cosying up to him, trying to get him to give me a tour but Irwin has always been completely silent about what he gets up to in his secret compound in the middle of the woods. It's been driving me crazy because, as you know, he's leaving France on Tuesday morning and without him here I won't get another chance. I even went out and took a sneaky look for myself and you'd think he was manufacturing nuclear bombs the amount of security he's hired. There are two fences, the inner one electrified. He has armed guards on twenty-four-hour patrol and guard dogs. I can't say I blame him. He's sitting on something that could be worth millions of dollars.

'Today was my last chance. I knew he was going to Menton this afternoon and when I met him on the *Mirabelle*, I really expected him to take me with him. It was more or less what he'd promised.'

'And if he had taken you in – what then?'

'I'm good at improvising. A few minutes on my own would have been all I needed. I know what I'm looking for and I've got a miniature camera. It's just a question of meeting the right people and taking the right shots. Anyway, it looks as if I'm going to have to fall back on an alternative plan.' She looked at Bond curiously. 'And the funny thing is, meeting you could be exactly the break I need.'

'You think I'm going to help you steal commercial secrets?'

'Why not? Maybe I can help you find out what's going on around here. You say this part of the world is poisoned. I agree. There's definitely something nasty in the air. Scipio may look like he's just walked out of a circus but he's extremely dangerous. Trust me, you don't want to go after him on your own.'

Bond was reminded of his confrontation with Jean-Paul Scipio and once again felt the liquid being thrown in his face. He still wondered why it had been water, not acid. Either way, describing him as dangerous was an understatement. He was a monster.

'Why did you meet him at La Caravelle?' Bond asked.

'I already told you,' Sixtine said. 'Scipio heard I was in Marseilles. He knew who I was. He invited me to meet him except it wasn't so much an invitation as a royal summons. There was no way I could refuse. He wanted to know that I wasn't up to anything that might interfere with his business.'

'What is his business? From what I understand, he's given up narcotics.'

'I have no idea. I didn't ask and he didn't say.'

'Did you tell him why you were here?'

'No. I make it a practice never to share information and certainly not in the way I have with you. I led him to believe that I was a gold-digger, trying to get my hooks into Irwin's fortune. And he believed me. It fits with his view of women. I don't think he likes us very much.'

She yawned and Bond glanced at his watch. It was only ten o'clock. He felt he had been in Antibes much longer. 'I should leave,' he said.

'I was hoping you'd stay.' She looked at him with laughter

in her eyes. 'I'm going to bed and you're going to come with me. I want you to make love to me again but more slowly this time. You make love like a schoolboy. I'm sure you've had plenty of girls, James, but you've never had a woman and you've still got a lot to learn.' He was about to protest but she stopped him. 'Don't say anything. We've talked enough. If there's more to be said, we can do it in the morning.'

There was a staircase opposite the kitchen and she climbed up with Bond following. The bedroom was exactly as he had imagined it would be, small and pretty with ormolu wall lights and an antique bed and two windows leading out onto the terrace that he had seen at the front of the house. She turned as he came in. 'No more talking,' she said.

It was only the next morning, as the sun came up, that they spoke again. Bond was woken by Sixtine slipping out of bed and padding bare-footed out of the room. When she returned, she was wearing a long, striped shirt with the sleeves rolled up and carrying something in her hand. 'I want you to have this,' she said. 'What I said to you last night, before we came upstairs, was unfair. I want you to have this as a souvenir of our time together. You can use it when you buy yourself some decent cigarettes.'

It was a flat square cigarette case made out of gunmetal. When Bond opened it, he saw that there were four words inscribed in the lid, but close to the edge where they were hard to see.

FOREVER AND A DAY.

'I bought it for Danny,' she explained. 'On the day we got married, he said he wanted to be with me forever but I told him that wasn't enough. I wanted forever and a day. I had this made for our anniversary but he was dead before I could give it to him. So I want to give it to you.'

'I thought you hated Danny,' Bond said, closing the lid.

'Did I say that? No. How can I hate him? He's part of my story and that story brought me to you.'

Bond reached out for her and as the first bright orange rays of the morning sun stretched across the wooden floor, she slipped into his arms, the two of them gently folding themselves into one another beneath the sheets.

15

Down to the Wire

The road from Menton is a gift to thrill-seekers. It climbs steeply through a series of hairpin bends with dazzling views of the deep blue Mediterranean Sea before plunging into the dense forests of the Alpes-Maritimes with olives, cypresses and pine trees taking over from the orange and lemon trees that have been cultivated on the slopes below. Apart from the tarmac and the occasional telegraph pole, it feels that nothing has changed here in a thousand years. Saracen fortresses, or the remains of them, still stand guard over rocky crags, and villages cling to hilltops with church bells sounding out from improbably large cathedrals. The houses are pink and yellow and white and green and many of them still lack electricity. It's a world apart from the coast of the Riviera. A train line runs up to the town of Sospel, tunnelling through the rocks that it was unable to bypass. But it is in a fast car with the roof down that you will fully experience the heat, the smell of herbs and wild flowers and the sense of calm that you have momentarily broken, the modern world rushing through the ancient.

Bond and Sixtine had enjoyed a late breakfast in Menton. They'd eaten eggs that had been warm in the hand when they were carried into the kitchen, bread baked that morning and strong Italian coffee. The town might call itself 'the pearl of France' but it was less than a mile from the border and enjoyed the best of both worlds. The sun was hotter than ever and the mountains had thrown an overprotective arm around the little community, preventing any breeze from reaching its tightly packed streets and alleyways. By the time they had finished their meal and paid the bill they were glad to climb back into the MG and to set off with the wind streaming over their shoulders.

Bond wanted to take a look at the plant where Wolfe Europe manufactured its new film stock and Sixtine had agreed to take him. It was still hard to believe that Irwin Wolfe was involved in any criminal activities but at the same time he certainly appeared to be at the centre of a web that stretched across the south of France. A British agent had been sent to look into the activities of the Corsican syndicates. He had been killed in Marseilles, close to a chemical company either owned or operated by Jean-Paul Scipio, a local gangster who had once controlled 80 per cent of the narcotics trade. When Bond had visited Ferrix Chimiques he had almost got himself killed, but he had learned that Wolfe was a customer there. It didn't matter that the chemical he was buying – acetic anhydride – seemed to be completely innocent. The link had been made. Scipio and Wolfe. Visiting the plant when it might not be possible even to penetrate the perimeter fence might seem like a waste of time but it was a Sunday, the weather was glorious and right now there wasn't anywhere that Bond would prefer to be.

The road took them through Castellar, one of the many *villages perchés*, where they were forced to slow down behind a donkey and a cart piled up with watermelons. The MG grumbled but the animal ignored it.

'One day,' Bond said, 'I want to spend a week with you in

a village like this. We'll sit in the sun and drink red wine and pretend there aren't any bad people in the world.'

'A week?' Sixtine looked at him scornfully. 'You'd get bored in three days.'

The donkey shifted forward. Seeing an opportunity, she touched the accelerator and sent the little car in a wide curve around it.

It was amazing how quickly the landscape swallowed them up. Still climbing, the road seemed to go into contortions as if trying to shake them from its surface, bending and twisting for no obvious reason, dog-legging and turning back on itself. They passed a few abandoned-looking stone cottages lost on the edge of a forest that stretched all the way to the mountains, blocking out much of the sky and turning the light green. Even the car sounded subdued, nervous about going too much further.

They almost missed the turning. Perhaps it was designed that way. There was a low sign with the letters 'W.E.' and an arrow, but it was the lane itself that gave the game away. The bitumen was brand new and the grass had been cut back to reveal the edges. Sixtine drove past and then pulled into a clearing between two trees. The car, only a few feet from the main road, was completely invisible and Bond remembered what she had told him. She had been here before.

'We'll walk from here,' she said. 'It's about half a mile but the lane only goes to Wolfe Europe so if they hear the engine, they'll know we're coming.'

Before they'd left Nice, Sixtine had driven Bond back to his hotel and he had changed into a short-sleeved cotton shirt, linen trousers and nubuck saddle shoes with crepe soles. He'd deliberately chosen shades of brown and grey so that he would blend in with his surroundings. He had also picked up his Beretta, now tucked reassuringly into his waistband.

He nodded. 'After you.'

They set off together, keeping a line of trees between themselves and the edge of the new lane. The ground was soft and spongy with a bed of pine needles and they were careful to make no sound. It was cooler inside the forest than it had been in Menton. A few bees droned around them, found them uninteresting and buzzed off. Birds rustled the leaves but remained unseen. But for the lane, it would have been easy to get lost. Every step they took offered a choice of a dozen identical directions.

After about ten minutes, Sixtine held up a hand and they stopped. 'There it is,' she whispered. 'They're still working, even though it's a Sunday. I don't think they ever stop.'

Bond looked through a gap in the foliage and saw a metal fence with the sun glinting on the wire. It was about ten feet high, disappearing through the trees on either side of the lane. There was a solid-looking barrier that rose and fell electronically and, next to it, a two-storey office and administration block made out of grey concrete with searchlights and radio antennae mounted on the roof. Two men were standing outside, both dressed in dark blue uniforms. Bond could make out the letters 'W.E.' on their jackets. It was more like the entrance to a high-security prison than a manufacturing plant, but the strange thing was that the men seemed to be guarding nothing at all. The lane simply continued further into the wood.

'The whole thing is shaped like a doughnut,' Sixtine whispered next to him. 'This is the outer ring. There's another quarter-mile of woodland and then a second fence. That's the electrified one. The actual plant is in the middle.'

'When did you come here?'

'Two weeks ago. Follow me. And take care where you tread.'

They turned left, heading away from the lane and moving clockwise round the fence. Every few yards, they passed 'Do Not Trespass' signs, printed bright red in both English and French and attached to the wire. Sixtine ignored them. She was looking for something and after about ten minutes she found it: a white cross scratched on a fir tree. The fence was right next to them and she went over to it.

'This is where it gets interesting,' she said.

Bond saw that the wire had been carefully cut at ground level. The join was invisible but one section could be lifted up like a cat flap. The gap was just big enough for the two of them to squeeze through. Now they found themselves inside the inner ring with the second fence somewhere ahead of them. The trees seemed even thicker here and the vegetation was wilder, the ground covered in nettles and moss with freakishly coloured mushrooms that looked like pustules, breaking out in clumps.

Sixtine held a finger to her lips and they continued forward in silence, taking care not to step on loose branches or anything that made a sound. After a few steps, Bond understood why. Sixtine pointed to the trunk of a tree and he saw a thick cable running up to a fan-shaped microphone. The entire wood had been wired for sound! She was right about what she had said. Irwin Wolfe had taken security to extremes. They were lucky that there didn't appear to be any cameras.

They continued more slowly after that. Bond was sweating. The air seemed very close, hemmed in by so many trees. Nothing else moved. Even the birds and the butterflies had been warned to stay away. Sixtine pointed at a thick clump of leaves, heart-shaped and a dark, bilious green. It was some sort of nettle and he knew at once that it was alien, that it had no place in a European wood. Sixtine put her lips very close to his ear and whispered: 'Gympie-gympie.' Bond knew immediately what she meant. It wasn't an easy name to forget, although he had heard it only once before at a briefing on jungle warfare in relation to Australia and Indonesia. Gympie-gympie. Also known as the mulberry-leaved stinger and the moonlighter. The most painful stinging nettle in the world. If the tiny silica hairs came in contact with your skin, within minutes you experienced pain that you would not believe possible, the sort of pain that would stab at every inch of your body with a series of electric jolts that could easily drive you into anaphylactic shock. The instructor had told the story of a serviceman who had unknowingly used one of the leaves as toilet paper during a training exercise. Thirty minutes later, unable to bear any more, he had shot himself dead.

And here it was, growing just a few miles away from the quietest and most genteel resort in the Riviera. Bond had no doubt that it had been brought to France and planted quite deliberately to punish unwary trespassers, and he had to ask himself – were such extreme measures really justified, simply to protect a replacement for Technicolor film? Plenty of industrialists kept secrets. Very few were prepared to maim or even to kill to protect them.

With a sense of dread and a growing knot in his stomach, he pressed forward. There was still no sign of the second fence but the forest had one last trick to play. Sixtine held up a hand, this time pointing down with the other. There was a tripwire, about six inches above the ground, stretching out in front of them before disappearing into the undergrowth. Intrigued, Bond followed it, carefully separating the leaves with a stick, not wanting to touch them with his hands. The wire was connected to a grey metal box that was fastened to a tree a short distance away. A miniature crossbow was attached to the side with a vicious, needle-sharp bolt pointing back. Anyone activating the device would have been crippled, shot in the ankle. Bond could imagine their pain and confusion as they stumbled back through the undergrowth, perhaps into the bed of killing nettles.

He'd had enough. He wanted to get out of there. Instead, they pressed on.

Bond heard the fence before he saw it – or rather, the 2,000 volts of electricity that were pulsing through it. There were no warning signs here. They weren't needed. Anyone desperate enough to come this far would certainly have hostile intentions and wasn't going to be put off by polite notices. They had emerged suddenly from the woodland. The ground had been cleared and trees cut down for about ten yards all the way round the compound, making it impossible to go any closer. Quite apart from the likelihood of further booby traps – and Bond wouldn't have been surprised if the area ahead of him was actually mined – they would be unprotected out in the open and all too easily seen. It didn't matter anyway. From here they had a reasonably good glimpse of the hidden world of Irwin Wolfe.

The main entrance, with a barrier and a security block identical to the one they had already seen, was over to their right. The lane emerged from the forest and finally led to a wide concrete area with two jeeps parked next to each other and a water tower to one side. The jeeps were Willys MBs, used by the French army, with Bren guns and ammo boxes mounted in the back. A short distance away from them, on the other side of the wire, they could make out the first in a series of long rectangular buildings made of dark wood on a brick base with slanting roofs formed from sheets of corrugated iron and windows deliberately designed to provide no view in or out. These were set in straight lines, each marked with a single letter painted white, like a POW camp. A single watchtower rose up in the far corner with two men silhouetted against the sky, one of them scanning the tree-tops through binoculars. The compound covered the same area as the mountain village they had passed.

'Seen enough?' Sixtine whispered.

'Wait!'

Everything was wrong. Armed jeeps. Guards. Electrified fences. The position – in the middle of a forest, miles from the nearest town. And there was something else. Studying the compound more carefully, Bond saw that it was split into two halves. A whole area was taken up with buildings that had been added more recently, constructed in a quite different style. They had no windows at all and they were air-conditioned, with large steel boxes clinging to the woodwork and bright, silver chimneys jutting out of their roofs.

Was this where the new film stock was manufactured? The lack of windows made sense. Undeveloped film would demand complete darkness. Bond detected a sharp, chemical smell in the air. A door had opened and a man came out wearing a white laboratory coat. He slipped off the protective mask that had been covering his nose and mouth and lit a cigarette. Bond had brought a Minox subminiature camera with him and fired off half a dozen shots. He nodded at Sixtine. There was no point staying.

The two of them turned to leave.

They were no longer alone.

Three men stood facing them, dressed in khaki and carrying light machine guns. They had emerged silently from the forest, creeping up on Bond and Sixtine while they were watching the compound. They had the same dark, whippet-like features of the Corsicans who had surrounded Bond at Ferrix Chimiques and he saw, with a sinking heart, that they were equally professional, keeping exactly the right distance between each other, ensuring they had a clear line of fire. What had given them away? Had their footsteps been picked up by the concealed microphones? Or perhaps there were other security devices that they'd both missed. Bond's mind was already racing. The Beretta was still in the waistband of his trousers but he would be dead before he could reach it. He would have to try another way.

He lifted his hands in the air and smiled. 'Good afternoon,' he said, speaking in fluent French. 'I wonder if you can help me. My wife and I went for a walk in the woods and we seem to have got lost.'

The men weren't buying it. One of them, the leader, spat into the grass, then said: 'Keep your hands in the air. You will come with us.'

'I really don't think you need to be quite so aggressive.' Bond was still playing the innocent tourist. Next to him, Sixtine looked terrified, as if she had never seen a gun before. 'We were following the lane and we took a wrong turn. You shouldn't be pointing those guns at us. I can assure you I'll be taking this up with the British consul.'

One of the men had a radio transmitter and brought it up to his mouth. There was a hiss of static as he made the connection. Bond realised that he had to act now if they were going to have any chance of getting out of this. If they allowed themselves to be escorted into the compound, it would be over. These men didn't work for Irwin Wolfe. He was sure of it. They must work for Jean-Paul Scipio. And

Bond had been warned. A second confrontation with the gangster would be his last. His hand edged round behind his back, reaching for the Beretta. He had to take them out before they called for back-up. There were three machine guns pointing at him. The odds were hopelessly against him. But if he dived to the ground and took out the two men on the right, leaving the man with the radio until last . . .

'Keep your hands in sight!'

One of them had seen what he was doing. The muzzle of his machine gun rose, the single black eye daring Bond to continue. Bond froze. His fingers were only inches away from the Beretta.

And then something silver glinted in the air, shining out against the dark background of the woods. It travelled so quickly that it had found its target before Bond knew what it was. The man with the radio grunted and collapsed, his knees folding underneath him. The handle of a knife jutted out of his neck. The other two turned just in time to face their own death. Two more knives span towards them. One of the men was hit in the throat, the other in his chest. Both crumpled and lay still.

Three more people stepped out of the woods. Once again Bond's hand crept round, reaching for the Beretta, but Sixtine had seen what he was doing and issued a one-word command. 'Don't!'

It was fortunate that she had reacted so quickly as he might already have fired. But now Bond realised that he knew the new arrivals. He had seen them before. One looked like a schoolteacher, young, with thick glasses and carefully combed hair. One was short and overweight and could have been a businessman although he no longer wore a gold signet ring. The third was shabby and unshaven, standing lazily with a crooked half-smile. The last time Bond had seen them, they had been sitting together, playing *vingt-et-un* in the Monte Carlo casino. They were Sixtine's syndicate. But how had they got here?

The youngest of the three – the schoolteacher – was examining the guards. He glanced up and spoke in English. 'This one is still alive.'

'Finish him, please, Marco,' Sixtine said.

The survivor was the last of the guards to have been hit. He was the one who had spoken to Bond. Marco calmly pulled the knife out of his chest and re-inserted it in his throat, pushing it in and twisting it at the same time. The guard's legs shuddered once. He made no sound.

'Are you all right, madame?' the businessman asked. Bond wondered what had happened to the woman who had acted as his wife. Or were they really married? With this group, anything was possible.

'I'm fine, thank you, Frédéric.' Sixtine looked around her. She seemed completely unfussed by what had just occurred.

'We will need to get rid of the bodies,' Frédéric muttered. 'We can bury them, if you like, in the woods.'

'No. I don't think we should disturb the ground in this wretched place. Find some of those bushes – the ones with the poison nettles – and throw them in there. With a bit of luck nobody will find them, at least not until we've finished. Then go back to Nice. I'll contact you there.'

'Would you like us to accompany you out of here, madame?' the third man asked. 'There are still quite a few unpleasant things between the two fences.'

'No, thank you, Georges. I can find my own way. Anyway, I have Mr Bond to look after me.' She turned to Bond and smiled. 'Have you seen enough?'

181

'More than enough, I think,' Bond said.

They left the three men to deal with the bodies and made their way silently and carefully back to the outer fence. Sixtine had marked the section that had been cut with another white cross on a tree. Bond lifted the flap for her as she crawled out. The two of them made their way back to the car.

'They followed us here,' Bond said as they drove back down the hill. At last it was safe to speak.

'Actually, they were already here. I asked them to wait for me and then follow us into the woods.'

'You didn't trust me?'

'I don't trust anyone, James. Not even the men I've slept with.' She stopped herself. '*Especially* the men I've slept with. But that's not why they were there. The boys always follow me wherever I go. They like to look after me.'

'They were playing cards with you in the casino.'

'Yes. Marco is actually very good at *vingt-et-un* and baccarat too for that matter. He could win on his own but he likes to indulge me.'

They reached Castellar after a few minutes and drove slowly through the narrow streets. This time there was no donkey to block the way. Bond thought about what he had seen; the old and the new buildings, the electric fence, the various traps in the forest, the guards with machine guns. He knew that he had to go back. He turned to Sixtine.

'Last night you said you thought you'd found a way into the plant – but that you might need my help.'

Sixtine nodded. 'That's right. But it's very high-risk and we'd have to be completely on our own.'

'Do you want to try it?'

'Absolutely.'

'Then tell me.'

16

Suicide Doors

It had taken Sixtine two weeks to find the baker who supplied the canteen at Wolfe Europe and another two weeks to persuade him to help her.

Paul Rémy was a nervous man. He had inherited the business from his father and dedicated himself to his work, getting up every morning at half past four to fire up the ovens and begin the lengthy, almost artistic process of creating the baguettes, croissants, *pain de campagne* and *fougasses* that would fill the window of his little shop on the Avenue Boyer in Menton. When he had first been offered the contract by the film manufacturer, it had seemed almost too good to be true: a guaranteed order three times a week and the kudos of being associated with a large international company. But he had come to dread his visits to the factory or whatever it was that was buried so deep in the woods. He did not understand why there had to be guns. He had been ordered to sign a confidentiality agreement. Why make such a big deal when all he was doing was delivering bread? Every time he drove in, he felt that he was entering a trap. Every time, he counted the minutes until he left.

And to make things worse, this strange, beautiful woman had suddenly appeared out of nowhere. She had offered him a huge sum of money to do something that would almost certainly put his life at risk. Why had she chosen him? He had been mad to speak to her at all.

The trouble was, Paul Rémy desperately needed money. He had fallen several months behind with the rent. Earlier that summer, one of the kneading machines in the *fournil* where he did his work had given up the ghost and the cost of its replacement had been exorbitant. There was a full-time patissier who was threatening to resign unless he got a rise. What was he to do? If he added even a few centimes to the cost of his products, his customers would desert him.

And then there was Jeanette. He had recently fallen for the pretty blonde girl who worked in the flower shop opposite and there was a problem here too. Jeanette was married to the owner of the flower shop. The two of them met regularly when the husband was away – either at the market or visiting his elderly parents. They talked constantly of running away together but that also required money. Jeanette had expensive tastes. Rémy knew he would have no trouble stealing her but keeping her would be altogether more difficult.

Which was why, that same Sunday evening after their visit to the factory, he found himself sitting in the tiny apartment above the shop, sharing a rough bottle of wine with the woman who called herself Madame 16 and the Englishman she had brought with her. A fan turned slowly in the ceiling but it only pushed the air around without cooling it.

'What can you tell us about Wolfe Europe?' the Englishman asked. He spoke excellent French.

Rémy spread his hands. 'Very little, monsieur. I see nothing. The place is full of *petits malfrats*. I have already told madame.' Small-time crooks. But Bond knew they were more than that. 'I come. I go.' He looked the Englishman square in the eyes. It was time to assert himself. 'I can take madame in the van with me. But that is all I can do. You must not ask for anything more.'

Sixtine had promised to pay Paul Rémy 200,000 francs to drive her into the compound. The guards had grown used to seeing him and never searched his van. There was plenty of space to conceal somebody underneath one of the shelves that lined the back. Sixtine would cover herself with sacks. While Rémy went into the kitchen with his loaves and cakes, she would slip out and find somewhere to hide. If by chance she was discovered, there would be no way anyone would know how she had got in. That was what they had agreed but now, it seemed, everything was going to change.

'This new plan is much better, Monsieur Rémy,' Sixtine cut in. 'You still have concerns that they will search your van even though they never have done so before. Then it's safer for you if you don't drive it. My friend will take your place. We will enter the compound at eight o'clock tomorrow morning. An hour later, at nine o'clock, you will telephone the police and say that the van has been stolen. That way, no blame will attach to you.'

'How can he take my place?' Rémy squinted at Bond.

'There is a similarity between you . . . the same age, the same dark hair. Wearing your coat and with flour on his face, nobody will notice. I will be in the back of the vehicle, as we agreed. It is possible that we will be able to enter and leave before anyone notices that we were there. But if for some reason we are apprehended, you need have no fear. We will say we stole the van.'

Rémy considered. 'How can I trust you?'

'Why would I lie to you? This is easier for you, Paul, because you won't be part of it. And since there will be two of us going into the plant, I will double the money that I offered you. 400,000 francs. What do you say?'

Bond saw greed and fear enter the baker's eyes, the two emotions at war with each other. Paul Rémy was about the same age as him. Although he had changed into his best suit, ready for evening Mass, he was still covered in white flour. Sixtine was telling the truth. Bond could take his place and nobody would notice. But would he agree?

'400,000 francs . . .' The baker had never earned so much money. He had never even spoken those words.

'If you'll agree now, I'll round it up to 500,000. All you have to do is to give us the keys.'

The next day, early on Monday morning, wearing a herring-bone worker's jacket and a cap, Bond sat behind the wheel of a Citroën H van, urging it up into the hills sur-rounding Menton. The van was a grey steel box with the familiar corrugated bodywork and the ugly, blunt cabin that made it look as if it had been chopped in half as it came off the production line. With its front-wheel drive and three-speed gearbox, it was crude and uncomfortable to drive – Bond could barely push it above thirty miles per hour – but at the same time it seemed reliable, an old work-horse. Bond hadn't shaved, allowing dark bristle to spread over his cheeks. He had also rubbed flour into his face and his hair.

Sixtine was beside him in the passenger seat. There was no point hiding yet. Only when they were in sight of the turn-off did Bond slow down and stop.

'If this goes wrong, get out as fast as you can,' she said.

'In this van, that's not very fast.'

'I know.' She was wearing a loose-fitting tussore shirt and trousers cut off below the knee. She took out a gun, a custom-made Baby Browning with an ivory grip, checked it and slipped it into her pocket. Bond approved. It was a small, light weapon, easily concealed and quickly engaged. A lady's gun.

'Once we're inside – even assuming we get that far – we're not going to have a lot of time,' Bond said. 'I know you want to take a look around and perhaps we'll find this secret formula or whatever it is you're looking for, but after what happened yesterday, Wolfe may well have racked up his security apparatus – and from what I've seen so far, he had a pretty efficient machine to start with.'

'Don't worry. I'm not going to hang around.'

She slipped out. The van had wide doors with the hinges at the back, not the front so that they opened the wrong way: suicide doors, they were called. Bond hoped the name wouldn't prove to be appropriate. The van rocked slightly as Sixtine climbed into the back and he heard the click as she swung the doors shut behind her. He pushed the van into gear and turned off down the lane towards Wolfe Europe.

He drove at a constant speed, passing through the green tunnel to the security barrier that he had seen the day before. This would be his first test and he felt his pulse racing as the two-storey building drew closer. At the same time, he reminded himself, this was the least dangerous part of Sixtine's plan. If the guards asked for identification or recognised that he wasn't Paul Rémy, it would be easy enough to talk his way out. 'I'm sorry, *messieurs*. Paul isn't well. He told me to come in his place.' But once he was past the checkpoint he would be trapped inside the enemy camp and, as he had discovered in the forest, with these people, anything could happen.

But to start with, things went his way. Even as the Citroën

H drew near, the first barrier was raised. The guards had recognised the van – they had watched it approach every other day at exactly the same time for months – and their eyes told them that the dark-haired figure hunched over the wheel must be the baker. Bond didn't look sideways as he drove through, keeping as much of his face concealed as possible. He was careful not to speed. He was delivering bread; that was all. That was how he should behave.

The lane continued through the wood with its deadly stinging nettles and booby traps although, looked at through the windows of the van, it seemed completely normal. Bond wondered what had happened when the three guards had failed to show up at the end of their shift. Was there a search party out looking for them now? If Irwin Wolfe or his people were expecting further trouble, they could be driving straight into a trap.

On the other hand, it had been less than twenty-four hours since the men had been killed. It was always possible that whoever employed them might think they had clocked off and gone home. No shots had been fired. The three men had simply disappeared.

Ahead of him, the electric fence loomed with the second checkpoint stark and menacing. There were more guards here – four of them – and the barrier stayed where it was as the van approached. Bond sank into his chair, allowing the collar of his worker's jacket to rise up. He wished he had lit a cigarette. It would have helped give the impression that he was completely relaxed and it would also have allowed him to hide more of his face with his cupped hand. It was too late now. He rolled down the window and called out cheerfully – in what he hoped was an approximation of Rémy's voice – *'Bonjour!'*

One of the guards glanced at him curiously, then seemed

to remember who he was and snapped out a command. The barrier rose. *'Merci!'* Bond waved a hand and continued forward, a single drop of perspiration drawing a question mark around his ear and then continuing down his neck.

He steered the van into the parking area beside the water tower. The jeeps, complete with their mounted guns and ammunition boxes, were still standing in the same parking bay where they had been the day before. One of them had its hood open and there was a man in overalls leaning into the engine. There was nobody else in sight. Bond got out. He opened the suicide door and spoke quietly. 'It's clear.'

Sixtine rolled out of her hiding place. She and Bond picked up trays of baguettes and walked quickly towards the nearest building. This was the kitchen. Rémy had sketched out a map of the complex – or the parts that he knew – before they had left. Bond kept his head down. He could feel the shadow of the watchtower looming over him and wondered if he was being observed through binoculars. Hopefully, the trays would speak for themselves. *I'm making a delivery. I've brought an assistant. There's nothing to be worried about.* He was glad when he reached the door and found that it was open. He and Sixtine moved inside.

The kitchen was industrial-sized. Huge tureens of soup or stew or something bubbled away on gas flames. The thick smell of cooking hung in the air. Chefs sweated in their chessboard trousers and white jackets as they chopped and mixed ingredients. Bond and Sixtine set down their trays and continued forward without stopping. They had to look as if they knew what they were doing. To hesitate would be to draw attention to themselves and that would invite questions. There was a door next to a wide serving hatch and, on the other side, a room with twenty long wooden tables and no decoration. Bond was already

189

picking up the work ethic of Wolfe Europe. You did your job, you ate, you finished, you left. There were no perks.

They passed through the dining room and into a corridor with whitewashed walls. Halfway along, Bond found exactly what he was looking for. There were two washrooms, one for men and the other for women, and a changing area where the staff could take off their outer garments before they ate. Half a dozen white coats had been left hanging on hooks and there were also square caps made out of white nylon. Without speaking, Bond and Sixtine slipped them on. Now, as they moved around the complex, they would look no different from anyone else.

They continued to the end of the corridor. Already they could hear the sound of machinery coming from the next building. They passed through a double door that formed an effective airlock. Bond noticed dust filters on the wall and a machine to remove dust from his shoes. The second door led into a much larger area with at least fifty people, all wearing protective coveralls, attending to different machines. The room was in half-darkness, which suited Bond well. It was hard even to tell the men and women apart and it was impossible that he and Sixtine would be recognised. Even so, the two of them kept moving. There was a steel gantry overhead and internal observation windows made of thick plate glass. Everyone was being endlessly observed by white-coated figures with protective goggles and clipboards. Nobody was talking. The people here were as well regulated as the machines.

Bond saw a clipboard lying on a table and picked it up. In an instant he had turned himself from a worker to an inspector and just holding it gave him the opportunity to linger. He examined the stainless steel panels, recording devices, platforms, ladders and overhead pipes. Knowing the final product, he was able to make some sort of sense of it all. In one part of the factory, emulsion was pouring down from an upper level, coating a roll of cellulose at least three feet wide. The cellulose was wound onto massive cylinders and then directed into the next metallic beast, a drying chamber that howled and shuddered as it fed. Moments later, the film base was regurgitated, cut into strips, then folded into rolls of yellow, protective paper. All the time, the machines hummed and shuddered. The lights flickered. The needles danced. Everything was connected to everything, and the end product, fulfilling the day's quota, was all that mattered.

Bond leaned over a woman who was inspecting a length of film through an infrared viewer. 'Everything all right?' he shouted, cheerfully, in French, making himself heard above the endless racket.

She nodded nervously, wondering why she had been picked out, then went back to her work.

Minutes later, Bond and Sixtine emerged through another set of double doors, into the fresh air. Here they were sheltered, out of sight of the watchtower. In front of them, some distance away, a man was stacking up crates behind the wheel of a forklift truck.

'What do you think?' he asked.

Sixtine shook her head. 'There's nothing there,' she said. 'It's a classic film-production facility. Wolfe isn't doing anything revolutionary. In fact, half that equipment is five years out of date.'

'Then let's try one of the new buildings.'

They walked across the compound to the section that had been built more recently, keeping close to the walls, still trying to look as if they knew what they were doing. Two men and a woman passed them. They were deep in conversation and didn't look at them. They came to an avenue, a clear space that divided one section from the other and saw another warning sign: PERSONNEL AUTORISÉ SEULEMENT. Authorised staff only. Bond heard footsteps and froze, pressing back against the nearest wall. Two guards with rifles walked past just a few feet away but failed to see them.

They crossed from one zone to another, leaving any sense of safety behind them. In front, they saw the first of the new buildings with an unmarked metal door. Bond noted that it fitted flush with the wall and had no keyhole. He cursed silently. It could only be opened from inside. He would have to find another way in. But just as he was about to move on, the door opened and a man came out, holding an unlit cigarette. Bond glanced at Sixtine who nodded. Together, they stepped forward. Sixtine reached the door before it swung shut. At the same time, Bond addressed the man, taking in the fact that he was Corsican.

'Do you need a light?' Bond asked.

'What?' The Corsican looked at him with dull eyes.

Bond hit him hard, twice, his fist crashing into his jaw, then into the side of his head. The man collapsed onto the ground and Bond dragged him quickly inside. It had been the safest thing to do but he was still annoyed. He had just put a time limit on how long they could stay here. Sooner or later somebody would notice that the man had disappeared. He would certainly come round in ten or fifteen minutes and raise the alarm. By then, he and Sixtine would have to be on their way.

But at least, for the time being, they were in. They continued down a brightly lit corridor with tiled walls and rubber flooring. Thick, snaking pipes suggested a sophisticated air ventilation system. Bond crept forward, passing half a dozen fire extinguishers lined up together. Everything about his surroundings – the extraordinary cleanness, the smell of chemicals – told him that this was different. There was something taking place at Wolfe Europe that was unconnected to film. Ahead of him were two swing doors with little glass portholes such as he might find in a hospital.

'What is this place?' Sixtine whispered.

Bond didn't answer. He moved ahead and pushed the door open. And there it was in front of him. It was the last thing he had expected and yet it made immediate sense: Irwin Wolfe and Jean-Paul Scipio and the *Mirabelle* and Ferrix Chimiques.

It should have been obvious from the start.

17

Hell's Kitchen

Everything was white: the walls, the work surfaces, the porcelain sinks, the protective clothes and face masks, the neon lights – even the air being blasted out of steel grilles after hidden machinery had chilled it and sucked it clean. The people employed here were a world apart from those working on the other side of the compound. They were phantoms, utterly silent, moving in slow motion as if performing a macabre dance among the test tubes and Bunsen burners.

Bond had walked into hell's kitchen. He could think of no other words to describe it. For this was the laboratory where Jean-Paul Scipio and Irwin Wolfe, in business together, had embarked on the mass production of high-grade heroin with an expertise and a sophistication that had never been seen before.

For the past twenty years, heroin production in the south of France had been a cottage industry. There were tiny villages all around Marseilles where run-down farmhouses and villas had been taken over and converted into makeshift factories that could be closed immediately, the moment the police got anywhere near. They might be tucked away in the basements or in disused kitchens with propane gas heaters fitted into stripped-down refrigerators for the drying process and old washing-machine engines converted into mixers.

194

The conditions would be filthy, the operators often so clumsy that it was a miracle they could produce anything of value at all.

It took twenty-four hours to produce twenty pounds of pure heroin and the process was complicated, fraught with dangers. If the morphine mix was overheated, it would explode. The fumes given off were enough to knock out an elephant and a leak could well kill everyone in the room. The purity of the finished product varied from batch to batch – and anyway it would be cut and recut many times before it reached the street.

Of course there were a handful of criminals who had proven themselves to be masters of their art. Antoine Guerini had been famous for the quality of his merchandise, while Joseph Cesari, who had learned his skills in Bandol, produced heroin so pure that it earned him the nickname 'Monsieur 98 per cent'. It was said that he could process an astonishing seventeen and a half pounds of morphine at a time. But these were the exceptions. The majority of heroin producers were amateurs.

James Bond knew that this laboratory was unique. What he was seeing took heroin production to an entirely new level.

The room was large, filled with equipment that was expensive and brand new: vacuum pumps, electric blenders, venting hoods, electric drying ovens and sophisticated exhaust systems. Close to where he and Sixtine were standing, still framed by the doorway, a man in a white jacket was leaning over the very latest reflux condenser, examining the contents through the glass, while next to him another man loaded gleaming flasks and test tubes into an autoclave, preparing them for sterilisation. There were shelves stacked with measuring cups, syringes, suction pumps, funnels and filter paper and Bond guessed that every item would have been accounted for down to the last strip of litmus. This was a meticulous operation, the IBM of narcotics.

And there was the final product. Bond saw four women in white coats, hair nets and plastic gloves looking bored as they packed the fine white powder into bags, weighing them on electric scales before sealing them. This would be the last stopping point on a journey that had begun in the opium fields of Turkey or Afghanistan. The morphine base would have been smuggled into Marseilles, probably in fishing boats, before being brought here. It had been refined in a solution of alcohol and activated charcoal until the precious flakes had begun to form. And where next? Bond thought he had a good answer to that question.

But it still made no sense.

The French authorities had been investigating and M had sent two agents down to the Riviera because the narcotics supply had come to a halt. They had all been concerned that the criminal activity was being replaced by something else. But looking at the evidence in front of his eyes, Bond could only conclude that the supply line had been brought to a deliberate halt while tons of the drug had gone into production. The obvious conclusion was that Scipio was stockpiling it. But to what purpose?

Bond had been standing at the edge of the laboratory for only a few seconds and even as these thoughts stormed through his mind, he realised that he and Sixtine were in the greatest danger. They had penetrated the very heart of the operation. They had unmasked a criminal enterprise working inside a respected, international business. Getting in had been one thing. Getting out would be quite another. What mattered more to Bond than anything else was that he should relay the information he had discovered back to M in London.

Standing next to him, Sixtine grabbed hold of his arm. 'This is crazy,' she whispered. She had also worked out what was going on. 'Wolfe is already a millionaire many times over. He's sick . . . maybe dying. Why would he want to get mixed up in narcotics?'

'Later,' Bond said. 'We have to go.'

It was already too late. A man wearing a long, white coat was walking over to them. From a distance he had looked like a doctor but as he drew closer Bond saw that he was unshaven, unfriendly, some sort of supervisor. He had the eyes of a shark. He already knew something was wrong.

He stopped in front of Bond and Sixtine and pointed down. *'Vos souliers,'* he said.

It was as simple as that. Everyone in the laboratory wore protective covers on their shoes. Bond and Sixtine had their stolen coats and caps but the man had noticed their feet were uncovered and that was what had brought him across.

Bond was about to answer but it was no good.

'Vos cartes d'identité!' the man demanded.

'Certainement!' Bond reached into his inside pocket as if about to draw out an ID card. Instead, he lashed out, his three extended fingers driving into the man's throat, cutting off the oxygen. Bond caught him as he collapsed and lowered him to the ground.

For just a fraction of a second he hoped that everyone in the room was so focused on what they were doing that they wouldn't notice what had just taken place . . . and indeed there was a moment of frozen silence while the work went on as before. But then half a dozen men came running towards him from all four corners of the laboratory and a moment later every alarm in the compound began to shriek.

Bond turned to run, then thought better of it. He twisted round and, taking out his Beretta, fired half a dozen shots, aiming not at the men but at the machinery. Whatever happened to him and Sixtine in the next few minutes, he was determined that he wasn't going to leave this obscene place intact. The first bullets smashed glass vials, the next fanned into the circuitry of the blenders and the centrifuges, severing the electric cables. The result was exactly what he had hoped for. There were two or three blinding sparks as the machines short-circuited just as the liquid from the broken vessels came splashing down. He could smell the fumes he had released. What happened next was inevitable. As the laboratory staff screamed and scattered, a great mushroom of flame billowed outwards, rolling over the surfaces and reaching all the way to the ceiling. At once, a sprinkler system burst into operation. A torrent of water cascaded down, drawing a curtain between Bond and the guards closing in on him. He fired off two more shots, emptying his gun, then left, pushing through the two swing doors.

Sixtine was already ahead of him. The strange thing was that she didn't even seem to be in a hurry. She had examined her options with the same concentration that she brought to a deck of cards before it was dealt and she already knew what she was going to do.

'The van,' she said. As they reached the corner, a guard appeared, rushing towards them. Sixtine had her own gun in her hand and shot him. 'Or one of the jeeps. There's no other way out of here.' She had finished her sentence, barely noticing the interruption.

'Right . . .'

'How are you for ammunition?'

'Empty.'

She grimaced. 'Then maybe you should have thought twice before shooting the hell out of that lab.'

They reached the next door and opened it cautiously. They were looking back out into the open air and there were people everywhere. There must have been a protocol that directed all the personnel to head for some general assembly point when the alarm sounded. And yet, for the first time, the enemy had made a serious miscalculation. If everyone had stayed at their work stations, if the compound had been clear, Bond and Sixtine would have been picked out easily. As it was, the pair could hide in plain sight. All they had to do was keep their heads down and move at the same pace as everyone else and they would effectively become invisible, disappearing into the crowd.

Sixtine had arrived at the same conclusion. She slipped her gun into her pocket and began to walk, keeping her face hidden. At the same time, the alarm abruptly cut out. It had made its point.

'Wolfe can't have known about this,' she muttered as they pressed forward. 'He's made a fortune out of film. Why would he risk everything to get into narcotics?'

'He can't *not* have known about this,' Bond returned. 'Hiding a heroin factory inside a film-production plant in the middle of nowhere . . . in a way, it's brilliant. But he must have cooperated. You're not telling me he never noticed?'

'It would certainly explain why he never brought me here.'

'And there's something else . . .'

'What?'

'The *Mirabelle* . . .'

But before he could explain what he had worked out, there

was a rush of three armed men pushing through the crowd and heading past them towards the laboratory. Bond broke off and he and Sixtine separated, knowing instinctively that the guards were looking for two intruders. They would be safer walking apart.

It was only when the baker's van was in sight that they came back together again and Bond saw at once that they couldn't use it. Someone must have noticed that it had been parked there far too long and a guard carrying a light machine gun was posted beside the front cabin, waiting for the baker to return. A short distance away, the man Bond had seen earlier was still working on the Willys MB French army jeep but even as the two of them approached, he slammed the hood and wiped his hands on a rag. Bond made his decision. He just hoped the mechanic had done a good job.

Ignoring the van, he continued as if heading for the kitchen area then, at the last moment, swerved to the right. The mechanic stared at him, aware that something was wrong. But too late. Bond grabbed hold of the side of the jeep and used it to lever himself into the air, both legs lashing out, his feet slamming into the man's head. The guard at the van saw what had happened and shouted out, bringing his machine gun round. Sixtine shot him in the chest.

The sound of gunfire changed everything. The factory workers scattered and now, finally, they were alone on the empty ground with the sun pinning them down like a huge spotlight, making them an obvious target. There were three gunshots from the watchtower, spitting up the dust close to their feet. Bond leapt into the driver's seat of the jeep and flicked the ignition switch. Sixtine scrambled in beside him, twisting round to fire at two men who were racing towards them across the concourse. One of them went down. The other veered away and took cover.

Sixtine reloaded.

Another gunshot slammed into the door and ricocheted with a loud twang. Bond wrenched at the gearstick and spun the jeep into reverse even as two more bullets hit the side panels. The mechanic was unconscious in front of him. The guard Sixtine had shot was lying face down to one side. Bond drew a savage arc in the dust, furiously manoeuvred the gears and sent the jeep hurtling towards the barrier and the way out.

'Get down!' he shouted.

There were two guards in front of him. They had come out of the concrete block and were emptying their pistols into the windscreen. Sixtine crouched down. His hands still gripping the steering wheel, Bond leaned sideways, taking partial cover behind the dashboard. The windscreen shattered. A second later, the jeep hit the barrier, smashing it. Bond felt the vehicle shudder once and then again as it rammed into the two men, batting them away. There was another gunshot from the tower, the bullet tearing into the canvas seat behind him. But then they were away, speeding up the lane, leaving the empty security block, the unconscious men and the broken barrier behind.

Bond and Sixtine straightened up. Bond had thought she might be shaken but she looked exhilarated.

'We need to head back to Menton,' she said. She looked behind them. For the time being, the lane was empty. 'If we go further into the hills, the road goes on for miles and they may be able to catch us. But if we go the other way, there's not much they can do once we get to the sea.'

She was right. The choice was between a corkscrew ride

into the mountains, climbing ever further into wasteland and forest, or a fast run down to a busy coastal road with traffic, police cars and plenty of witnesses. The jeep seemed to have shrugged off the injuries inflicted by all the gunfire but Bond would feel more confident if it was heading down-hill. How long would it take before the guards came after them? The engine coughed and he cast his eye at the fuel gauge. It was touching red: the tank was almost empty. That was one twist of the knife he hadn't considered.

Branches and leaves raced past them in a jumble. With the glass shot out in front of them, the wind hammered into their faces, sending Sixtine's hair flying. She had reloaded her Browning and twisted round in her seat, ready to use it. But for the time being, they were still alone. The outer bar-rier and concrete administration block rose up ahead. Two more guards were waiting for them but they were young and nervous. They had begun firing too soon, quickly emptying their guns, and could only hurl themselves out of the way as Bond slammed the jeep through the barrier and onto the last section of the lane. A minute later, he reached the main road and spun round without stopping, the tyres howling as they bit into the concrete.

Bond was beginning to relax. The jeep was handling per-fectly even if it must be wolfing down what little fuel remained, and Castellar, the first village, was only a few miles away. It was beginning to look as if they had made it to safety. What next? He would report to M that evening and afterwards the whole thing could be handed over to the French authorities. The plant would be closed down, Irwin Wolfe arrested. Finding Scipio might be more difficult but that wasn't his business. Basically, he had done exactly what he had been told.

He might even ask for a leave of absence. Why not? He wanted to take Sixtine to a big city that he knew well, somewhere he would be on his own territory. Rome perhaps. The Hotel Majestic in the Via Veneto. Dinner at Alfredo's with its famous fettuccine, a midnight stroll along the Tiber and then, later . . .

'James.'

He heard the worry in her voice and glanced in the mirror. He saw them at once. They were half a mile behind, only specks, but already closing in. Not cars. Motorbikes. At least three of them. He could hear the distant roar of the throttles. Inch by inch they were expanding in the mirror. Maybe he had two or three minutes before they caught up.

He stamped on the accelerator but the jeep was already doing the best it could. They had reached Castellar! Now the die was cast. The road swept them along, giving them no alternative but to follow the hill down into the village centre. There were no turn-offs. They were hemmed in by olive trees and vegetable gardens on one side and a high stone wall with a church on the other. They spun round a corner between tumbling bushes and a sheer drop to the terraces below, the wheels kicking up a miniature storm of gravel and dust. The further they went, the narrower the road became. The motorbikes were filling the mirror now. Black BMWs. Bond could make out the hunched shapes of the riders leaning over the windscreens.

No! There it was ahead of him, the worst bad luck. The wretched donkey with its cart filled with melons, the same one that he had seen the day before, once again blocking the way! Its owner was tugging at the reins, urging it to move forward but the animal seemed to be in no particular mood to cooperate. Bond swore. He couldn't slow down but there was no way around it. One side of the road consisted of houses packed tightly together with balconies, outdoor staircases and brightly coloured washing hanging out to dry. No alleyways. No openings. The other was barred off by a long line of metal bollards with the hillside beyond, a series of gardens and orchards dropping away steeply to the next bend in the road. The village was suddenly busy. There were women shopping, old men outside a café playing backgammon, children chasing each other round the tables. Two stalls had been set up, one selling cheese, the other *saucissons*. Just to add to the atmosphere, a grandfather was sitting on a stool playing an accordion. All it needed, Bond reflected bitterly, was a couple of cockerels and a few baskets of geraniums and he could have made a fortune selling the postcard.

He slowed down. The motorbikes were right behind him. There were five of them in all: black and silver, as mean as hornets, whipping along with their glittering chrome and exposed drive shafts. Some of the riders had taken out guns, balancing them against the hand grips. He suddenly became aware that Sixtine had left her seat and was clambering into the back. Looking over his shoulder, he saw her jerk open the ammunition box and pull out a magazine clip. She rammed it into the gun and pulled back the cocking handle. Bond's hands tightened on the steering wheel.

Seconds later there was a burst of gunfire that sounded deafening at close quarters. The nearest two riders were blown out of their seats, their bodies cartwheeling through the air as their machines toppled and slid away beneath them. At the same time, the street ahead of the jeep emptied as if hit by a tornado. People ran in all directions. The donkey whinnied and jerked forward, scattering the melons. Children were grabbed and swept into doorways. As Sixtine let loose with a second burst, Bond shouted 'Hang on!' and stamped down on the accelerator, swerving to avoid the tumbling melons. The jeep leapt forward, hitting a table outside a café, sending glasses and a deck of cards flying, then crashed through the cheese stall. He heard screaming but the whole village had become a blur. His eyes were fixed on the road ahead. The shooting stopped. As Bond steered the jeep out of the other side of the village, Sixtine climbed back next to him.

'It's jammed!' she shouted.

'It did the job!' Bond replied.

It hadn't quite. Two motorcyclists remained, dropping back, warily keeping their distance now but still not letting the jeep out of their sight. Bond was determined to lose them and took the first hairpin bend at breakneck speed, the wheels of the jeep almost leaving the ground as they slalomed across the surface of the road. Before they'd had time to recover, he'd swung them viciously the other way, anticipating the next corner. The jeep rocked from side to side as if protesting the punishment it was being given. Briefly, the front fender came into contact with the wall at the side of the road. There was the scream of metal tearing and Bond had to fight for control to stop the whole thing turning over. The engine coughed a second time. The needle was now well into the red. Bond swore quietly. They must already be running on fumes. How much further could they go before grinding to a halt? He twisted the wheel and they rounded the second corner and plunged down, the road steeper than ever.

The Mediterranean lay ahead of them, a dazzling blue that stretched out from the haphazard contours of the shoreline to the straight certainty of the horizon far away. Bond gunned for it, going hell for leather. He wanted to be out of the hills, perhaps even out of France. There was a thought! If he could make it to the Italian border, there would be police in patrol cars. He wondered what they would make of a fully armed jeep, riddled with bullet holes, trying to leave the country. Well, let them arrest him. Right now, a night in jail – locked behind solid doors and surrounded by police – sounded almost attractive.

'They're dropping back,' Sixtine exclaimed.

It was true. The two surviving motorcyclists seemed to have lost heart. The distance between them and the jeep had doubled. Even so, Bond didn't slow down. He glanced at the speedometer. Sixty-five miles per hour. Almost as far as the speedometer was able to go. Two more bends and they would be down at sea level. They had got away with it!

'When we get into Menton, I'm going to buy you—' Bond began.

'James!'

She had seen them carefully spaced out on the road ahead. He saw them too. A dull shade of silver. They were shaped like pyramids but with four separate protruding spikes made out of thin-gauge steel. Each one was about four inches long. They were inspired by medieval caltrops, devices used to cripple horses, but when the Germans had dropped them on airfields and roads in the last war, they had referred to them as crowsfeet. He recognised them only when it was too late.

He was already braking but the jeep had driven over them and the tyres exploded, the rubber torn to shreds. He lost control at once. It was as if the steering column had been severed and the wheel span uselessly in his hands. They were either going to crash into the hillside or be thrown over the edge of the cliff. Now it was in the hands of the gods.

'Brace yourself!' Bond shouted.

Sixtine was already clutching the dashboard with one

hand, the other curved round the edge of the broken wind-screen. He had one last image of her, resolute and unafraid. Then the jeep came to a corner and, unable to turn, launched itself into the air. For a tiny eternity they hung there, sus-pended in space. Bond saw the sea rushing towards them, replacing the sky. It came closer and closer, a blue wall that suddenly looked as solid as steel. He felt himself tipping for-ward and pressed his hands against the steering wheel, pinning himself in his seat. They fell and they fell, every-thing silent now in the last moments before the end.

They hit the sea with all the force of a missile strike. Bond was aware of the water erupting around them. Without the windscreen to protect him, his head was torn backwards, almost separating from his shoulders. At once he was sucked under. The jeep that had saved them had now become an instrument of death, threatening to lock them in its grip as it sank. At the last moment, Bond had managed to gulp down some air but he knew he had only seconds to get back to the surface. Water filled his vision. He was aware of angry bub-bles erupting all around him. He tried to free his legs but they were pinned under the steering wheel. He could feel the pressure building in his ears as he was dragged ever deeper and twisted and writhed, desperately trying to escape. And what of Sixtine? She was no longer next to him. If Bond was going to die, he would die alone.

He bent himself forward and jack-knifed over the steering wheel. He felt the blunt edge of the windscreen slicing into his stomach, his thighs and then, finally, his ankles. He was free! How deep was he? There was no air in his lungs and he wanted to breathe. No. Keep your lips closed. Feel for the right direction. Swim, damn you. It can't be too far.

Bond could imagine the jeep continuing silently below

him, disappearing into the void. He began to swim, one hand above his head, forcing himself upwards, his eyes closed. It seemed an impossibly long way. He kicked out six times before he felt his fingers break through the surface, the rest of him following a second later, gasping for air, water streaming down his face. He looked around him. Sixtine was there. She had made it out. He swam over to her.

'Are you OK?'

She nodded, too exhausted to speak.

Bond turned round. With the tyres of the jeep in ribbons, they had left the road and driven off the cliff about thirty yards above them. Looking at the distance they had fallen, Bond was surprised they had managed to survive. He guessed that the metal bodywork of the jeep had, at least to some extent, protected them. The water was warm. There was a ribbon of sand and shingle running alongside the foot of the cliff but no swimmers, no one in deckchairs. Everything had happened so quickly, it was possible that nobody had seen it. They were on their own.

'Can you swim back?' Bond asked.

Sixtine was treading water. 'I can't think of any other way to get there,' she said.

They set off together. The beach was very close. It didn't take them long to reach the edge of the water and then to drag themselves onto the sand. For a moment they lay there, panting, feeling the warm sunshine on their backs. Bond was relieved. It could have been a lot worse. In a way, the entire operation had been clumsy and ill-judged: driving into the compound without any real plan and no back-up, aimlessly stumbling around, crashing their way out. It might have told them what they needed to know but they had been lucky to escape alive.

The crunch of footsteps on the shingle made him look up. There were two men, both of them dressed in waxed leather jackets, holding guns. They had climbed off their motorbikes, leaving them parked on the edge of the road. From behind him came the sound of an outboard motor. Bond turned and saw a four-seat speedboat cruising towards them. It was manned by the two thugs he had already encountered at Ferrix Chimiques. Carlo and Simone. Those had been the names Scipio had addressed them by. The one with the broken nose stood at the wheel. The other was cradling a rifle. Bond glanced at Sixtine and saw in her eyes what he already knew for himself.

It could have been worse. And it was.

18

Number Four

It was a tourist-class cabin for the class of tourist who didn't demand too much in the way of space and comfort. One day, more than 600 of them would discover the charms of the *Mirabelle*, the cruise liner that Irwin Wolfe had named after his first wife. There were two berths, one above the other, two wicker chairs, a chest of drawers and a sink. The floor area was just big enough for two people to sit together in comfort but if they wanted to move they would need to plan a route around each other. The toilet was across the passageway, shared with the cluster of six cabins that surrounded it. There was a porthole but it didn't open and it wasn't big enough to provide much of a view.

It was less than twenty-four hours since Bond and Sixtine had been brought here. They had arrived separately. It had been made clear that if one caused any trouble, the other would pay but, drawing up in two cars, surrounded by men with guns, there had been no chance of that. Scipio's two hired hands – Carlo and Simone – had accompanied Bond. They hadn't spoken to him again but their very presence had confirmed what he already knew. They worked for Scipio. Wolfe owned the *Mirabelle*. Scipio and Wolfe were in this together. But there was still something missing from the picture. This wasn't just a case of narcotics smuggling, even if the amounts involved were enormous. What was their common aim?

All night long, the *Mirabelle* had been preparing for its departure. It had taken more than twelve hours simply to fire up the furnaces. Finally, just before sunrise, Bond had been woken by a distant rumbling and a series of vibrations coursing through the cabin. He swung himself off the bunk and went over to the porthole. There was no view. He and Sixtine had been deliberately placed on the seaboard side, away from the port of Nice. It occurred to him that there were plenty of people looking for them. Sixtine's team would know that something was wrong and Reade Griffith must surely have noticed that Bond had disappeared. The last time they had spoken had been on the Friday evening before Wolfe's party. Might he have alerted his people at the CIA? Bond thought it unlikely.

And anyway, it was too late. Looking out of the porthole, Bond saw that they were moving. Wolfe had told him the *Mirabelle* was going to weigh anchor on the Tuesday morning and here it was, exactly on schedule. The ship would conduct a week of sea tests off the coast of France and then continue to America for its gala reception. And he and Sixtine were to be unwilling passengers – supercargo – at least for part of the trip. Nobody knew where they were. Bond wasn't expected to report back to London for another twenty-four hours and he hadn't told Reade Griffith where he and Sixtine were heading either. As far as the CIA man was concerned, the two of them would simply have vanished into thin air.

'We're on our way.' Sixtine's voice came from behind him.

'It looks like it.' Bond watched her climb down from her bunk.

'So what now? Maybe they'll throw a launch party. We might even get invited to the captain's table.'

'It'll make a change from beans and potatoes.' That was all the food they'd had so far, brought in on a tray by a scowling crewman.

Bond could feel movement under his feet now, a very slight swaying as they left the harbour and headed into open sea. The fact that they had left the port only made their situation more perilous. While they were moored, there was always a chance that they might break out and find someone to help them. Now that had become impossible. The cabin on the *Mirabelle* was a prison within a prison and the great expanse of the sea gave it the solitude and the inescapability of a Devil's Island. Worse still, they were alone. There were no other passengers and Bond had no doubt that everyone who worked on the *Mirabelle*, from the captain down to the cabin boy, would have been paid or coerced to do exactly as they were told. Two shots in the night, two bodies overboard. It would have no significance at all in the great emptiness of the ocean.

Sixtine came over to him and looked out of the window. He put an arm around her. 'Listen to me,' he said. 'Whatever happens, you have to survive. It may be that Wolfe has a soft spot for you. He was talking about marrying you only a few days ago. And Scipio knows who you are. He won't want to go to war with you. What I'm saying is, don't worry about me. If you can find a way out of this, you have to take it.'

'Don't be ridiculous, James. For a start, Wolfe is a horrible man who doesn't care about anyone. He's not going to give me a break and it certainly won't have helped our relationship, his finding me with you. As for Scipio, maybe I can talk him round – but I doubt it. No. If we're going to find a way out of this, as you put it, it's going to be together. It seems to me our best bet will be to get to the radio room. I can get a message to my group or we can send out a general Mayday alert. Otherwise, it's just going to be on deck and overboard and let's hope it's not too far to swim!'

'They've kept us alive,' Bond said. 'There must be a reason for that. Maybe they need us for something.'

Sixtine shuddered. 'You may be right,' she said. 'But I'd prefer not to find out what it is.'

It was another eight hours before they heard the lock being turned and the door opening. The same men who had brought them to the *Mirabelle* had come for them a second time.

'Out!' the man with the broken nose grunted.

'Which one are you?' Bond asked. 'Carlo or Simone?'

'Just move . . .'

'A shame. It would be nice to know your name when I kill you.'

As before, the two men knew where they were going. They led Bond and Sixtine out of the cabin and along a corridor that stretched out ahead of them with what looked like a mile of brand-new carpet, unused handrails, door after door with chrome handles and numbers in the mid-hundreds, glowing lamps set at precise intervals in the ceiling, the countless fire extinguishers that Bond had noticed before. The air was warm. The vibrations were ever-present but seemed more distant. Wolfe had boasted that the ship was fitted with anti-roll stabilisers and Bond had to admit that he could no longer feel any movement under his feet at all.

They went up the stairs and out onto the deck. Bond saw the coast of France, with the hotels, the apartment blocks and shops fighting for space close to the sea and the green hills rising up serenely behind. He guessed they were at least a mile away. It might just be possible to swim ashore but there was no chance of jumping now. He would be dead, riddled with bullets, before he had even reached the side.

A second staircase led up to the promenade deck, which would one day be reserved for first-class passengers. This was where Wolfe had greeted him when he first came on board. When the *Mirabelle* actually came into commission, there would be an officer positioned at the top on the other side of a discreet barrier, making sure that everyone knew their place. But nobody stopped them as they made their way up and then back inside, into the first-class dining room. Now that they were at sea, there was something eerie about the cruise liner; a sense of the *Marie Celeste*. The dining room had more than fifty tables, doubled and trebled by their reflections in the mirrored walls. Marble columns cut the room into different sections but the identical chairs, the low ceiling and the thick, red carpet reaching from corner to corner only emphasised that this was one vast space. It was another reason why Bond would never have considered taking a cruise – unless he was at gunpoint. For all its plush, this was a food factory, nothing less. Breakfast, lunch, dinner, two sittings of each, too much food, with the band playing mood music, day after day. It wasn't for him.

They passed through the dining room and into the ballroom, one man ahead of them, four more behind. Here the carpet gave way to acres of walnut and their feet tapped out a rhythm of sorts . . . more a funeral march than a waltz. Another door led into the bar – the Wolfe Bar – that Bond had already visited. Wolfe himself was waiting for them, settled into a velvet armchair with a low, dark wood table in front of him and two more chairs facing. Jean-Paul Scipio was sitting at the bar with a triangular glass lodged in his massive hand and surrounded by the glittering stones of his many rings. The liquid inside it was a creamy white with something – nutmeg perhaps – sprinkled on top. A brandy Alexander? His translator stood next to him. Bond felt himself being carefully examined as he moved into the room. The cannibal king savouring his next meal.

'Sit down,' Wolfe said. It was not an invitation. It was a command.

Bond chose one of the chairs opposite him. The American millionaire looked uncomfortable, out of sorts. This time, there was to be no 'Jim', no 'baby girl'. He was wearing a grey flannel suit and a wide silk tie – it was all business tonight. Bond noted with interest that he was doing his best to avoid looking at Scipio. There was a sort of disdain, as if the Corsican gangster was a butler who had risen above his station by joining the family for drinks.

'Irwin . . .' Sixtine had gone straight over and was crouching beside him, her eyes wide and tearful. 'I don't understand what's happening. I was just interested in your work. That's all. I didn't mean . . .'

'I know who you are,' Wolfe cut in. 'According to Scipio, you're as crooked as he is. From the very start I wondered why you were getting so close and cosy, but I was happy to play along with it. Why not? You're an attractive woman. Well, you can put a sock in it now. I know your business and I've got a good idea what you were up to. It's a damn shame because I don't see how you can get off this boat alive, but we'll come to that later. For now, take a seat. What can I get you to drink?'

'I'll have a bourbon with a little water and ice,' Bond said. 'But before that, there's something you need to know. Miss Brochet has got nothing to do with me. We hadn't even

215

met until a few days ago. Send her back to the cabin and you and I can say what has to be said. But leave her out of it.'

'She's here and she's staying,' Wolfe replied, curtly. 'I think the phrase is – she's made her bed and she can lie in it.'

'I'm not going anywhere,' Sixtine muttered petulantly. 'I've been stuck in that cabin long enough, thank you.' She sat next to Bond. 'And I'll have a bourbon too.'

The barman started fixing the drinks. The translator was already whispering into Scipio's ear, repeating everything that was being said. Scipio gazed ahead, his eyes fixed on Bond.

'I guess you want to know what this is all about,' Wolfe began.

'I know what it's all about,' Bond said. 'And for what it's worth, so do my superiors. I think you'll find there's quite an unpleasant reception waiting for you when you dock in New York. You may have a nice boat and plenty of friends in high places but American customs officials take a pretty dim view of heroin smugglers and, at the end of the day, it turns out you're just another dime-a-dozen petty criminal. Your business affairs must have taken a turn for the worse if that's the only way you can think of to make money – but that's not my problem. Wolfe America, Wolfe Europe . . . from now on it's going to be Wolfe Alcatraz. Your business is finished and so are you.'

To his surprise, Wolfe broke into laughter. It was an unpleasant sound, like a dog barking. 'Is that what you think?' he demanded. 'You think I'm in this for the money? Do you have any idea how much money I have? Do you really think I need to make any more of it? I'm seventy-three years old. Even if I was in perfect health, I'd only live another ten or fifteen years and as it is, I'll be lucky to have half of that.'

He tapped the side of his head. 'I have something inside

my brain. The doctors call it an ependymal tumour, which strikes me as a very fancy name for something that's growing where it shouldn't. The fact is, it's going to kill me. There's nothing I can do, no treatment I can buy. I've spoken to doctors all over the world and they talk about drugs and surgery but I can see it in their eyes. I'm a goner and I might as well get used to it.

'It was diagnosed a year ago and, you know, that was what set me thinking. I thought about the war and about the two boys I lost. It was a stupid war, an unnecessary war. What would it matter to us if the Nazis kicked you British in the ass? As a matter of fact, I actually knew President Woodrow Wilson when he brought in the Neutrality Acts back in the thirties and they were meant to keep us out of exactly this sort of situation. A European war . . . not an American war.'

The drinks arrived. 'I'd like a cigarette, if you don't mind,' Bond said.

'It's a dirty habit but you might as well go ahead.' Wolfe nodded and one of Scipio's men handed Bond a packet of Lucky Strike.

Bond offered one to Sixtine, who shook her head. 'America didn't exactly enter the war,' he said as he lit his cigarette. 'Your country was attacked on 7 December 1941. Or maybe your brain tumour has knocked that particular detail out of your memory.'

'I think I know my history rather better than you, Bond. Pearl Harbor was the end result of a series of hostile manoeuvres by the United States that began ten years before – when the Japs invaded Manchuria in 1931, to be precise. Once again, it was none of our business but our politicians didn't approve. So what did we do? We threatened them with a blockade. That led to them dropping out of the League of

Nations, the second Sino-Japanese War and eventually to the Tripartite Act with Germany and Italy. The Japs didn't become our enemy overnight. It was our aggression and interference that drove them to it.

'Anyway, Roosevelt didn't need an excuse to go to war. He'd been wanting it all along. He had said as much in his commencement address to the University of Virginia on 10 June 1940 – they called it the "stab in the back" speech and in my view they got it exactly right. A few months later, he brought in the Lend-Lease Act, which went against everything that had gone before, providing your country, France and the Soviet Union with $50 billion worth of supplies. And of course, those supplies had to be protected by American ships and American lives. So don't talk to me about Pearl Harbor. It was a European war and it should have stayed in Europe, but we threw ourselves into it long before December 1941.

'We're doing the same thing right now in Korea. You tell me – what has the North Korean People's Army got to do with us and why should it bother us if a whole load of gooks want to kill each other over the 38th Parallel, a line that was created artificially in the first place and which doesn't actually exist? But even now, while you and I sit here in first-class comfort, young American soldiers are dying far away from home leaving American parents feeling like I felt when they told me that my two boys had been cut down on the sand.'

Wolfe was sitting rigidly in his chair, breathing heavily. Bond could see a pulse throbbing on his forehead and it made him think of the malignant growth somewhere beneath. Wolfe had a glass of water. He lifted it and took a gulp.

'You should take it easy,' Bond said mildly. 'You're going to make yourself ill.'

'I *am* ill.'

It amused Bond, how easy it was to rile the American.

'I have been thinking a great deal about my legacy and what I can do to change the way my country is heading,' Wolfe went on. There was a rasp in his voice. 'We are coming to the belief that we can solve all the problems in the world and, as we become ever more powerful, with ever greater weapons, we don't see what's happening. We don't see that we risk becoming monsters! Look at Hiroshima and Naga-saki. Believe me, I have no love of the Japs. But I never thought I'd live to see a day when we would sit back and kill tens of thousands of people, including women and children, simply to assert our superiority.

'Something has to change. What the United States of America needs is a wake-up call, or what you might think of as an injection of common sense. And that is exactly what I am intending to give them.

'I will not tell you how I came to meet Mr Scipio here or how I got into business with him. Working in Marseilles, I was obviously aware of the Corsican syndicates and their power. I learned a great deal about the narcotics business and it became clear to me that it's going to change the world. In fact I would go so far as to say that, with or without my intervention, drug addiction is going to become the driving force of the twentieth century. People are going to get ill. People are going to need treatment. People are going to turn to crime. That's the future whichever way you look at it – but maybe it can become a force for good. This is the thought that has occurred to me. If America becomes more inward-looking, if it is made to look after its own, then maybe it will re-examine its position in the world and as a result the world will become a better place.

'On this ship are concealed more than 12,000 pounds of

what is known as Number Four heroin – between 90 and 99 per cent pure. To put that into perspective, the average heroin addict uses less than half an ounce a day and in most cases the drug has been contaminated with many other substances. I do not intend to make money from this consignment, Mr Bond. That is why I laughed at your suggestion just now. What I am providing might be called the greatest loss-leader of all time. Although I have paid Scipio a fair market price for his product, I am going to pretty much give it away. Of course, this will eventually bankrupt me. It is financial suicide. But I am dying anyway and I have no friends and, thanks to Mr Roosevelt, no family.

'Can you imagine the transformative effect that so much high-grade heroin is going to have on American society? There is already a huge network of dealers across the country, but soon the new product will flow relentlessly into every town and every community and at a price so ridiculously low that it will make at least one encounter with the drug irresistible. One, of course, will lead to another. I intend to create a nation of heroin addicts, Mr Bond, a million future customers for Mr Scipio.'

Bond saw the translator whisper this last sentence into Scipio's ear and the man's enormous face rearranged itself into a smile. Wolfe's plan was hideous, an act of self-destructive lunacy, but whatever happened, Scipio would reap all the benefits. Wolfe had facilitated the manufacture of high-grade heroin. He had paid for it. And he had provided Scipio with a business opportunity that would last for generations.

'It is, of course, only the weakest who will succumb to the temptation I am placing before them: the uneducated, the delinquent, the petty criminal. I find some consolation in that. Families who look after their young people won't have anything to fear. But soon the streets will be littered with victims. As the prices rise and the supply begins to fall, there is sure to be an unprecedented crime wave. The government will be forced to concentrate all its resources on its own back-yard and it simply will not have the money or the energy for another Omaha Beach, another Okinawa, another Pusan. It will start trying to help its young people instead of killing them, nursing itself rather than policing the world.

'In doing this I will have built a memorial to my sons. At the same time, I will go to my grave in the knowledge that I have changed the future of American history so that other sons will be saved.'

He fell silent. The translator spoke for another few seconds, catching up with the end of the sentence. Finally, it was over.

Bond finished his bourbon. He glanced at Sixtine, who had listened to all this with growing incredulity and who was sitting very straight, her face pale.

'I have to say, it will make interesting reading in the *Lancet*,' Bond said, finally. 'I wonder if doctors were aware that an ependymal tumour could actually cause the sufferer to lose every trace of his sanity?' He leaned forward. 'You really think that by condemning hundreds of thousands of young people to the living hell of heroin addiction, you can make your country a better place?'

'I'm creating a tunnel. But it will lead them to the light.'

'You're creating a completely useless and self-destructive nightmare which will be of benefit to no one except Fat Boy over there, and he must be laughing at you from behind the folds of his face. It won't work anyway. There were drug addicts all over America in the thirties and the forties.

221

Marijuana, methamphetamines, cocaine . . . it made no difference to the entry to the war. You're going to create chaos. That's for sure. But you're deluding yourself if you think any good is going to come out of it.'

Wolfe got stiffly to his feet. He looked drained. 'Then think of it simply as revenge for what happened to my boys,' he said. He turned to Scipio. 'I'm done with him. You can do what you like. Don't kill the woman . . . not yet. She and I have still got things to say.'

Scipio waited until Wolfe had walked out of the bar. Then he slid himself off the bar stool, carefully transferring his enormous weight to his legs. The translator handed him his shooting stick. Slowly, he took a few steps forward. The smile was still on his face.

'Meester Bond,' he said.

19

Pleasure . . . or Pain?

Scipio rapped out a command and his two men – Carlo and Simone – dragged one of the bar stools into the middle of the floor.

'May I ask you please to sit down here?' This time, the words were translated into English for Bond to understand.

Bond got slowly to his feet. Out on its own, in the middle of the polished wood floor, the stool had the same dark invitation as a gallows or an electric chair. It was made of brown leather on tubular steel with two low armrests. Bond didn't like the look of where this was going, but he was surrounded by five men, at least two of them with guns, and knew he had no choice. Clamping down on a rising sense of unease, he walked the short distance over to the stool and sat down. Scipio stood in front of him. The two of them were now the same height.

But before anything could begin, Sixtine spoke.

'Scipio!' she said. 'You know who I am. You know how much money I'm worth. Listen to me now.' She waited for the translator to catch up. The light glimmered in his wire-frame spectacles as he spoke, masking his eyes. He was wearing the same drab suit and narrow tie as before. As ever, he was standing close to Scipio, translating now from English to Corsican, delivering the message while seeming to

223

take no interest whatsoever in its contents or anything else that was happening around him.

'You have made a mistake working with Irwin Wolfe,' Sixtine went on. 'You know that he's sick. He's dying so he doesn't care what happens in the future – but he can still bring you down with him. But it's not too late. If you will let Mr Bond and myself leave, I will pay you 100,000 American dollars. You can have the money in diamonds or any currency that you prefer. There is also the heroin on this boat . . . more than five tons of it. Wolfe wants to give it away but you could sell it on top of what he has already given you. You are an intelligent man. Surely you can see that you have no need for Irwin Wolfe. Let us go. Get on with your business. You're making the wrong enemies here.'

Sixtine fell silent. A few moments later, the translator finished her last statement and stood there, waiting for what might come next. Scipio shook his head, the red crease of his old wound showing briefly as his chins swivelled left and right.

'*Innò. Sò Corsu!*'

'No,' the translator explained. 'I am a Corsican. In my country, a man's word is his bond. Do not speak to me again, madame.' The translator paused and Scipio waggled an elephantine finger in her direction. 'We sat together in a bar in Marseilles and it was then that I warned you . . . you should stay away from this part of the world. It is regretted . . . it is greatly to be regretted that you did not take my advice.'

Scipio turned to his men and spoke rapidly in his high-pitched whispering voice. The translator listened in silence, then addressed Sixtine directly. 'Mr Scipio has given instructions for you to be dragged out of here and locked up if you speak again,' he explained with a note of apology. 'You will be hurt quite significantly.' He turned to Bond. 'He also wishes you to know that Madame 16 will be shot if you make any move at all. You must sit where you are and take what is given to you. Do you understand?'

'Please tell Mr Scipio that I understand completely and that whatever happens to me in this room will be paid back tenfold. I work for serious people. They know I am here. You have already killed one of our agents. If you kill me, you will spend the rest of your life running.' He turned a cold eye on Scipio. 'Or in your case, waddling. I hope you know the Corsican for that word.'

Bond could not tell how much of what he had just said was translated. Just for once, the translator looked discomfited as he repeated the lines. But Scipio was unconcerned, the great, round ball of his head pale and impassive against the coloured bottles that lined the bar.

'The last time we met, I also gave you a warning, Mr Bond. I said the same thing that I said to her . . . to madame. Stay out of my affairs. To be honest with you, I was quite expecting you to ignore me. It may surprise you, but I was also very pleased. I did not think for one minute that you will . . . that you would return to England and I hoped also that you and I would meet again and that on a second occasion I would be able to do what I wished, without restraint. We have arrived at that occasion. You interest me, Mr Bond. You are young, good-looking, resourceful . . . you are in many ways a first-class secret agent. You are not unlike the man who was here before . . . your predecessor. I killed him. I shot him three times. But I never got to know him. This time it is going to be very different.'

Scipio glanced at his translator and rapped out a sentence.

'Mr Scipio says he will kill your friend if you try to resist,' the translator said.

'You've already told me that,' Bond said. 'But you seem to have forgotten that the man you work for wants her alive.'

The words were translated.

'I do not work for Irwin Wolfe,' Scipio muttered. He took a step forward so that he was close to Bond. The eyes beneath the gossamer eyebrows examined him minutely. Then Scipio reached out with two fingers and stroked the side of Bond's face. Bond recoiled in disgust. He could feel all his muscles tensing, preparing to strike out. He forced himself not to move. Out of the corner of his eye he could see Sixtine sitting in the oversized velvet chair, strained and afraid. One of the guns was trained on her. The other was on Bond.

The fingers continued their obscene journey over Bond's lips, under his chin. Now they were resting on his chest. Bond felt the nausea rising in him. The hand was a pink, alien animal, probing him, looking for where to bite.

But then Scipio smiled and stepped back.

'Let me tell you what I am going to do to you, Mr Bond.' Scipio's voice was thick with pleasure, with the knowledge of his absolute power. The translator was indifferent. 'I am going to change you. I am going to make you into my creature. We have almost a month together on this boat, more than enough time to break you completely. And as you have heard from Mr Wolfe, the method . . . the way in which I shall achieve this is all around us. When I leave the ship . . . the *Mirabelle* . . . at New York, you will follow me obediently as a dog follows his master. You will be a heroin addict, Mr Bond. Given the purity of my product, this will happen more quickly than you can believe. Even one week from now, there will be no need to secure you. You will spend every minute waiting for your next injection. Your body and your mind will demand it, and everything else – Madame 16, your former life, your precious secret service – you will have forgotten. A week after that, you will come to me on your knees and beg me to give you what you need. And maybe, in return for your complete . . . for your total submission, I will.

'But this is what you must understand. This is what will destroy you and in the final . . . ultimately make you mine. You will not know what I am going to do, whether I will provide you with pleasure . . . or pain.'

Bond was so gripped by what he was hearing that he was not prepared for what came next. Almost lazily, and yet with a speed that took him by surprise, the fat man swung his fist through the air, crashing it into the side of Bond's head. It was like being hit by a battering ram. Bond was almost thrown off the bar stool. He would have fallen except that Scipio had caught him with his other hand, held him for a moment and then punched him again, this time in the stomach. Again, Bond was blasted backwards, the breath exploding out of his lungs and his own blood dancing behind his eyes. He had never been hit so hard. Scipio let go of him, leaving him gasping for air. Bond saw him clasp his hands, bringing the various jewels together as if in a gesture of celebration. Then the bullets of flesh and bone became a blur as they came pounding once again into the side of his head. There was a brilliant burst of light and he was propelled sideways, this time falling onto the floor.

It wasn't over. Taking his time, Scipio kicked him again and again, the leather toecaps carrying all the weight of the gigantic legs, pounding into his flesh. And all the time, the translator watched, silent, with nothing to do. Bond glimpsed the other men. They seemed to have multiplied but it was more likely that it was his vision which had fractured. Unable to stop himself, he let out a groan and rolled onto his side, bringing in his knees to protect himself. Scipio stood over him and stamped down. Bond not only felt his rib crack – he heard it.

'Stop it!' Sixtine called out. Her voice was far away. Bond's heart was beating in his ears, blocking the sound. 'That's enough! You're going to kill him!'

Silence. Bond lay floating in a pool of agony.

He heard words but did not understand them. Scipio was talking, not to him but to his men, giving orders.

The translator crouched beside him and explained. 'You are to be taken now to your cabin. Your friend will come with you also. The pain is over for the present. Mr Scipio is sure that it will have been familiar to you. But he is going to introduce you to a type of pleasure which . . . he is sure it will be new to you and which you will never forget. Do you have anything to say?'

Bond swore. He could taste blood in his mouth.

Carlo and Simone closed in and jerked him to his feet. Bond wanted to fight back but he was exhausted by the beating. One side of his chest, where the rib had been broken, was on fire. He knew that his face was badly bruised. One of his eyes was partly closed. There had to be a way out of this. He thought back to the forest outside Wolfe Europe. Any minute now, Sixtine's people were going to burst in. They would explain that they had been on board the *Mirabelle* from the very start. Bond looked round, half expecting to see the stiletto knives spinning through the air. There was nothing. No last-minute cavalry.

The two men dragged him across the floor. He had one last sight of Scipio walking back to the bar. The barman slid a drink towards him . . . another brandy Alexander. 'I'd watch those calories if I were you,' Bond said but the words were muttered through swollen lips and nobody heard. And then he was gone, back through the ballroom and the dining room with all its glitter and pomp, out onto the deck and finally downstairs to the cabin. He was thrown onto the bed and at once Sixtine was with him, holding his head in her hands.

'James!' She was trying to hide it but he knew she was afraid.

'Don't worry,' he whispered. 'We'll find a way out . . .'

A third man came into the cabin carrying a small Gladstone bag, which he set down on a table. Bond recognised the oily hair, the bad skin, the shabby little moustache. It was Dr Borghetti, the man Wolfe had introduced as the ship's medic. This time he didn't even pretend to be friendly. He opened the bag and took out various items, laying them neatly on the table. First there was a syringe, an ugly-looking thing, slender and about four inches long, made of stainless steel encasing a glass cylinder beneath the plunger. Next to it he placed a spoon, a candle, a ball of cotton wool and a glass, which he filled with water from the sink. Finally, he removed a packet of waxed paper that he carefully unfolded. It contained a small heap of white powder.

'Could you get him ready, please,' he said, speaking in English.

Bond could feel his strength returning and wondered if he could fight back. It was surely now or never. But as two of the men moved into the room, two more took their place at the door and he knew that, in the confined space, any resistance was hopeless.

As if reading his thoughts, Borghetti added: 'I am sure you will not try anything stupid, Mr Bond. Not if you care about the well-being of the lady. You must accept what is being done to you. It is the beginning of a life-changing journey. Your first experience of heroin. Soon your life will be unimaginable without it.'

'One day I will kill you,' Bond said, matter-of-factly.

'I don't think so.'

Bond was gripped on both sides. One of the men took his shirtsleeve and ripped it apart so that it hung in two strands on either side of his arm. At the same time, Borghetti lit the candle. He tipped the powder into the spoon, then added some water, using the syringe to suck it out of the cup. He took great care in ensuring he had the right amount. Bond could only watch with a grim fascination as he continued the process. He held the spoon over the flame, stirring the mixture with the needle until it had dissolved. Finally, he dropped a ball of cotton wool into the preparation and sucked it back into the syringe. He nodded at the two men. He was ready.

'You are about to leave the real world and find yourself in a very different one. Having Madame 16 with you will, I am sure, only add to the pleasure. Please do not attempt to struggle. It will do no good.'

It was impossible anyway. The first man had clasped his arm, forcing it forward so that the bare wrist was exposed.

Borghetti came over to the bed.

Sixtine started to rise but the man with the broken nose brutally pushed her back, bringing his gun round so that it aimed at her stomach.

'Don't!' Bond said. He was speaking to her, not to Borghetti.

He looked down and saw the syringe with its hideous load drawing closer. He saw the needle touch his wrist and felt the prick as it penetrated the skin. Borghetti pushed further, finding the vein. He pressed the plunger. The heroin swirled downwards, entering his bloodstream. The syringe was empty. Borghetti removed it. Bond saw a bead of bright red blood on the puncture wound. Sixtine cried out as if she was on the edge of tears and, ignoring the gun that was being aimed at her, rushed forward and grabbed hold of him.

'It's done,' Borghetti said. He blew out the candle and placed it, along with the syringe, back in his case. He left the rest. 'He will be helpless for the next eight or nine hours,' he said. 'Even so, one of you should remain outside all night.' To Bond, he added: 'I will be back tomorrow.'

The two men released Bond, who fell back into Sixtine's arms.

Borghetti was the first out of the cabin. Smirking, the others followed. The door slammed shut. The key was turned on the other side.

Bond and Sixtine were alone.

20

Bad Medicine

Sixtine had worked out what she was going to do. Long before the door had closed, she had set about her work.

To the men who were watching, it appeared that she had grabbed hold of Bond; a frightened woman who thought she was going to lose her man. In reality she had done more than that. The torn sleeve of his shirt was hanging loose and even as Dr Borghetti was collecting his things, she had grabbed hold of it, wrapping it around his upper arm, effectively turning it into a tourniquet. Now she tightened it further and tied a knot. Bond was in shock, still dazed from the violence done to him. He was only half aware of what was happening.

'Don't move,' she whispered. She touched her hand against his head, trying to reassure him. 'I'm going to have to hurt you. It's the only way.'

Borghetti had left his glass behind. Sixtine picked it up and, holding it carefully in her palm, smashed it against the wall. The piece that remained was jagged, shaped like a knife. Without hesitating, she picked up Bond's hand and stabbed the point into his wrist, exactly where the syringe had entered moments before. Bond cried out, but there was a part of him that seemed to understand what she was doing and he didn't move as a jet of crimson blood spurted out. Sixtine was cradling him, holding his arm, trying to keep the flow out of his sight. She watched, trying to damp down her fear as the blood formed a gleaming pool on the floor.

She had worked out what she had to do but there was no way of calculating it precisely. It would have taken fifteen seconds for the heroin that had been injected into Bond to reach his heart and after that there would have been nothing to stop it disseminating through his system and entering his brain. The makeshift tourniquet had prevented that happening and the deliberately inflicted wound – what medieval doctors would have called bloodletting – would hopefully remove much of the poison from his veins. The trouble was that if she let him bleed too much, she might kill him. Too little and the whole exercise would be pointless. It was also impossible to quantify how much blood had actually been drawn. Looking down, Sixtine felt sickened. Bond was a healthy man in prime condition and his heart was pumping furiously. Already the cabin looked like a slaughterhouse. But she knew the appearance was deceptive. Even the smallest cut will look worse than it really is and in her time she had treated gun wounds that looked lethal but that had turned out to be fairly minor. She felt revolted by what she had been forced to do – cutting him. But the truth was that he could easily lose a whole pint without coming to any harm. Blood donors did it every day.

All she wanted was the contents of one arm.

'Try to relax, James,' she whispered. 'I'm going to take off the tourniquet.'

The blood flow had dwindled, the last drops falling like evil rain onto the puddle below. This was the moment of truth. Sixtine untied the shirtsleeve then tore the fabric free, bunching it up and pressing it down on the wound that she herself had inflicted. As blood flowed back into the arm, she kept the pressure firm and constant. Her aim now was to stop the bleeding. How much of the heroin might she have removed? Half of it? More? There was no way of knowing. All she could do was wait.

Meanwhile, the invisible army stormed the fortress of Bond's consciousness.

Although Bond wouldn't have known it, his brain was already in overdrive, combatting the effects of the beating he had received at Scipio's hands. It had its own pain-relief mechanism and was furiously sending out messages to the bruised flesh and the broken bone, using his entire central nervous system as a conduit, trying to calm things down. Gleefully, the heroin took over. It was ten times more powerful than the brain, ten times more effective. Pain? What pain? It was as if a heavenly chorus had exploded inside him. Everything Scipio had done to him was wiped away. Just a few moments ago he had felt Sixtine tying something round his arm and there had been another bolt of pain as the glass had cut into his wrist. Why had she done that to him? He had forgotten. But it didn't matter any more. The wrist was no longer connected to his arm. The arm was no longer connected to his shoulder. His entire body had fragmented and he could feel each and every one of his molecules spinning gloriously in the ether.

'I will provide you with pleasure . . .'

That was what Scipio had said, but it wasn't even close. What Bond was experiencing went far beyond any pleasure he had ever known, more gratifying than any food or wine he had ever tasted, more pleasurable than all the women he had ever slept with. It was like the rush that came with the first cigarette he smoked every morning, only a thousand times more powerful and longer-lasting. For the first time in his life, he understood what it meant to be himself – and it was clearer, simpler, more certain than anything he could have imagined or been told. He was the greatest spy who had ever lived. He was the world's most successful killer. Why should he have had a moment of doubt creeping into Rolf Larsen's bedroom in Stockholm and sticking a knife into his throat? It was what he had been born for.

He was James Bond, a boy standing on the icy slopes above Chamonix, breathing in the ice-cold air – and no matter that this was where his parents would die. They had left him this dazzling white world and it was his to command. He was Commander Bond, a war hero, feeling the rush as he parachuted into the Massif Central – and he actually saw it again, the curve of the Earth, the perfect blue sky . . . all of it his. He was the man every woman wanted to sleep with, starting with that first conquest when he was just sixteen years old and still at school. Every time was perfect, no one better. He was James Bond 007, rewarded with the number that placed him above the law and turned him into someone people would fear and respect in equal measure.

His entire life had become a kaleidoscope, shifting and disintegrating with every turn. He skied. He swam. He drove the fastest cars. He was invulnerable. He would live forever. He did not consider these things. They were not thoughts so much as raw emotions. All he knew was that he was happier than he had ever been. Indeed, he was discovering real happiness for the first time.

The first effects of the heroin injection lasted only five or ten minutes but to Bond it was a celebration that went on for eternity. After that he settled into a warm sense of comfort and well-being, aware now that Sixtine was holding him and knowing, also, that the two of them were prisoners on a steamship that was heading to America and that he was going to be killed. But even that didn't matter. It had been threatened before and somehow it never happened. He would find a way out! He drew Sixtine closer to him, revelling in her softness and the scent of her skin. He wanted to make love to her right now but at the same time holding her was enough. It wouldn't bother him if he never moved again.

Or again.

Or again.

Hours, days, weeks went by and then, quite suddenly, he felt himself sliding back down the hillside to normality with all its doubts and uncertainties and although he didn't want to go there, he couldn't stop himself. He had thought he would never feel pain again but now an unwelcome visitor, it began to insinuate itself, starting in his wrist, first throbbing then hammering all the way up his arm. There was something wrong with his chest. He turned sideways and cried out as the broken rib made itself known. His vision, which had been perfect, darkened at the edges and he remembered the blows to his head, which must have caused all the swelling he could feel around his face. His lips were cracked. His mouth was completely dry. And someone was talking to him.

'You're coming out of it. It's all right, James. You're with me again. I'm looking after you.'

It was Sixtine, speaking softly, close to his ear. Bond had no idea how long he had been here but remembering what had happened and the danger he was in, he felt his senses locking together.

'How long?' It was all he could do to bring the two words together in a question that made sense. Already he knew that both their lives depended on the answer.

'I managed to get some of the heroin out of you, James. I had to hurt you but there was no other way. And it's worked. I've bought us time. They said it would be eight or nine hours but it's been less than three. Just don't try to move for a minute. What you've been through . . . it's been horrible. But you're going to get back your strength.'

'I'm OK.' But he wasn't. He turned his head and saw the blood, now dark and sticky, on the floor. He was hit at once by a hammer blow of nausea. 'Going to be sick . . .'

He couldn't stand up on his own. Sixtine helped him to his feet and supported him as he stumbled over to the sink where he stood for a minute, resting with his hands on the porcelain, avoiding looking at himself in the mirror. When he had recovered a little, she ran the tap and splashed water over his head, using her cupped hand to allow him to drink just a few sips. Bond was feeling atrocious. He was finding it hard to breathe. He was sweating. The muscles in his chest and stomach were in spasm, made more painful by his broken rib. Part of him was astonished by the speed of his descent from the heroin-induced euphoria he had been feeling just moments ago to this abyss. What person in their right mind would want to make this journey if they knew that it would always lead to this destination? But that was just the point, of course. A second injection was the easiest way out, then a third and a fourth until the demand was continuous. Bond had been addicted to many things for as long as he could remember but he had always considered addiction to be one of life's pleasures, whether it was alcohol, cigarettes or women. This was different. He had felt himself being torn apart. It was a lesson he swore he would never repeat.

'How are you feeling?' Sixtine asked.

'Not good. Need time . . .'

'James, we don't have time. We have a window of opportunity. An hour, maybe two. You have to get yourself back together.'

He nodded. 'Ten minutes. Cigarette . . .'

She lit a cigarette for him and he sat down on one of the wicker chairs, not looking at the blood, focusing on the injection of nicotine quieting him down. At the same time, he took stock. He would be able to move but not to run. Sixtine had badly cut the wrist of his right arm and even if he managed to get hold of a gun, it would affect his aim. He was dizzy from blood loss. He could still feel the drug wreathing itself inside his head, clouding his thoughts. Any sense of invulnerability had well and truly vanished. On the contrary, he had become a liability. He would only hold Sixtine back.

As if sensing his thoughts, she spoke. 'We're going to break out of here together. First of all out of this cabin, then off this boat. You and me, James. We're going to do it together. Don't you dare argue with me.'

Bond nodded. The taste of the cigarette was an old friend. It was helping to restore him. 'We can't just . . . swim,' he said. He still had to keep the sentences short. 'Too far out. And I want to stop them. All the heroin. Tons of it. Sink the ship.'

'Sink the ship?' She stared at him. 'How are we going to do that? Forgive me, but I forgot to pack a hand grenade.'

Bond's thought processes were still disjointed. He had to force himself to concentrate. There were things he had learned – sabotage techniques – working in the secret service during the war. He thought about the fire extinguishers he had seen at the Wolfe Europe compound. And there was

something else. What was it? Oh yes. The boxes being carried on board the *Mirabelle* when he had visited that first
time, a century ago. And Wolfe telling him: '*We're going to
have a party like you wouldn't believe.*'

Somehow, it all came together.

'I have an idea,' Bond said.

21

The Dark Blue Sea

It was soon after midnight that the hammering began – and with it a voice from the other side of the door.

'Help me!' It was the woman. She sounded desperate. 'Someone . . . please. He's stopped breathing. I think he's dead.'

Two guards, not one, had been stationed in the corridor – and for a moment they were unsure what to do. They had been instructed not to enter the cabin until the morning. Then they were to take the Englishman back up to the promenade deck for another beating at Scipio's hands. Still in shock from the first heroin injection, the pain would take him well past the point of endurance. They had seen this before. The last time Scipio had prescribed the same course of treatment, his victim had become a jabbering idiot in only a week.

'Is there anyone there? Please!'

It could be some sort of trick. But the woman sounded genuine enough, close to hysterics. And they had heard what the doctor said. The spy would be semi-conscious for at least another five hours. Right now he would be out of his head, unable even to stand. On the other hand, if something had gone wrong, if he'd had some sort of reaction to the drug that had been injected into him and his heart had stopped beating, Scipio would be furious. They knew what his plans for Bond involved.

Everyone else was either working in the engine room or asleep. The men had to make the decision for themselves and in the end it wasn't difficult. There were two of them. They both had guns. An unarmed woman and an unconscious spy weren't going to present a challenge and anyway, they would proceed with extreme care. They unlocked the door and went in.

The sight that met their eyes was every bit as grim as they might have imagined – although imagination was something they had never had in great supply. Sixtine was on her knees beside the door, her whole body limp, tears streaming down her face. Bond was lying prostrate on the floor. He seemed to have struck his head when he fell. There was blood everywhere. It was impossible to see if he was breathing but it seemed unlikely. His muscles were locked together, his arms stretched out, his fists clenched.

'He fell!' Sixtine sobbed. 'There was nothing I could do. He just fell and he lay there. You killed him.'

Was he dead? One man stayed by the door, covering Sixtine, while the other continued further into the cabin, moving forward to examine the body. He had no doubt that Sixtine was right and that Bond was beyond help. The quantity of blood spoke for itself.

So he was careless as he leaned down to check for a pulse. In the blink of an eye, he saw Bond's lifeless arm suddenly twist round – but before he could react it was already too late. Bond rolled sideways, driving his fist upwards in a savage blow that dislocated his opponent's jaw and smashed him into unconsciousness. The man at the door swung round, aiming at Bond, at the same time taking his attention off Sixtine. At once, she seized hold of his arm and, dragging it towards her, bit hard into his wrist. The man howled and dropped his gun. Bond was already on his feet, rushing towards him. The man was aware of two pitch-black eyes, filled with a ferocity that was truly animal. Sixtine was on her feet. She jerked upwards, twisting his arm behind his back and almost breaking it. As he bowed down involuntarily, Bond kicked out, his toecap slamming into the man's head. Sixtine let go and he collapsed.

Bond stood catching his breath, swaying on his feet. Even this short burst of action had been almost too much for him. Sixtine knew that what he had been through in the last few hours – the beating, the injection, the makeshift surgery – would have finished most men. Bond was fighting back but the situation was still almost hopeless. They were out at sea. There must be at least fifty crew members on the boat and all of them were on Scipio's payroll. For the time being, they had the element of surprise but that could change the moment someone came to relieve the two guards on the door. Sixtine was certain that their best course of action was to get over the side and swim for the shore, and she said as much.

Bond shook his head. 'No. It's too dangerous. We don't know how far out we are. We might not make it.'

'What then?'

'Tie these two up. Then follow me.'

Sixtine knelt beside the man who had been guarding her. She took his head in her hands and twisted it sharply, breaking his neck. Bond stared at her. 'I don't have any rope,' she said. 'And we're running out of time.' Before he could protest, she did the same for the second man. Bond was too exhausted to argue. Somewhere in his fuddled brain he realised that he had known their names. They were Carlo and Simone. He never had discovered which was which.

'So, where are we going?' Sixtine demanded.

'Baggage Room. R deck. Aft . . .'

'Why?'

'Trust me.'

Locking the door behind them, they slipped out into a long, empty corridor, softly lit by the night-service lamps set at intervals between the multiple doors. Bond could hear the distant hum of engines and felt the vibrations beneath his feet. It was hard not to feel trapped in the warm, claustrophobic atmosphere, surrounded by so much metal. He and Sixtine both now had guns. Bond had taken a weapon – and also a shirt – from one of the two dead men. But he still felt very exposed. If someone appeared fifty or a hundred yards ahead, they would be seen at once, targets at the end of a long shooting gallery. There was nowhere to hide. The entire ship was a vast network of interconnecting spaces, stairways, corridors, doors and arches. They had no way of knowing what lay ahead. Bond wasn't even sure he would be able to shoot straight. His mouth was dry and his vision blurred. His heart was pounding. The heroin was still in his system and he knew that it might be weeks before he was finally free of it. Thank God for Sixtine. She knew what she was doing. She was the most extraordinary woman he'd ever met.

They reached a stairwell and climbed down, sinking further into the bowels of the ship. Bond couldn't be sure after his brief tour but he thought R deck must be immediately beneath the level where they had been held. Fortunately, there were plenty of signs to direct them and sure enough the letter R was printed on the wall one floor down. They followed a second corridor almost identical to the one above, although the carpet was a different colour, perhaps designed to help guests find their way back to their cabins. Every ten yards, they came to a fire extinguisher. It was what Bond had noticed before. Irwin Wolfe seemed to have a phobia about fire.

Their journey took them through the tourist-class restaurant, simpler and more austere than the one Bond had seen in first class, the tables without cloths and shrouded in shadows. The lack of any life or movement was unsettling. The ship was like an abandoned city with only the constant hum of the engines to remind them they were actually moving. They passed a shop, a smoking room, a pantry, a vegetable store and finally a kitchen with different-shaped knives hanging on hooks above the polished worktop. Bond would need those for what he had in mind. He went in and helped himself to a couple, slipping them into his belt.

Despite the ever-present signs, the various sections of the ship looked very much the same in the half-light. Bond knew they were heading aft but there were dozens of doors to choose from. Which one was the baggage room? It could be on either side or somewhere concealed in the middle. It might take passengers days to find their way around. His life depended on his managing it in a matter of minutes.

He stumbled onto it at the very back, surrounded by offices for the ship's baker, the restaurant manager, the storekeeper and the stewards. The baggage room was labelled and it wasn't locked. He opened the door and turned the light on. And there it was in front of him, exactly what he was looking for.

Irwin Wolfe had told him there was going to be a gala reception when they arrived in America and had boasted about the $1,000 he had spent on fireworks. As it happened, just as Bond had come on board the *Mirabelle*, he had seen them being delivered and heard the purser yelling out the delivery instructions. There were about a dozen large boxes clearly marked FEUX D'ARTIFICE stacked up in front of him, isolated in the dry, empty surroundings of the baggage room. For a major display in the harbour of New York, some of the fireworks would be huge. They would be packed with explosive gunpowder along with all the other chemicals used to create the sparks and colours that would burst over the city skyline.

Sixtine had worked out what was on his mind. Bond wanted to produce a single explosion, one big enough to sink the *Mirabelle*. He planned to send Wolfe's heroin to the bottom of the sea and possibly even Wolfe with it. The means to do it were right here in front of him. 'OK,' she said. 'You want to make a bomb. That's not such a bad idea. But where are you going to put it? In the furnace?'

Bond shook his head. 'That won't work. We have to smash the cooling water system . . . the inlet valve.'

'Do you know where it is?'

'I can find it.' Bond had served on ships. And as a lieutenant in the Special Branch of the RNVR, he had also learned how to destroy them.

'Will it work?'

'It might.'

Sixtine stared at the boxes of fireworks piled high in the storeroom. 'There's plenty of gunpowder here. But you're going to need some sort of casing.'

'One of the fire extinguishers.'

'OK. But just out of interest – how are you going to get it open?'

'Wait here.'

Leaving Sixtine in the baggage room, Bond went out into the corridor. A few moments later, he returned carrying one of the many red cylinders that he had seen lining the ship's corridors. He rolled it on its side.

'They've got too many of these,' he explained. 'There must be hundreds of them. And I saw the same models at the compound – when we were at Wolfe Europe. They've got to be the answer . . . how he's going to do it.' All the time, he had been examining the metal surface – and with a smile, he found what he was looking for. The mechanism couldn't have been simpler. The base, in its entirety, unscrewed.

But there wasn't water or sodium bicarbonate inside the cylinder. Bond took out a bulging plastic bag and held it in his hand. He and Sixtine had seen dozens more of them being prepared in the heroin laboratory and here they were, carefully packed into the shell, ready for the crossing to America. Irwin Wolfe had boasted of 12,000 pounds of the drug on board. That was the equivalent of 600 fire extinguishers with twenty pounds in each. When they arrived in New York, nobody was going to search the ship. On the contrary, they were going to welcome it with a celebration and they were going to miss what was sitting there, right in front of their eyes. Dirt-cheap heroin for anyone who wanted it. All too soon everyone would want it.

Bond felt sickened remembering the tiny quantity that had been injected into him and the devastation it had wreaked inside his mind. He clawed at the plastic, tearing it and allowing most of the contents to cascade between his hands onto the floor. Then he threw what was left into the far corner. It was a small gesture but one that made him feel better in himself.

'You're going to have to help me,' he said, handing her one of the knives he had taken from the kitchen. 'We need to cut open the fireworks. And we'll need a fuse . . .'

'It's one o'clock, James. How long have we got?'

'Your guess is as good as mine. Let's get on with it.'

He and Sixtine tore the lids off the cartons, revealing the brightly coloured fireworks inside, packed together in straw.

There were cannons, rockets, mortars and zip-bangs, each one industrial-sized, fat boxes filled with explosive. Using the knives, they sliced them open. Bond had cut a piece of cardboard into the rough shape of a funnel and he used it to pour the gunpowder into the empty fire extinguisher, packing it in as tightly as he could. The fireworks had come complete with one-minute fuses. He fed one into the nozzle, then screwed the base back on. What he had, he hoped, was an effective bomb. He wondered how he would explain himself to Sixtine if all he managed was an attractive display of pink sparks.

'How many of these are we going to need?' Sixtine asked.

'One should do.' Bond looked at his watch. It was a quarter past two. Their work had taken them over an hour. He thought about the men they had left behind in the cabin. Was it too much to hope that they were meant to stay on guard duty for the whole night? Bond had locked the door and taken the keys. But the moment they were found to be missing, someone would raise the alarm.

'Did you bring your lighter?' he asked.

'I have it here.' She took it out of her jacket pocket. 'They left it with my cigarettes.'

'Very considerate.' With an effort, Bond hoisted the fire extinguisher onto his shoulder.

'Let me take it,' Sixtine said.

'No. I can manage.' He grinned at her. 'When this is all over, I'm going to take you to Rome. I'm going to take you to the Piazza Navona and buy you the biggest ice cream you've ever eaten, and then we're going to go back to the hotel and drink martini cocktails the way you like them and stay in bed for a week.'

'I'll take you up on that,' she said. 'If we get out of here alive . . .'

They went back out into the corridor. Nothing had changed. Inside a cruise ship like the *Mirabelle* night and day were interchangeable and the atmosphere would always have this blank, sterile quality. They made their way past the various offices until they came to a staircase that led them down two more decks. The further down they went, the less luxurious their surroundings became. Finally, they reached a door marked CREW ONLY and pushed it open. At once, they were greeted by a waft of warm air that smelled of oil. The sound of the triple expansion engine leapt up in volume. It was accompanied by the whirr of the fan-assisted ventilators and the disjointed clanking of steel.

This was the hidden world of the luxury cruiser.

There were at least three separate spaces: the engine room, the boiler room and the generator room. But with so many pipes, so much machinery, it was impossible to tell where one ended and the other began. The entire area rose up through three decks, connected by wide metal stairways, gantries and more of the submarine-style hatches that Bond had noticed when he was shown round. Everything was brutal, harshly lit, intensely hot, utterly lacking in luxury. The air was being circulated but with little effect. Bond was standing on the uppermost level, his eyes already smarting as he made his way down, breathing in the fumes that leaked out of the twin Lobnitz & Co. boilers.

The *Mirabelle* was cruising gently off the coast of France. Had it begun the transatlantic crossing, there would have been forty or fifty people at work and the noise would have been deafening. Instead, the engine room was eerily empty with just a few figures in overalls absorbed in their work – and nobody noticed as Bond and Sixtine continued past the air pipes, the turbines and the main condensers.

Bond carried the fire extinguisher on his shoulder, hiding his face. Sixtine stayed close to him, using him as cover. There was little chance of his being recognised, but a woman in the engine room would have drawn attention to them at once. They didn't speak. They had to look as if they knew what they were doing, do it, and then get out of there as quickly as possible.

But where was the bloody inlet valve? Bond knew that it would resemble a very ordinary circular tap on a pipe about twelve inches in diameter. It would be connected to the hull, drawing in a constant stream of seawater that passed through the engine, removing the heat from the cylinder heads, the exhaust valves and the turbochargers. If this had been a corvette or a battle cruiser, he would have been able to go straight to it. But it was a brand-new, purpose-built cruise liner. Bond barely recognised half the machinery around him. Although he would never have admitted it to Sixtine – she had followed him all the way without question – he would need a great deal of luck if he was going to find what he was looking for.

'You do know where you're going?' Sixtine whispered. It was as if she had read his thoughts.

'Of course . . .'

He broke off as a mechanic brushed past them, carrying a bucket full of rags. For a fraction of a second, Bond was tempted to ask him for directions – at gunpoint, if need be. But then he saw it. Luck was with him after all. The inlet valve was stuck between two platforms in the bilge area, tucked away against the curving sheet of metal that was the outer wall. Was it possible that the makeshift bomb would be strong enough to blast out the rivets and welding that held it all together? Bond doubted it, but it didn't matter. The valve was thirty feet below sea level. Roughly translated, that meant it was taking in water at thirty pounds per square inch. Break the pipe and it would be the start of a deluge that would sink the ship fairly quickly unless the hydraulic doors were closed immediately. And Bond had ideas about that, too.

The mechanic who'd just passed them had stopped. He turned round and examined them, a puzzled look on his face. 'Who are you? What are you doing here?'

Sixtine took out her gun and shot him in the leg. The sound of gunfire was almost drowned out by the noise of the engines . . . but not quite. Pandemonium broke out all around them with engineers and crewmen running in different directions above their heads. Nobody knew where the shot had come from. That there had been a shot was enough.

Bond knew he had to act fast. He swung the fire extinguisher down and rested it between the hull and the inlet valve with the fuse trailing towards him. Sixtine handed him her lighter.

'Ready?' he asked.

She nodded.

'We have one minute.'

'To go where?'

'The generator room.' He lit the fuse.

Another man appeared. Bond looked up and was surprised to see Dr Borghetti walking towards them, still dressed in his whites. What was he doing down here in the middle of the night? Perhaps one of the engineers had been taken sick, or he could have been on his way to check on Bond. Either way, it didn't matter. Sixtine shot him, quite deliberately, aiming for his stomach. She stood and watched as he crashed down in front of them, then began to writhe on the unforgiving metal. Bond knew that she wanted him to suffer. There was an icy anger in her eyes.

'Just what the doctor ordered,' she muttered quietly.

They had wasted precious seconds. As the fuse sparked and hissed, Bond and Sixtine backed away, making for the nearest ladder leading to a hatchway on the deck above. It was the fastest route to where Bond needed to go next. He had seen the generators when they had first entered the engine room. There was a fire axe on a wall and he snatched it. That would come in useful too.

They reached the ladder and climbed it. By the time they had made it to the next level, climbing through the circular hatchway, Bond was seriously worried. Surely sixty seconds had passed by now? What would he do if the bomb failed to go off? He cursed himself for not having thought to bring a second fuse. Well, no matter. A torn strip of rag would do it, perhaps soaked in oil. And if he blew himself up in the process, at least he would have the knowledge that he had sunk Wolfe, Scipio and 12,000 pounds of heroin. The boy stood on the burning deck and all that.

Beneath them, the bomb exploded. The blast was incredibly loud, echoing off so much metal. Looking down through the gantry, Bond saw the bright red fireball as it erupted. Bizarrely, it was also coloured with brilliant streaks of blue, green and silver, and sparks danced in the air as the various compounds contained in the fireworks were ignited. It was, he thought, the most beautiful explosion in the world. But had it done its job? He saw the answer almost at once. The inlet valve had been shattered. A huge snake of water was bursting out of the pipe, leaping ferociously into the engine room. A klaxon had begun to sound and a series of red lights, set high up on the walls, were suddenly flashing.

Bond was still gripping the axe. He and Sixtine came to a complicated wall of electrical machinery with dozens of switches, valves and gauges. There had been a man in white overalls sitting on a stool in front of it, but he took one look at them and ran. Bond knew that this was the main switchboard. He would have to be careful. He wanted to knock out the breakers and destroy it – but ideally without electrocuting himself in the process. There were half a dozen master switches, each presumably controlling a different area of the *Mirabelle*. Using the blunt end of the axe, he carefully demolished every one of them. Then, for good measure, he swung the axe into the largest glass panel. There was a satisfying starburst of white and yellow sparks. Half the lights in the engine room went out. The ventilators stopped working. All the dials on the switchboard swung to zero.

He had done what he could. It was time to go. His entire body – his head, his stomach, his throat – felt like hell. His broken rib was on fire. The cut that Sixtine had made in his wrist had opened and he was bleeding again. God knows what he must look like. He just hoped he had the strength for what would be the most difficult part. Scipio and his men must have realised what was happening by now. He and Sixtine had managed to creep in. They would have to fight every inch of the way out.

Still holding the axe, he ran back the way they had come, making for the bow of the ship. Once again the corridors yawned emptily ahead of them, this time shrouded in the dull glow of the emergency lighting. It was the semi-darkness that saved them. They were about halfway down when three of Scipio's men appeared, heading for the engine room. The men didn't recognise Bond or Sixtine until it was too late. Bond's gun-hand spoke and two of the men went down. But they were replaced a moment later by more men behind them. The corridor was blocked. There was no way forward.

'Help me!' Sixtine had grabbed hold of a heavy fire door, which she was struggling to close across the corridor. Bond seized hold of it and together they swung it shut. There was no lock but Bond slid the axe between the handles, effectively bolting it. Scipio's men were on one side. They were on the other. They had wasted time and there was no choice but to go back the way they had come.

Something strange was happening. The *Mirabelle* was beginning to tilt. It was only very slight but Bond already had the sensation of leaning sideways and he realised with disbelief that his improvised bomb must have done more damage than he had thought. Perhaps it had blown a hole in the side after all. And with the electricity cut and all the safety devices neutralised, there was nothing to stop the ship filling with water and capsizing. How long would it take? The *Titanic* had gone down in two hours and forty minutes but at least it had been able to close the bulkheads between its sixteen compartments and the pumps had actually worked. Thanks to Bond, that wasn't the case here. The *Mirabelle* might sink much faster. Either way, he and Sixtine had to find a way out of this gigantic metal coffin, which meant getting onto the deck – and fast.

And they still had to take care. There could be fifty men looking for them. They had no real idea where they were going. Bond was exhausted. They only had half a dozen bullets between them.

Quite suddenly, beneath them, there was an explosion, much louder and more ominous than the one Bond had caused. It was immediately followed by a shaking so violent that Bond and Sixtine were thrown against the walls and then to the ground. The emergency lights flickered. The klaxon stopped. Bond was dazed and his injuries were screaming at him but he managed to work out what must have happened. Gallons of cold water had poured into the engine room, hitting the boilers filled with high-pressure steam, and this had caused the second, much larger explosion. Now the passageway was tilting more seriously. Bond could hear a mournful grinding. It was the sound of Irwin Wolfe's $2 million steamship tearing itself apart.

Bond and Sixtine got to their feet and clung to each other for a moment.

'Up,' Bond said.

'And out,' Sixtine agreed.

There was nothing more to say. But their progress was more difficult now. Bond continued forward like a drunkard, about to collapse on his side. He had to lean on Sixtine for support. They came to the end of a corridor and turned a corner in time to see a horrendous sight. At the far end, about thirty yards away, a torrent of black water almost floor to ceiling was rushing towards them like a living thing, hunting them down. It was impossible to see where it had come from. A whole section of the *Mirabelle* had disappeared behind it. They could only turn and run the way they had come, aware of the flood that must be inches behind them and that would crash down and devour them if they so much as paused for breath.

Somehow, they found another staircase and clambered up – but it still didn't take them to an outside deck. Another corridor, more doors. But no portholes, no way out. And somehow the water had already reached them. It was around their feet, licking their heels, rising incredibly quickly. Another corner. They hurried round and even though their every instinct was to keep moving, they stopped dead in their tracks. It was the most bizarre thing Bond had ever seen.

Jean-Paul Scipio.

It was impossible to be sure how he had got there but Bond suspected that, after the first explosion, he must have hurried down to the engine room with his translator to see the damage for himself. The ship would have already been flooding at that point, the seawater rushing in through the broken valve. But then there had been a second explosion, perhaps cutting off the main staircase. He and the translator had been forced to take the ladder and Scipio had got stuck. It was the only possible explanation.

That was what Bond and Sixtine were seeing now. The great bald head was missing its wig, which had floated away on the water that now coursed over the carpet. His shoulders and part of his chest had made it through. His arms were on either side of him, his palms under the water, straining to free the rest of him. But that was all there was. It was like a magic trick that had gone horribly wrong, a man cut in half. He couldn't go up. Nor could he go down. And very soon he would drown. The water was all around him. It was already lapping at the pink scar across his throat. Inch by inch, it was rising over his several chins. In less than a minute it would cover his mouth, then finally his nose. He was actually watching himself drown.

Now he stared at Bond, his face distorted with fear.

'*Aiutatemi!*' he gasped.

'Help me,' the translator translated.

Sixtine took out her gun and fired a single shot. One of the lenses in the translator's glasses shattered and blood streamed out of what had once been his eye. She aimed at Scipio and pulled the trigger a second time but the gun was empty.

'Leave him,' Bond said.

They turned. The water reached Scipio's lower lip. He screamed at them. Gleefully, the water poured into his mouth.

Finally, the next staircase brought them out to the main deck. By now the *Mirabelle* was listing badly, and they had to fight to stop themselves from sliding into the sea. Behind them they saw lifeboats being clumsily lowered in a tangle of ropes. It was the middle of the night but the moon was out, giving everything the silver nitrate sheen of an old film. Bond wondered what had happened to Irwin Wolfe. Was the millionaire still in his cabin? Had he drowned in his bed? Or perhaps, seeing the sinking of his ship and the end of all his plans, he had simply jumped overboard. Bond was still tempted to find him. After what had been done to him, there was a part of him that didn't want to leave a single one of them alive.

Somebody shouted. Even in the darkness, with all the mayhem around them, he and Sixtine had been seen. Black shadows without faces were making their way towards them along the sloping deck. He saw the white pinpricks of gunfire and seized Sixtine. Bullets ricocheted around them, splintering the wood and hammering into the railings as they ran forward and jumped. The sea was still a long way beneath them. Time seemed to have suspended itself. They were next to each other, trapped in mid-air, an easy target for the people firing at them. There was more gunfire. Then, finally, their feet broke through the water. Bond felt a fresh bolt of pain in his chest as the broken rib was jarred once again. He screamed and almost blacked out but the water revived him. It was swirling all around, driving him upwards. He let it carry him to the surface and broke through, gasping for air. Already he was searching for Sixtine and saw her close by, the moonlight reflecting in her hair. They had done it! They had actually got away with it!

'Are you OK?' He swam over to her. Every movement hurt but he no longer cared.

'Yes.' Her voice sounded weak. Bond guessed she had been winded when she hit the sea.

'We have to move. The ship's going down. We don't want to be caught in the suction.'

Together they swam – twenty, thirty strokes – knowing that the further they went, retreating into the darkness, the more invisible they became. Scipio was dead. His men would be fighting for a place in the lifeboats. Surely no one would care about them any more. But it was only when they were a safe distance away that they turned and looked at the *Mirabelle*, silhouetted against the night sky. It was already low in the water, slanting at an impossible angle. A few pinpricks of light blinked behind the windows and the portholes but otherwise it was a great, dying beast, sinking into its grave. There were more lights on the lifeboats that surrounded it and they could hear men shouting uselessly at each other, planning their evacuation. The two funnels were no longer steaming. The boilers were drenched, any fire extinguished. There was a part of Bond, perhaps the naval commander in him, that felt a touch of sadness for the stricken cruiser. She had been beautiful. She wasn't to blame for the way she had been used.

They were still too close. Bond knew that when the ship finally disappeared, everything around her would be sucked down with her – even the lifeboats if they didn't get away soon. And there was another, more pressing question. Where were they? If they were in the middle of the Mediterranean, then all of this would have been for nothing. They would still drown.

He twisted round and saw the lights of buildings along the coast. In the darkness, it was impossible to tell exactly how far away they were but Bond figured that the distance couldn't be more than a mile. He was in bad shape. His breath was coming in dagger thrusts. The salt in the water was attacking the open wound in his wrist. It was going to be touch and go. But with Sixtine's help, he was sure he could make it.

And what of her?

She was close to him, still and silent. 'We can't stay here,' he said. 'It may take us an hour or two to reach the coast but if we take it slowly, we should be OK. Stop for rests. Let the tide take us in.'

'James . . .'

She was going to tell him something that he didn't want to hear. Instinctively, he knew it.

'If you feel tired, you can hold onto me,' he insisted.

'I can't come with you, James.'

The sea was suddenly icy cold. He put his arms around her and drew her against him. She didn't resist but now he saw the pain in her eyes. When he took his hand out of the water, he saw that it was covered in something black. It was the colour of blood in the moonlight.

'You can do it,' he whispered. His voice caught in his throat. 'You have to.'

She was strangely calm. 'We beat them,' she said. 'There were so many of them and just the two of us but we got away with it.' She shuddered. 'Something hit me when we went over the side . . .'

'I can get you back. I can swim with you.'

'No. You're going to have to finish this on your own.' They were still clinging onto each other, hanging in the water like lovers. Her voice was beginning to drift away. 'I'm sorry, James. Don't be angry with me.'

'I could never be angry with you.'

She smiled. 'It wasn't meant to be forever. But at least we had our day.'

'Sixtine . . .'

'You must go now. You mustn't . . .'

She died.

He saw the moment when the life slipped out of her eyes. Still he held her, refusing to accept that she had gone. Behind him, he heard a great cracking sound as unimaginable forces seized hold of what was left of the *Mirabelle* and broke it apart. The bow was almost vertical now. It was beginning the final plunge. He knew he had to let Sixtine go with it.

He released her and watched her slide away from him, gently carried beneath the surface of the dark blue sea. The water washed over her face as if erasing her. Her hair was billowing around her and she looked serene, as beautiful in death as she had been when they were together. Finally, she disappeared from sight.

Bond uttered a single sound, something between a snarl and a sob. Then he turned and began to swim towards the shore.

22

Death at Sunset

Like some gigantic bird of prey, the Boeing 377 Stratocruiser came dropping out of the sky over Los Angeles, its wings stretching out and its wheels searching for the two-mile strip of concrete runway. The palm trees on either side bowed briefly in obeisance as it roared past, disappearing into the heat haze. It was midday and the sun was at its most intense, the air thick with the fumes of oil and methanol. The wheels made contact. The pilot slammed the engines into reverse thrust and with a howl of rage the great beast allowed itself to be steered back into captivity. As it reached Hangar Number One, an armada of little vehicles congregated from every direction: baggage tractors, container loaders, dollies and service stairs. By the time the plane had reached its destination, it was surrounded. The twenty-eight-cylinder engines were switched off. The four propellers slowed down and shuddered to a halt.

The door was unsealed and a blast of warm air came rushing in. James Bond, seated close to the rear on the upper floor, was the first to feel it. For the past twelve hours – the last leg of the journey from New York – he had sat silently in the pressurised, air-conditioned stillness of the cabin (the woman next to him, on the other side of the aisle, had soon given up any hope of conversation). Now the noise, the heat and the smell of the airport reminded him where he was and why he had come here. He could already feel the sweat patches underneath his shirt. His sense of discomfort was made worse by the bandages tightly strapped across his chest. The broken rib was already healing but it would be a while before he was fully fit.

A week had passed since he had returned to London from the south of France.

M had been pleased with the way things had gone. 'You've taken out the number-one trafficker in the narcotics business and you've sent five tons of his product to the bottom of the ocean . . . best place for it. This will deal a major blow to the international syndicates and with a bit of luck it will allow the Americans to get on top of the problem of heroin addiction. The truth of the matter is that once the war ended, they could have eliminated it altogether if they hadn't allowed themselves to get sidetracked. Maybe this will give them a second chance.

'You also achieved exactly what you were sent out to do. When you confronted Scipio, he told you that it was he who killed our man.'

'Yes, sir. He was quite clear about it.'

'Then I'm very glad he's been dealt with.' M always chose his words carefully. Violence and death were often part of his remit. But that didn't mean he had to articulate it, here in this office.

'I was wondering about Wolfe, sir.'

'Yes. I'm afraid that part of it didn't work out quite as well as we might have hoped. He managed to get into one of the lifeboats and they took him ashore. He was driven down the coast to Perpignan and slipped over the border into Spain. He was on a plane back to the US before anyone could speak to him. Now he's resurfaced at his home in Los Angeles and we're not going to be able to do very much about him . . . not officially, anyway. He's surrounded himself with expensive lawyers. Claims that he knew nothing about Scipio or the drugs or you, for that matter – and unfortunately, as to what happened on the *Mirabelle*, it's your word against his. The police raided the factory outside Menton but again he's pleading ignorance. According to him, it was all down to Scipio.'

'So he's not going to be prosecuted?'

'I've spoken to our friends in the CIA but they've been surprisingly unresponsive. They've made it clear that they want to handle things their own way.'

M's voice was bleak. If the *Mirabelle* had made it to New York it would have been the start of an epidemic that could have decimated the country. He would not have enjoyed being cold-shouldered by the Americans after everything Bond had done.

'I did want to ask you about Joanne Brochet,' M went on, a little softer now. His clear grey eyes were examining Bond carefully. 'I understand that, contrary to what we believed, she was actually very helpful to you.'

'Yes, sir. I certainly couldn't have got away with it without her.' As he spoke, Bond's thumb pressed against the wound on his wrist and the bandage wrapped around it.

'And she died.'

'Yes. For what it's worth, she died helping me and I'd like to think you'll amend the records to show that, although she had gone into business for herself, she was never an enemy of this country. Quite the contrary. I learned something of her experiences during the war. We owe her a great deal.'

'I'll see to it. And that son of hers, the one in the

Bahamas. I understand that he's with relatives but we'll make sure he's looked after.'

Bond nodded, satisfied.

'Is there anything else?' M asked.

'I'd like to take a week's holiday, if that's all right, sir,' Bond said. 'The doctor patched me up but the rib still hurts like blazes and it'll be a while before I'm fully operational.'

'Absolutely.' M lit his pipe. He seemed to be searching for the right words, as if he had something difficult to say. 'As a matter of fact, I was wondering if you might like to spend some time on the west coast of America. I've been thinking about this man, Irwin Wolfe. We obviously can't involve ourselves in CIA business, but I'll be damned if I'm just to sit back and do nothing. I wondered if you might like to have a word with him?'

Bond thought for a moment. 'Yes, sir. I'd like that very much.' He paused. 'Although I don't think a loaded revolver and a glass of whisky would be something Mr Wolfe would consider.'

M smiled. 'I'm not surprised. I'm afraid the Americans don't quite have our sensibilities when it comes to these matters but at the same time, it can't hurt letting him know we're not giving up on him, and at the end of the day all the lawyers in California won't protect him from justice.'

'That's a lot of lawyers,' Bond muttered.

'Just see what you can do. You might find it personally helpful coming face to face with him again. And I want you to understand that whatever results from such a meeting has my full sanction.'

So there it was. M was effectively giving Bond carte blanche. The visit would be unofficial. Bond could take whatever action he saw fit.

'I want you to know that you handled yourself extremely well, 007,' M concluded. 'You fully justified my decision to promote you to the Double-O Section. Enjoy your week off. You deserve it.'

Loelia Ponsonby had made an international call before Bond left and had spoken to one of Irwin Wolfe's assistants. Although at first there had been a great deal of reluctance at the other end, a meeting had finally been arranged at the film mogul's Los Angeles home at seven o'clock on the evening of his arrival. Bond was surprised that Wolfe should have agreed to see him, but then what did he have to lose? He was dying anyway. And he would doubtless be protected.

At the airport, Bond presented the passport provided for him, made out under a false name. He collected his luggage and made his way through customs, presenting himself to a young, enthusiastic man in a grey uniform shirt.

'How long are you here for, sir?'

'A week.'

'A business trip?'

'I'm seeing a friend.'

'Oh. A special occasion?'

'It might be.'

There was a car waiting for Bond at the airport and he drove himself up La Cienega Boulevard to the hotel he had booked for the few days he actually planned to remain in the city. The Beverly Wilshire suited his needs exactly: grand and comfortable, close to the best shops and restaurants, it was somewhere a wealthy Englishman travelling on his own wouldn't be noticed. It also had an Olympic-sized swimming pool which he would use twice a day, coaxing his body back into shape.

Once he had been shown to his room, Bond took a long,

hot shower followed by an icy cold one with needles of water pounding down on his shoulders and back. He had ordered a negroni – made with Gordon's gin – from room service and drank it on his terrace, allowing the sunshine to dry him, wearing only a towel. Feeling refreshed, he wrapped a new bandage round his wrist, got dressed again and called down to the valet to bring round his car. Before he left the room, he opened the hinged compartment concealed in the base of his travel bag and took out the .25 Beretta that he had brought with him from England. He loaded it, slipped it into his back pocket and left.

Sunset Boulevard runs for twenty-two miles, all the way from downtown Los Angeles to the Pacific West, but there is a specific point where it stops pretending to be an ordinary east–west thoroughfare and becomes something quite different; the home of movie stars, moguls and assorted millionaires. You know you have entered the world of Billy Wilder's famous film just after you turn the corner at Doheny Road. Suddenly, you've left the shops and the offices, the huge billboards and the traffic behind you. Even the houses begin to disappear, lost behind high walls and clumps of cedar trees. More and more space stretches out between the various entrances with their gates, mailboxes and perfectly maintained front lawns . . . or front yards as the Americans call them. The air smells different, more countrified. You soon get the feeling that you are not in Los Angeles at all.

Bond drove for about half an hour, following the twisting road towards the village of Westwood and the University of California at Los Angeles, before he came to the address he wanted. He saw a pale yellow wall with a fantastical metal gate – all birds and flowers hammered out in silver. The front yard was crowded with evergreen sumacs, which put Bond in mind of the deadly nettles he had encountered at Menton. These plants, too, were far from their natural habitat, the brilliant crimson leaves exploding in the evening sun. He pulled up to the gate and got out of the car, noticing a television camera trained down on him. He found an intercom box with a single button and pressed it. After a long wait, he heard a burst of static as he was connected.

'Yes?' The voice was distant, metallic.

'My name is James Bond. I have an appointment with Mr Wolfe.'

'Come in.'

Bond heard a buzz and the gate slid open, revealing a pink tarmac driveway beyond. He got back into the car and drove in.

There was no sign of the house. He was surrounded by a garden so extravagant that it might have been used to illustrate a Victorian fairy-tale book or a Bible. Everything was green and heavy, a mass of different leaves blocking out the light, flowers of every shape and size bursting out of the earth, over-ripe and odorous. It was the garden of a man who wanted everything and had the money to get it. Statues, lamps, hedges cut into the shapes of pyramids and elephants, palm trees, rose bushes, cacti, conservatories and greenhouses . . . they had all been jammed together into not quite enough space, so that the overall effect was stifling. In the mirror, Bond saw the gate sliding shut behind him and felt completely trapped.

He drove round a corner and passed the obligatory tennis court, the one well-defined space in all this clutter. It hadn't been used for a while. The net was sagging and weeds sprouted out of the clay. And there ahead of him was the house, built in the style of a Spanish hacienda, two or three times larger than any similar house in Spain. According to the records, Wolfe lived here alone – but even when his wife was alive, with a cook, a butler, a tennis coach and half a dozen friends it would have been surplus to requirements. How many bedrooms did it have? Eleven? Twelve? The walls were thick and white, curving and rippling as if struggling to hold back the interior. Many of the windows were stained glass. The roofs were square, circular, rectangular . . . all made from Spanish tile. There was nothing welcoming about this house. It seemed to be hiding from the world.

Bond parked between a turquoise Buick Roadmaster – the latest model with its two-piece, convex windscreen – and a black Pontiac Chieftain. The first car was more likely to belong to Wolfe, he thought. So what about the second? A bodyguard, perhaps. It was unlikely that the millionaire would have agreed to see him on his own. He walked to the front door, his feet crunching on the gravel, and pulled the heavy iron bell chain. He heard the bell ring out inside the house but nobody came. He looked behind him and saw the sun sinking behind the trees. It wouldn't be dark for a few hours.

He rang a second time. Still nothing. Annoyed now, wondering if Wolfe had decided not to see him after all, he reached out and touched the door. It swung open. There wasn't a single sound coming from the building. Bond hadn't seen any gardeners working in the grounds. Everything was still. If it hadn't been for the monosyllabic voice that he had heard on the intercom, he would have thought the place deserted.

He stepped inside, into a cavernous hall with wooden floors, exposed beams, a minstrel's gallery with a twisting rail. Just like the garden, there was too much clutter in the room, too many antique tables, too many faded tapestries covering the walls, too many clocks, potted plants, oil paintings in gilt frames. An arched doorway led down into what might have been a kitchen area. Other doors, dark wood, were closed. Ahead of him, a grand, double-width staircase invited him up to the second floor. Halfway up, he was faced by a nineteenth-century banjo clock fighting the silence with its sonorous ticking. Its hands, twisted into overly ornate shapes, pointed to six forty-five. It was ten minutes slow.

Bond had already decided to take advantage of the situation and began to explore the different rooms, moving from the study to the dining room, to the library, to the sitting room, to the bar. The floors were uncarpeted – either wood or tile – but his footsteps made no sound. It was darker inside than out. All the furniture and bric-a-brac seemed to swallow up the light. Everywhere, in every room, Bond saw photographs in gold and silver frames and Wolfe appeared in nearly all of them, sometimes with a woman – presumably his dead wife, Mirabelle – sometimes with two young men who must have been his sons, but most often with celebrities; film stars and politicians. There was Wolfe in a dinner jacket, Wolfe in swimming shorts, Wolfe on horseback. Just no sign of Wolfe himself.

Bond went upstairs. He took out the Beretta and held it in front of him, knowing instinctively that there was something wrong, that something bad had happened in this house. The silence, punctuated only by the banjo clock, was too oppressive, the lack of any sort of welcome a statement in itself. He did not call out. He had already announced his arrival at the gate and whoever had answered knew he was there.

He reached the first floor, where a carpeted corridor stretched into the distance with old-fashioned candelabras overhead and arched windows high up on either side. Two floor-to-ceiling doors stood open at the far end – surely the master bedroom – and he made for them, with the uneasy feeling that he had become a player in somebody else's game and that – although he should have had the advantage – he was being sucked into this against his will. He stopped in front of the doors and pushed them wider open. No sound came from the other side.

He'd guessed correctly – it was the bedroom. Bond stepped into a wide chamber with high ceilings and windows looking out onto a swimming pool. The bed was a four-poster, the sort of thing that might find its way into a museum, or which might have been bought from one. It had an oak frame with gold ornamentation and a canopy that was a heaving sea of antique, mauve satin. Pillows and cushions were piled up against a velvet, studded bedhead. It was, Bond decided, a nightmare of a bed – made more so by the man who was lying in it, a gun lying in his open palm, blood seeping out of the hideous wound in the side of his head.

Bond had got here too late. Irwin Wolfe had shot himself. That at least was the picture that presented itself to him. The dead man's eyes were still open, staring glassily into the mid-distance. He was wearing pyjamas and a silk dressing gown. The sheets, stained dark with his blood, were bunched around him. The hair that had impressed Bond when he had first met the millionaire at the house in Cap Ferrat now seemed to be in full flight from his head, sprawled across the pillows. His skin was grey. He was the most corpse-like corpse Bond had ever seen.

So if Wolfe had killed himself, who had answered the intercom?

The answer to that question came a moment later as a

hand with a gun stretched out from behind the door, point-ing in his direction, and a gravelly voice said: 'We really shouldn't make a habit of this.'

Bond had raised his hands. Now he turned his head and smiled. 'I was rather hoping we'd run into each other again. But I have to say you've taken me by surprise.'

'I'm the one who's surprised, James. What the hell are you doing here?'

'Can I put down my hands?'

'Of course. Just don't hit me again.'

The last time Bond had seen Reade Griffith had been over a bourbon at the Hotel Negresco in Nice. As the man stepped out of the corner where he had been concealed, Bond recog-nised the neatly cut dark hair and blue eyes of the CIA agent. He lowered his hands and slipped the gun into his jacket pocket. 'I don't need to ask what you're doing here,' he said.

'Supporting and defending the Constitution of the United States against all enemies foreign and domestic,' Griffith replied, quoting the CIA oath. He grinned. 'As a matter of fact, Wolfe asked me to come out to the house. Quite ironic when you think about it. He had this idea that he might need protecting.'

'From me?' Bond sounded innocent.

'I can't imagine why.'

'And you'd been given orders to take care of him.' Bond glanced at the dead man sprawled out on the bed.

'Wolfe was an embarrassment. He was also an enemy of the country. We like to keep things tidy. This seemed the best way.'

'Suicide.'

'The easy way out.' Griffith paused. 'Out of interest, why did you want to meet him?'

'My people wanted to put pressure on him. I think the idea was to achieve exactly what you've accomplished.'

'Then you owe me a drink.'

'I owe you more than that. I was hoping to see you again. I'm sorry we didn't catch up before I left Nice.'

'Yeah. I heard you killed Scipio and closed down his entire operation. That's quite an achievement.' Griffith put his own gun away. Bond noticed it was the same US Army Remington that he had carried at the Rue Foncet. 'So where are we going to have that drink? There's a place I know down in Westwood . . .'

'That sounds good.' Bond thought for a moment. 'But before we head off, there is one thing I wanted to ask you.'

Bond took out his gunmetal cigarette case and extracted a cigarette with three gold bands. This particular mixture of Turkish and Balkan tobacco had been recommended to him by the man at Morlands, the cigarette maker in Grosvenor Street that Sixtine had told him about. It was stronger than he was used to but he already preferred it to the Du Mauriers he had been smoking before. He glanced inside the lid, then closed it.

'You were working for Scipio all along,' Bond said.

He lit the cigarette.

Reade Griffith frowned but made no attempt to deny the accusation. 'I wouldn't put it quite that way,' he said. 'I was working for the CIA. But that meant cooperating with Scipio. Yes. How did you know?'

Bond had been warned from the start. The report he had read in London had made it clear that the CIA had chosen to support the Corsican crime syndicates in return for their help combatting the communists in the Marseilles docks – even if it had been something that Reade Griffith had denied. But it had still taken him a while to work it out.

271

'When I first met Sixtine, she knew who I was. My name, my number, my recent history – everything. I assumed she must have got the information from her own network, and that of course was very disturbing. But later on, she told me that it was actually Irwin Wolfe who had warned her about me. So the question was, who had told him?'

'That wasn't me.'

'No. But he was working with Scipio. So someone must have told Scipio, who had then passed the information across. And that person could only have been you. Nobody else knew I was there.'

'I hope we're not going to fall out over this, James.'

'Not at all. You were doing your job. I understand that. And the truth is, I should have seen it. When you and I drove to the dock at La Joliette, the man sitting at security asked to see my ID. He checked me out but he ignored you. There had to be a reason for that and the reason was simply that he knew who you were. He had seen you before.' Bond paused and blew out smoke. 'We lost a man at La Joliette. I'm going to assume you were there when it happened.'

'I didn't have anything to do with his death and I'm sorry that it occurred.' Reade Griffith shook his head, remembering. 'The thing was, he'd worked out something of what was going on. The connection with Ferrix Chimiques, for example . . .'

'That was why he had the invoice,' Bond said. 'I have to congratulate you. You completely blindsided me on that.'

'Did I?'

'It was an invoice for thirty gallons of acetic anhydride. You told me it was the principal component of photographic film.'

'It is.'

'I know. But as it happens, it's also used in the production of heroin. At the start of the process an equal amount of morphine and acetic anhydride are heated together. The chemical is known as a heroin precursor.' Bond had checked it out when he got back to London. He was annoyed with himself for not having done so before. He had allowed Griffith to spoon-feed him the lie.

'Your guy was smart but he still got it all wrong,' Griffith continued. 'He decided that Sixtine must be working with Wolfe. It made sense. She was a major operator and they were practically living together. He needed information and he decided he could get it from Scipio. After all, he'd seen the two of them sitting together in that café in Marseilles. He'd even taken photographs. He figured he could persuade Scipio to tell him what she was up to.

'For what it's worth, I warned him against it but he asked me to set up a meeting on neutral ground. I said I'd come along just to make sure that everyone played fair and that's why he wasn't packing a gun. I arranged the meeting at La Joliette . . . white flag and all the rest of it. I was genuinely trying to help. The only trouble was, Scipio hadn't read the rules. When he realised your guy knew too much, he took out a gun and shot him three times in the chest. It all happened so fast, there was nothing I could do. It's like I told you the first time we met: you can't trust these people.'

'Scipio knew I was coming to Ferrix Chimiques. You told him.'

'I also told him not to hurt you, buddy. That's why it was water and not acid in that flask they threw in your face.'

Bond had worked that out too. Scipio had almost admitted as much when they had met that second time, on the *Mirabelle*. He had said that he wanted to deal with Bond – 'without restraint'. Those two words had told Bond someone must have been protecting him when he was at the chemical factory.

'There's one thing I don't understand,' Bond said. 'Irwin Wolfe was planning a lethal strike on your own country. American gangs sell about 600 pounds of heroin every month across the United States. Wolfe was delivering twenty times that amount and he was giving it away almost free. Was Scipio so important to you that you were prepared to go along with the consequences? Or were you planning to stop the *Mirabelle* when it arrived?'

'I knew nothing about the *Mirabelle*,' Griffith said. 'I didn't know what was going on in Wolfe's head. Scipio didn't tell me. But why would he? For him it was a whole new business opportunity. I have to say, my government is very grateful to you, James. You saved us from a whole load of trouble. I hear you're being recommended for a Medal of Honor. You certainly get my vote.'

'That's very kind of you.'

Griffith glanced at the dead body that had been a silent witness to the entire conversation. 'Let's get the hell out of here, James. And make sure you take that cigarette butt with you. We want to leave things nice and clean for the police and the paramedics.'

Bond didn't move.

'You're not sore with me?' Griffith asked.

'There is just one other thing I want to know,' Bond said. 'Did you know that Sixtine and I were on the *Mirabelle* at the very end, when it went down?'

'No. I didn't. What happened to her?'

'She died.'

'That's too bad.'

'Yes. It is.'

Bond's hand had slipped, casually, into his pocket. When he took it out, it was holding the Beretta. In a single movement, without hesitation, he turned and shot Reade Griffith in the middle of the forehead. The CIA agent stared at him as if in disbelief, blood trickling down between his eyes. Then he pitched forward.

Bond moved quickly. Lifting him up by the armpits, he dragged the dead man closer to the bed and left him there. He took the gun out of Irwin Wolfe's hand, noticing that it was a Webley & Scott .45. He wondered, vaguely, why that weapon had been chosen. But it didn't matter now. Using a handkerchief, he wiped it clean, then pressed it into Reade Griffith's hand. He removed the CIA agent's gun and slid it into his pocket. Finally, he wiped his own gun with the handkerchief and placed it in Irwin Wolfe's hand, closing the dead man's fingers around the trigger.

When he had come into the room, he had been presented with the scene of a fake suicide but he had transformed it into something else. Reade Griffith had been sent here to kill Irwin Wolfe. He hadn't realised that the older man was armed. In the end, the two of them had shot each other. That was what it would look like. Of course, the CIA would be suspicious but they wouldn't be able to ask too many questions, not without admitting why he had been there in the first place. Nobody knew anything about Bond. He was travelling under a false name. They didn't even know he was in America.

He finished the cigarette he had been smoking and pinched it out. He slipped the butt into his top pocket, then wiped the ashtray clean. He hadn't touched anything in the room. He had left no fingerprints. He took one last look around, then left, walking out of the silent house. The police and paramedics would arrive eventually but by then Bond would be long gone.

He climbed back into the car, thinking about the man he had just killed. Reade Griffith had lied to him from the very start and had been lying all along. He had been hopelessly compromised by his relationship with Scipio and had been blind to the consequences. Whatever he might say, he had been responsible for the death of a British secret agent. He had almost certainly told Scipio about Monique de Troyes, the girl who worked at Ferrix Chimiques, and had caused her death too.

And it had been thanks to him that Sixtine had died.

Once again Bond saw her, one last time, slipping away from him into the blue.

Slowly, he drove back through the overcrowded garden, heading for the gate. He knew that although he had been given a licence to kill, it hadn't extended to this. There would be no official report. He would never speak of it again. He had committed murder. Pure and simple.

Ahead of him, a sensor picked up the movement of the car and the electric door swung open, revealing Sunset Boulevard on the other side. Bond drove out, leaving behind him the memory of what he had just done.

He felt nothing.

Acknowledgements

I am enormously grateful to Ian Fleming Publications Ltd and the Ian Fleming Estate for inviting me back a second time. As someone who grew up with James Bond – the books before the films – it's a dream come true to write about the world's most enduring spy, though a huge challenge to come anywhere near to the brilliance of Fleming's writing.

As ever, though, I have been helped – firstly by Fleming himself. Much of the chapter 'Russian Roulette' is based on one of the outlines he wrote for an American television series which in the end never happened. (Another of these outlines, 'Murder on Wheels', appeared in my first Bond novel, *Trigger Mortis*.) Curiously, Fleming also refers to the story of the *Aleksandr Kolchak*, which he claims is based on fact, in his collection of travel journalism which was published as *Thrilling Cities* in 1963. I'm afraid I rather brazenly raided the book for my description of the casino at Monte Carlo in the same chapter. It follows that many of the attitudes expressed are Fleming's, not mine.

Once again I have to single out Corinne Turner, who has been a constant supporter and friend at IFE, as well as Jonny Geller at Curtis Brown (who represents Ian Fleming) and my own agent Jonathan Lloyd, who helped steer me through moments of doubt. It's been a pleasure working with Jonathan

Cape and I particularly want to acknowledge the work of Ana Fletcher and David Milner, who separately edited the text, each with an eagle eye, and saved me – many times – from myself. It might be unusual for an author to thank his cover designer but, along with the title, there is nothing more important to the success of a James Bond novel and I think Kris Potter got it exactly right.

Forever and a Day required a great deal of research that the internet could not supply and I am particularly grateful to Joe Forrest, who came up with sensible answers to some impossible questions and convinced me that some of the more daring escapes in this story might work. To get a working knowledge of the *Mirabelle*, I went to Southampton and visited the SS *Shieldhall* – the largest working steam ship in Britain – and I want to thank Nigel Philpott and Graham Mackenzie for giving me so much of their time and expertise.

There were many books that helped me. I've mentioned *James Bond: The Man and His World* by Henry Chancellor before. It's a great resource, as is the website 'literary007.com'. I acquainted myself with blackjack by reading Edward O. Thorp's *Beat the Dealer*, and Alfred W. McCoy's *The Politics of Heroin* and Meyer & Parssinen's *Webs of Smoke* provided all the background I needed to describe Scipio's activities. A special thank you to Andrew Lycett, who drew my attention to Shame Lady, a name that Fleming flirted with for his home in Jamaica. He eventually chose Goldeneye.

Last year, I offered the opportunity to appear as a character in the book at an auction to support the Old Vic (a charity which receives no Arts Council funding) and I would like to acknowledge the extraordinary generosity of two bidders. The auction was won by Reade Griffith, who appears under his own name in Chapter Five onwards. Joann McPike also made a substantial donation and the character of Joanne Brochet, Madame 16, is inspired by her. Brochet is the French for pike.

Finally, I might have been able to write this book without the help of my assistant, Alice Edmondson – but certainly not on time. The manuscript was read by my brilliant wife, Jill Green, and my two sons, Nicholas and Cassian. As usual, their suggestions were vicious but invaluable.

Ian Fleming has played a huge role in my life. He wrote the first adult books that I ever loved and the films saved me from some of the darker corners of my childhood. I dedicate this book to his memory . . . not, of course, that he has any chance of being forgotten.

Ian Fleming

Ian Lancaster Fleming was born in London on 28 May 1908 and was educated at Eton College before spending a formative period studying languages in Europe. His first job was with Reuters news agency, followed by a brief spell as a stockbroker. On the outbreak of the Second World War he was appointed assistant to the Director of Naval Intelligence, Admiral Godfrey, where he played a key part in British and Allied espionage operations.

After the war he joined Kemsley Newspapers as Foreign Manager of the *Sunday Times*, running a network of correspondents who were intimately involved in the Cold War. His first novel, *Casino Royale*, was published in 1953 and introduced James Bond, Special Agent 007, to the world. The first print run sold out within a month. Following this initial success, he published a Bond title every year until his death. His own travels, interests and wartime experience gave authority to everything he wrote. Raymond Chandler hailed him as 'the most forceful and driving writer of thrillers in England.' The fifth title, *From Russia, with Love*, was particularly well received and sales soared when President Kennedy named it as one of his favourite books. The Bond novels have sold more than sixty million copies and inspired a hugely successful film franchise which began in 1962 with the release of *Dr No* starring Sean Connery as 007.

The Bond books were written in Jamaica, a country Fleming fell in love with during the war and where he built a house, 'Goldeneye'. He married Ann Rothermere in 1952. His story about a magical car, written in 1961 for their only child Caspar, went on to become the well-loved novel and film, *Chitty Chitty Bang Bang*. Fleming died of heart failure on 12 August 1964.

www.ianfleming.com

The James Bond Books

Casino Royale

Live and Let Die

Moonraker

Diamonds Are Forever

From Russia, with Love

Dr No

Goldfinger

For Your Eyes Only

Thunderball

The Spy Who Loved Me

On Her Majesty's Secret Service

You Only Live Twice

The Man with the Golden Gun

Octopussy and the Living Daylights

Non-fiction

The Diamond Smugglers

Thrilling Cities

Children's

Chitty Chitty Bang Bang

About the Author

ANTHONY HOROWITZ, one of the UK's most prolific and successful writers, may have committed more (fictional) murders than any other living author. His novels include *The Word Is Murder*, *Magpie Murders*, *Trigger Mortis*, *Moriarty*, *The House of Silk*, and the bestselling Alex Rider series for young adults. As a screenwriter he created the television series *Midsomer Murders* and the BAFTA-winning *Foyle's War* on PBS. His other television work includes *Agatha Christie's Poirot* and the widely acclaimed miniseries *Collision* and *Injustice*, and the BBC series *New Blood*. He regularly contributes to a wide variety of newspapers and magazines, and in 2014 was awarded an OBE for services to literature. He lives in London.